Getting Rich

Previously published Worldwide Mystery title by
MONIQUE DOMOVITCH

GETTING SKINNY

MONIQUE DOMOVITCH

Getting Rich

W RLDWIDE®

TORONTO • NEW YORK • LONDON
AMSTERDAM • PARIS • SYDNEY • HAMBURG
STOCKHOLM • ATHENS • TOKYO • MILAN
MADRID • WARSAW • BUDAPEST • AUCKLAND

Recycling programs
for this product may
not exist in your area.

Getting Rich

A Worldwide Mystery/August 2015

First published by Carina Press

ISBN-13: 978-0-373-26957-0

Printed in U.S.A.

In memory of Charlotte and Jackie Chan,
two little dogs with big attitudes.
I miss you both

the opportunity of a lifetime

I SHOULD BE SKINNY, damn it. And if life were fair, I *would* be skinny. After all, as the owner of a gourmet restaurant specializing in low-calorie meals, by now I'd had four months of unlimited access to dozens of wonderful gourmet dishes, each of which was under five hundred calories. So, I should have lost my damned love handles and be thin as a rail, right?

The problem was that after a hundred and twenty days of diet meals, there were times when the mere thought of another low-fat, low-sugar and low-cal dish was enough to send me screaming all the way to the nearest fast-food joint, wanting—no, *needing*—serious calories.

This explained why I had braved the icy roads on my way to work this morning, all the way to the drive-through of the nearest Burger Heaven. It was only eleven-fifteen, but when it came to food, my appetite knew no schedule.

The old Buick ahead of me drove away and I inched over to the pick-up window. A blast of frigid winter air tore through my smart car as a gap-toothed girl handed me my bag. She recited its contents, sounding bored. "That's one double-decker with extra cheese, one super fry, and one jumbo diet drink, right?" Suddenly her uninterested stare turned into a squint. She pointed at me, now wide-eyed.

"You're that girl in the ad," she squealed.

I managed a crooked smile, snatched the bag from her hand and pressed the accelerator, lurching forward.

Shit, shit, shit.

What were the chances? I hated when that happened. Not that it did very often. I wasn't famous or anything, but my picture had been seen by hundreds of thousands of Torontonians. Not because I was beautiful, but, as my girlfriend and partner Toni explained, because I was attractive in a non-threatening sort of way. That was Toni's way of saying I was plump—not model thin—which made me perfect for the before and after pictures to advertise the low-cal restaurant she and I co-owned. That was the only modeling I'd ever done—hardly worth boasting about.

Back when our restaurant first opened, I'd thought that our excellent food and charming decor was all we needed for customers to discover us and start coming in by the droves. It wasn't long until reality hit, that we had to do something else and fast, or we'd go bust. The something I'd come up with was the low-cal menu idea. It made sense, as I'd pointed out, considering our name, Skinny's on Queen. And then, because I'd recently lost twenty pounds, Toni had the bright idea of using my pictures—one of me fat and one of me twenty pounds thinner—in an ad campaign. After a blitz of advertising flyers dropped all over the city, business turned around, and I finally started getting paychecks. Hallelujah.

On the not-so-good side, I couldn't as much as stand in line at the Dairy Queen anymore without worrying about being recognized. If word got back to Toni about yet another of my diet infractions, she would not be thrilled since—as she so liked to remind me—I was the face of Skinny's on Queen.

My stomach in a knot, the burger's mouthwatering aroma no longer seemed nearly as appetizing. Half a dozen blocks later I zipped into a parking spot just the right size for my tiny car, pocketed the key and stared down at the bag on the passenger seat. I debated. Should I scarf down the burger here and now, or chuck it?

Toni was already talking about a new ad campaign, which meant an updated picture of me. How embarrassing would it be if my new *after* picture looked worse than my old *before*. I couldn't risk that, I told myself with unusual determination. I climbed out of the car, tightened my coat against the November cold and marched off toward a trash bin, bag in hand. A few yards away, I was about to drop it in, when an idea came to me. Surely I wasn't the only person on a diet who would kill for a hamburger. I hoofed on to the restaurant.

The bell above the door tinkled, announcing my arrival. Charles, our wonderful sous-chef, came hurrying out from the kitchen, wiping his hands on a bar towel.

"Morning, boss," he said, and then frowned, noticing the eye-catching logo on the Burger Heaven bag. "What have you got there? Don't tell me there's nothing on our menu you would have preferred to *that?*"

"Oh, for heaven's sake, you've been spending way too much time with Toni." I dropped the bag on the nearest table as I slipped out of my parka. "Tell me something, Charles. How often do you eat hamburgers?"

"Me? Why?"

"You're naturally thin, and you don't have to watch your diet. I'm just curious. On average, how many burgers a month would you say you eat?"

He shrugged, frowning as he counted in his mind. "Uh, I don't know—maybe half a dozen." My jaw dropped. And then, looking guilty, he added, "Okay, maybe more like ten or twelve."

"You eat about a dozen burgers a month? That's… that's an average of three a week." I was *so* jealous. "Does Jennifer eat that many too?"

Jennifer was Charles's new girlfriend, a tall and slender blonde he'd recently talked us into hiring. In all fairness, we'd needed the extra help and she was proving invaluable in the kitchen. The girl could multitask better than anyone I'd ever known.

"I think she eats more than I do," he replied.

"More than you?" Life was so not fair. "Well, that proves it."

"That proves what?"

"You know what I miss the most since I've been watching my weight?" In truth, the only weight watching I'd been doing was daily peeks at the numbers on the scale as they kept climbing. "Hamburgers. There are days when I'd sell my firstborn to the devil for one."

He chuckled. "Good thing you don't have kids."

"You know what our menu needs? A good low-calorie burger. I know it isn't exactly a gourmet dish, but maybe we can create a really upscale *Skinny* burger."

"A low-cal burger? Let's see." He counted on his fingers. "Beef, cheese, bread—none of those are exactly diet foods." He bobbed his brows. "But you're right. If we can find a way of making it, we'd have a new hot item."

"Don't worry. We'll figure out a way." I picked up the bag again and headed for the kitchen, pausing at the swinging door. "We've turned more challenging dishes than burgers into low-cal meals."

In the kitchen I was greeted by a blend of delicious aromas. Charles had put Jennifer to stirring at the stove. She threw me a beaming smile. "Hi, Nicky."

Marley, our assistant, was at the counter chopping vegetables, his dreadlocks gathered in a bun under a hairnet, and Scott, our dishwasher, was stacking clean dishes onto the open shelves. Even Jake, our headwaiter—actually our only waiter—was putting clean dishes away.

"How are we doing? Is everything ready for the lunch crowd?" I asked. Just using the word *crowd* gave me a kick. It wasn't so long ago that we were thrilled when we served six or eight customers a shift. Now we were averaging over thirty people at lunchtime alone. Granted, our dinner clientele was still meager, but eventually that would improve too.

Charles walked over to the stove and peeked into the pot Jennifer was stirring. His hand landed on Jennifer's back and a tender look passed between them. "The Alfredo sauce is simmering. I've got two dozen individual crustless quiches in the oven."

Since the introduction of our Skinny menu, our three most popular dishes remained our quiches, our Skinny Fettuccine Alfredo and our Skinny Caesar salads. We had to keep a ready supply of those at all times.

He continued. "The romaine is washed and dried. The dressing is done and the special of the day—" he indicated another pot, "—is chicken mulligatawny."

"Yum." I plopped my burger bag on the plating counter. "How soon can you get going on the Skinny burger idea, Charles?" He turned from the stove.

He frowned. "Does it have to be a *beef* burger?"

"Hmm." I thought quickly. "How about we test a few different versions and then decide which one we should adopt?"

"Good idea." He tapped his wooden spoon on the edge of the pot and set it in its rest. He came over and opened the bag. He snatched the burger and unwrapped it. "Do you want to include fries?"

"Burger *and* fries, what a treat. If you can manage to still keep the dish under 500 calories I say go for it."

His eyes got that faraway look they always did when he began considering options. Charles liked nothing better than a challenge, which was one of the many reasons he was so valuable to us. Another reason, one I didn't like to admit, was that he could almost outcook even me. He was that good.

I grabbed an apron from the hook by the door. "Has anybody heard from Toni yet?" At that very moment, she appeared in the doorway, wearing a leopard-print shrink-wrap dress, five-inch heels and a wide smile.

I blinked. Toni, arriving on time?—that was unheard of.

"Why are you all looking at me that way?" she said, giving her blond mane a toss. "Is it my new dress?" She walked a few steps runway style and twirled. "How do you like it?"

"A better question would be, why are you here so—" I frowned, my eyes locking on her breasts. They were ginormous.

Seeing the confusion in my eyes, she burst out laughing. "How do you like them?"

I glanced around quickly and, yes, the guys were all staring bug-eyed at her chest too.

Toni gave a little shoulder wiggle. "Are they all right? Too big? Too small?" Her smile widened. "Will somebody say something?"

Charles found his voice. "Nice," he said, blushing.

Toni slipped a hand into her V-neck and pulled out two apples. "I've been thinking of getting a boob job and thought I'd see what everybody thought first."

"Please don't," I said. "You look great just the way you are. In fact, sometimes I have to remind myself that it's not your fault if you're tall, slim and gorgeous. You were born that way."

"I know," she said, fanning herself. "It's a blessing and a curse." She smiled wanly and winked. "So, seriously, do you think I should do it?"

"No," five voices exclaimed at once.

"Well, I guess that settles it." She dropped the two apples on the plating table. I waited for her to turn her back, picked them up and threw them in the nearest trash can. There was something very unappealing about apples that had masqueraded as boobs.

The bell above the entrance door tinkled, announcing the first lunchtime customers, quickly putting an end to the conversation. Jake hurried out front and the rest of us jumped into high gear. I plopped on my chef's hat, got a box of shitake mushrooms from the walk-in fridge and began chopping. At the plating table, Toni was wrapping the apron ties around her waist. She looped it around three times before tying the ends into a bow in the back, and the apron still looked too big on her.

She threw me a smile. "Like I said, a blessing and a curse."

"Wish I had to live with that kind of a curse," I snapped back. My eyes wandered over to Jennifer. Every woman around me was tall, thin and gorgeous, damn it.

For all the complaining I did about my weight, I knew I had it pretty good. To most people, my life probably seemed perfect. I mean, here I was, not even thirty and I owned a pretty little Victorian semi-detached, which I had lovingly restored to a warm and cozy home. And I already co-owned my own business. Thank goodness, the restaurant had turned around, because I was also the owner of many overextended credit cards, which I was slowly paying off. If those paychecks stopped coming in, I would so be in deep shit.

THE DAY WHIZZED by in a frantic rush of grilling, baking, steaming and roasting, and suddenly it was ten-fifteen. The lunch shift had been packed, but once again the dinner crowd was sparse—normal for a Wednesday. Now, one couple remained and they had just asked for the bill. I peeked out from the swinging door to see Jake escorting them to the exit. I looked around. "Where's Toni?"

Charles looked embarrassed. "She hurried out about an hour ago—"

"I don't believe it," I exclaimed, unamused. She had sneaked out so quietly that I hadn't even noticed. "She had a date with Steven, didn't she?"

He shrugged. "She said she'd be back with some kind of a surprise before you left."

"A surprise? Any idea what it might be?"

"Not a clue."

The real surprise would be if she showed up before we left.

"Everything is done," Scott said. "Do you mind if we take off?"

I looked around. The kitchen was clean and tidy once again. The counters were spotless, the dishes and glasses stacked neatly and sparkling on the shelves. The floor had been swept and mopped. "Okay, let's call it a day. Good job, everyone. See you in the morning."

Jake, Marley and Scott were going out the back when the bell above the entrance door chimed. I looked at Charles. "I thought you locked up."

"Of course I did," he said, looking as worried as I was.

I slipped off my stool and went to the door. To my surprise, it was Toni. She stood in the entrance looking around, as if confused. "Toni, you came back," I said. "Toni? Are you all right?"

She turned to look at me and I stopped short. This wasn't Toni. But this woman—whoever she was—looked so much like her that the two could have been twins.

She smiled tentatively. "You must be Nicky." She

walked over with her hand extended. "Oh, what the hell. I feel like I already know you," she said, taking her hand back. Grinning, she leaned forward, brushing her lips against my cheek.

From up close I could see the differences. She wasn't quite as tall as Toni, and her features, although lovely, were not as refined. Her hair was slightly darker, her eyes brown instead of blue. "Oh my God, you look so much like—"

At that moment Toni stepped out from behind the coat-rack, laughing. I must have looked stunned because she pointed at me and doubled over, laughing even harder.

"I wish you could see the look on your face. It's price-less." She came forward. "Nicky, meet my sister, Judy Donaldson. Judy, this is Nicky."

I tried to regain my composure. "But you—" Toni had told me she was an only child, orphaned at the age of three when her parents passed away. She'd been raised by her maternal grandparents, later inheriting their fortune when they died in a car crash.

"I know. I always thought I was an only child," she said, guessing the question going through my mind. "Imagine my surprise when Judy contacted me and announced that she and I were sisters—half sisters to be exact."

"But she—"

"We share the same father, but different mothers. Judy is a year older, from a relationship my father had before he and my mother married."

"But how—"

"We were raised by different grandparents. After our parents died, I went with my mother's parents and she went with our father's."

"But why—" Clearly I wasn't able to form a com-plete sentence.

This time, Judy explained. "From what I was told, To-ni's grandparents were dead set against Toni's mother marrying my father. He came from a middle-class family. He already had one child—me—and only eked out a living as an artist. And they regarded him as a phi-landerer—not exactly the kind of match wealthy parents would want for their beloved daughter. So, when he and Toni's mother died, Toni's maternal grandparents took her in, and I went to live with Grandma and Grandpa Spen-cer. It wasn't until Grandma died and I went through her papers that I found out about Antoinette."

Toni grimaced and said lightly, "I hate that name. It makes me feel like I'm about to get my head chopped off."

Judy chuckled. "Sorry, Toni."

I was watching the interaction between these two. They obviously liked each other. Whenever they glanced at each other their eyes lit up. "Have you met Steven?"

"No, not yet," she replied.

"I'll introduce them soon," Toni said. There was a hint of worry in her voice. "I wouldn't be surprised if he thought I'd been seeing another man."

Judy shook her head. "I wouldn't blame him if he did. After all the sneaking around you've been doing since we met, anybody would imagine the same thing." She said to me, "I told her she shouldn't keep me a secret. But she wanted to make sure I really was who I said I was. All anybody has to do was look at me to know we're related." She chuckled. "But she insisted on DNA tests. Can you believe it?"

Actually, I did. Toni was a very rich woman. And she was also suspicious by nature—at times bordering on paranoid. During her entire ten-year marriage to Steven she had carefully kept her net worth a secret from him. According to her, that was the only way she could be sure he was with her for love and not her money. It would have been just like her to suspect Judy of being some sort of scam artist.

Noticing the blush creeping up Toni's neck, I changed the subject. "Where did you grow up?"

"In Ottawa." She shrugged. "I searched for Toni for three years before finding out that her grandparents changed her name from my father's—Spencer—to their name—Gordon. Once I knew that, it took me no time to track her down."

Charles had been listening to the story with as much fascination as I had. He suddenly remembered his manners and held out his hands. "Here. Let me take your coats." He hung them and then guided us to a nearby table, asking, "Can I offer anybody a glass of wine?" He looked at Toni for approval.

She jumped up. "I'll go get a bottle."

Judy called after her. "Please don't open a bottle on my account. I can't stay very long." She turned to me. "I have to go back to the hotel. I promised my husband I'd be back early. Poor guy, I keep leaving him alone all the time."

Toni came cha-cha-ing back from the kitchen carrying a tray. "Here's to taking life with a grain of salt… plus a slice of lemon…and a shot of tequila. Margaritas for everyone."

Judy's eyes grew wide. "Oh my God, margaritas. Just give me a small one."

While Toni poured, Charles cleared his throat. "I should let you ladies talk." He looked at me. "If you don't mind, I'll take off now. Jenny's still in the back waiting for me."

"Of course, go. I'll see you tomorrow."

He returned to the kitchen, and a moment later I heard him and Jennifer leaving by the back door.

"I'm so happy to meet you at last," Judy was saying. "Toni told me all about you, your lovely home and your boyfriend."

I nodded. "He might be going out of town to work on his manuscript with his editor."

"Do we have time to meet him before he leaves?"

"Maybe. Why don't you and your husband come here for dinner? If you make it soon, before he leaves, you'll both get to meet him."

"Sounds good. It must be difficult for you to find time together. You work such long hours."

"That's one advantage of living next door to each other."

Toni cut in. "And when she says next door, she means *right* next door. Nicky's house is a semi-detached. Mitchell lives on the other side."

I laughed. "It's true. I can even hear his phone ringing from my place."

Judy chuckled. "What a great arrangement. It's even better than living together. He's there when you need him but you can still have your own space. I was telling my husband that Mitchell's an author. Richard is so impressed. He loves to read, especially mysteries. You'll have to tell me the title of his book. I'll make sure to buy it."

I made a mental note to repeat this to him. He would be flattered.

Toni turned to me and changed the subject. "You should see my niece. She's adorable—six years old and a real sweetheart. I just love her to pieces."

Toni thrilling about her relationship with a child was something I never thought I'd see. "So you're an aunt."

She nodded, chuckling. "All the pleasures of being a parent and none of the hassles—I can do as much spoiling as I like, and just hand her back when she's being naughty."

Judy beamed with pleasure. "And she sure has been doing a lot of spoiling. Celia is crazy about her auntie. Toni must have bought out the entire toy department of The Bay. Our room is filled with dolls. There are so many, we can barely move around. I have no idea how we'll get them all home."

"Do you still live in Ottawa?"

"Yes, but hopefully not for long. I'm trying to convince Richard we should move here. He's an accountant. I think he could find work very easily in this city, don't you? After all, this is the financial capital of Canada. There couldn't be a better place for him to carve a career. But it couldn't be until the end of June. We don't want to pull Celia out of school in the middle of the year." She glanced at Toni and then lowered her eyes shyly. "My whole life I missed having siblings. Toni is the only family I have, and it's important to me that Celia gets to know her."

"Celia just went back to Ottawa. She's staying with an aunt until Judy and Richard go back." She reached over and placed her hand on Judy's. "I'm sure he'll agree to move here. And if he doesn't, we'll just have to put our heads together and come up with some way to convince him."

Judy smiled, but her eyes held uncertainly.

"Tell him I have two very nice guest bedrooms and when you decide to take the leap, you can stay with me until you find a permanent home. There's plenty of room." Toni snapped her fingers. "I know. I'll go shopping for a child's bed tomorrow, so Celia will have a bedroom ready for her."

Judy shook her head. "Please don't go to any expense on our account."

I was a bit surprised that Judy and her husband weren't already staying with Toni, especially since they seemed to only be here for a short visit. On the other hand, although the condo was large, some people felt uncomfortable living in another person's home.

"I have a guest room," I said. "My house isn't big or as luxurious as Toni's apartment, but it has a small backyard, and I'm only a block away from Trinity Bellwoods Park. If you decide to move here, you can stay with me until you find a place. Your daughter would be able to play outside."

"That's really nice of you. It would still be months away, but I might take you up on that." Judy took a sip of her drink. "I didn't expect everyone to be so welcoming."

"Why wouldn't we be?" I asked. "Isn't it the most natural thing in the world? After all, you and Toni are sisters."

Toni smiled, embarrassed. "Let's just say that I didn't exactly greet her with open arms."

Judy laughed. "I know I teased you about that, but the truth is, in your situation I would have done the same thing." She looked at her watch, exclaiming, "Oh my goodness. Is it eleven-thirty already?" She hopped to her feet. "I have to get back. Richard will be worried. I'm surprised he hasn't called me."

Toni got up. "I'll give you a lift to your hotel."

"Don't bother, I can grab a cab. It'll be just as fast—faster. I noticed the taxi stand across the street. That way you and Nicky can gossip about me when I'm gone." She laughed. "That's what I would do if I were you."

"Don't forget to tell Richard about my offer," Toni said, getting up and giving Judy a hug. "I mean it. You could stay as long as it takes to find the perfect place. Let me know what he says."

Judy hurried to the coatrack. She slipped on her coat

and took off, blowing us kisses. We watched her run across the street and hop into a cab. Toni and I returned to polishing off the rest of the pitcher of margaritas.

"She's nice," I said. "What's her husband like?"

"I haven't met him, but I suspect he might be a bit of a control freak. She's always so worried about not getting back too late. Tonight was the perfect example. She was looking forward to meeting you for weeks, but from the moment she got here she was nervous about how late she would be getting back to the hotel."

"Maybe it has nothing to do with her husband. If she's a year older than you, that means she wasn't very young when her daughter was born. A lot of mothers who have children later in life become overprotective. She probably hoped to give her daughter a call before she went to bed."

Toni shot me a dirty look. "If *she* isn't very young, what does that make *me?*"

"That makes you much more beautiful and younger looking than her."

She searched my eyes. "Do you really think so?"

I nodded. "Much," I said, and Toni's irritation melted away. I looked at my now-empty glass. "How was your weekend with Steven?"

A few months ago, when Toni and her ex began show-ing signs of reconciling, nobody could have been more surprised than I was. In retrospect, I should have known she wasn't over him. Any woman who does that much griping about an ex had to be still carrying a torch. Since their reconciliation, she seemed happier than I'd ever known her.

Toni hesitated. "Steven's been acting a bit strange lately."

"What do you mean?"

"Oh, in little ways—for one thing he seems quieter,

almost secretive. And I have a feeling he won't be very happy when he finds out I have a sister and a niece."

"I don't get it. Why would he be upset because you have a sister?"

She gave me a sardonic smile. "Because he won't be the primary beneficiary to my estate anymore. I've decided to leave most of my money to my sister and my niece. Something tells me that when he finds out, he won't be thrilled."

"I thought he had no idea how much money you have." When they'd divorced, he'd even given her a generous settlement—something he wouldn't have done had he been aware of her true financial situation.

"Well...he didn't. But then I goofed." She traced a perfectly manicured finger down the stem of her glass and scowled. "I'd been living by myself since our divorce. So naturally I stopped storing all my papers in a safety deposit box. I started keeping them at home, in my desk drawer. Steven stayed over one night and the next morning, while I ran out for croissants, he went looking for an envelope. And—" she let out a long breath, "—came across my investment statement."

I had a quick memory of how intimidating Steven could be. I'd once seen him cross examine a hostile witness in court, and had I been in the witness box, I'd probably have been reduced to a stuttering, blubbering fool. He had to be tough, after all he was a criminal defense attorney and his roster of clients counted some of the worst criminals in the country—embezzlers, robbers, murderers, even some members of organized crime. I imagined him in a heated argument with Toni. "Uh-oh. That couldn't have been much fun."

She grimaced. "You can say that again. To say he wasn't happy is putting it mildly. I had a lot of explaining to do."

I could understand why he might have been upset. I would have been too, under the circumstances. A lie by omission is still a lie. Not to mention that large divorce settlement he'd paid. He probably felt he'd been conned—which he had been.

"Did you know that the second most frequent cause of divorce is disputes about money?"

"Really?" I said. "What's the first?"

"Marriage," she said, without cracking a smile. "That was one hell of an argument. He kept going on and on about honesty and trust. I tried to explain that the only way I could be certain he was not with me for my money was by keeping my inheritance a secret. Luckily, I still had a copy of my old will. I showed him that he'd been my sole beneficiary during our entire marriage, and he calmed down a bit. And I promised him, now that we're reconciled, I would have my will redrawn, naming him as my sole beneficiary."

"That sounds reasonable."

"But just between you and me, I don't get it. Statistically, women outlive men by six to eight years. And he's ten years older than I am. I'm going to outlive him by at least a dozen years. Why it was so important that I put him in my will I'll never figure out." She bit her bottom lip, looking worried. "I had an appointment with my estate lawyer last week to do just that, but after meeting Judy, I postponed it. The thing is, Steven doesn't really need my money. I don't understand why it even matters to him. He may not be rich, but he's successful. He has enough to be comfortable for the rest of his life."

Toni didn't consider having enough money for the rest of his life as being rich? Wow. The rich really were different.

"Judy, on the other hand, hasn't got two nickels to rub

together," she continued. "I don't think her husband earns very much as an accountant if she's worried about the cost of raising a child."

My eyebrows went up. "You didn't change your will? And Steven is under the impression that you did? Won't he be even more upset when he finds out?"

She raised her glass and, in one quick swig, polished off the remainder of her drink. "I expect he'll blow a fuse."

home with three buns in the oven

I PARKED ON the pad behind my house and hurried around the side to the front, glancing at Mitchell's window as I pulled out my keys—no sign of him. I swallowed my disappointment and walked in. I was greeted by the hysterical barking of an overjoyed Jackie Chan, my three-pound Yorkie. She came galloping down the hall.

Yap, yap, yap, yap! Translation? "You're back! Oh, thank goodness you're back. I was afraid you'd never come back!" Jackie Chan was frantic with joy. She leaped into my arms and I buried my nose in her neck—a futile effort to avoid her energetic tongue.

"It's okay, Jackie. It's okay. I love you too." I put her back down. "How are your babies, little girl?"

She took off. I hurried to the mudroom behind the kitchen. There, in a large crate, two teensy-weensy doggies were pawing madly at the wire door. Underneath, half a dozen wee-wee pads were in dire need of changing. How could such tiny dogs produce so much poo?

"Phe-ew, you guys stink," I muttered, picking up a bunch of clean pads from the nearby box.

Four months ago Jackie had run away from home one night. She came back the next morning with a bun in the oven, or rather, three buns in the oven. For two months I was the proud owner of three puppies. Then, a week ago, a friend had adopted one of the little females, and—if I was to believe her—Toni would soon take the little male off my hands. I sure hoped she was sincere, but the dog had been ready to go for a few weeks now and she was still procrastinating.

The timing for the litter to be born couldn't have been worse. Having a houseful of untrained doggies too young to take outside in this cold was a challenge. Even Jackie was too small to brave the frigid weather for more than a few minutes. To make matters worse, until they were two months old, pups were too young to be adopted, and of course by the time the little ones were ready to leave I was totally in love with them. But, as much as it had been heartbreaking to see the first one go last week, it had also been a relief.

I opened the back door and stepped outside carrying the two pups. Jackie followed and did her usual mad sprint around my postage stamp of a backyard, did a quick pee and then ran back in. The two pups sniffed the ground, unsure what to do. At last, the little male, Trouble, raised his leg and peed on my boots—once again proving he deserved his name.

"No, Trouble, not on my feet," I muttered, shaking my foot. The little female, Sugar, trotted off toward a flower bed and squatted. "See," I said to Trouble. "That's where you do it."

He ignored me and galloped up the stairs. I gave Sugar her two minutes, picked her up and followed inside.

After making sure their water bowls were full, I checked the phone for messages—nothing. I hadn't heard from Mitchell in a couple of days now, which was somewhat unusual. It brought out all my insecurities. I knew Mitchell was a good guy. We'd been dating for a few months—long enough to call it a relationship, but not long enough to feel completely safe.

OVERNIGHT THE WEATHER had grown colder. By morning the mercury had dipped to below zero and the sidewalks were covered with a thin dusting of snow. I glanced out the window and decided to drive to work, even though I could have used the exercise.

"Morning, boss," said Jennifer as I walked into the kitchen. In the short time Charles's girlfriend had been working for us, I had grown accustomed to her cheery disposition and friendly manner. The atmosphere at work had always been pleasant, and now she added to it.

"Hi, Jennifer. Hi, guys." I walked over to the counter and snuck a peek at what Jennifer was preparing. She had a row of cookie sheets covered with diced butternut squash.

"I tossed them in olive oil and salt and pepper," she said. "They're ready to go into the oven."

"Good job." I walked on. A few feet away Charles was assembling our signature Skinny pizzas, one of our regular menu items.

"Before I forget," he said. "Toni called. She said she was spending the day with someone and would only come in for the dinner shift—but that if you blew a fuse, I should call her back and let her know." He studied me. "Are you going to blow a fuse?"

I was tempted to, but since I knew who the "someone" was—Judy—how could I? "No. It's okay. She doesn't play hooky all that often. This time I'll let her off easy."

But when dinner came around, there was still no sign of her. It wasn't until the evening was almost over that she suddenly popped in by the back entrance. She gave me an apologetic smile and slipped off her coat. "Sorry I'm late."

"Late! You're not late. You were absent all day."

"I wouldn't have come in at all except I need a minute with you."

I pulled off my chef's hat and smoothed a strand. "Uh-oh. I know that tone. What is it?"

She grinned. "Don't worry. It's good news." She pulled out a bottle of chardonnay from the wine cooler, snatched two glasses from the shelf above the plating table, and gestured for me to follow.

I plopped down into my usual seat at the back corner table of the dining room and waited.

"Don't look so worried," she said, handing me a glass. "Trust me. You are going to love me." Whenever Toni said something like that, I just knew she was about to clobber me with bad news. She took a sip of her wine. "You've heard of *Lauren Live*, right?"

I puckered my brow. "Of course." *Lauren Live* was the number-one talk show in the country. "Who hasn't?"

Toni leaned forward excitedly. "Well, I have a friend who works at Global TV. She phoned last night. It seems that one of the guests scheduled for tomorrow morning has cancelled, and you and I got the spot." Her voice rose to a feverish pitch. "We're going to be on TV."

"What?" I had a sudden vision of myself looking chubby and tongue-tied in front of an audience of millions. "You call that good news?"

Toni's smile crumpled. "Of course it is. This is an incredible opportunity. Think of the publicity. Viewers from all over the country will hear about Skinny's on Queen. We'll get so many bookings we'll have to turn customers away."

I cleared my throat. "You're right. It is a great opportunity. *You* do the interview. You'll be much better than I could ever be. You have tons of television experience."

Unlike me, before becoming a chef and restaurateur,

Toni had been a *real* model. She'd appeared in dozens of television commercials, had been interviewed on camera, and had even once played a small role in a movie.

She shook her head, jaw set determinedly. "I am telling you right now, Nicky Landry. You are not squirming your way out of this. We both have to be there. Don't forget, your face is on all our advertisements." Her eyes shone with excitement again. "You can talk about the twenty-five pounds you lost since we developed our Skinny menu."

"You and I both know I didn't lose that weight because of our menu—at least not all of it." The first fifteen or so pounds I'd lost was following what I liked to call my heartbreak diet, after the breakup and subsequent murder of my then-boyfriend. *Don't ask.* As if that hadn't been difficult enough, the stress had become even worse when the police pegged me as the prime suspect. Me. Imagine! It was the first time in my life I'd actually lost my appetite. No wonder the pounds had melted away. What Toni didn't know was that I had since gained back much of that weight—nine pounds to be exact.

I swallowed hard. "I've never been on television. I wouldn't know what to say." Just the thought of all those people watching was already sending me into hyperventilation.

"Come on, Nicky. You have to be there." She picked up her glass. "Besides, you can't back out. I already said yes for both of us."

"That's why you waited until now to tell me, isn't it?"

She smiled, gulped down the rest of her wine and rose from the table. "You'll thank me later." She fished into her purse and pulled out a piece of paper. "Here's the address. Be there tomorrow morning at seven sharp." She disappeared into the kitchen. A moment later I heard the back door open and close.

I stared morosely into my wine. Toni was right. It was an incredible opportunity, one we couldn't pass up. But what in the world could I wear that would make me look thinner on TV? Suddenly, my thoughts were interrupted when the front door opened and a disheveled woman wandered in.

I jumped to my feet and hurried over. "I'm sorry. We're closed for the evening."

The woman stood her ground. There was something unnerving about the way she stared at me.

I smiled uncertainly. "You'll have to come back another day."

"Nice place you got here," she said, and then to my surprise, her face contorted into a mask of fury. She pointed a finger at me, yelling, "It's just too bad you'll have to give it back!"

"What are you talking—"

She cut me off. "Don't imagine for one minute that you're getting away with it. I am going to get even with you if it's the last thing I do."

She was going on so loudly that Charles and Jennifer appeared in the kitchen doorway, looking from her to me, worried. I shook my head slightly, but Charles either didn't see or disregarded my silent message.

He strode over purposefully, taking a protective stance next to me. "What's going on here?" he demanded.

The woman jutted out her chin. "This bitch stole my restaurant from me."

"Your restaurant?" He searched my face. "What is she talking about?"

I shook my head, as confused as he was. "I don't know any more than you do." I spotted the demented gleam in her eyes. As she went on, I became convinced the woman was mentally ill. "Perhaps I could give you a reservation for some other evening," I said pleasantly, looking for a way to calm her. "Would you—"

She took another step forward, jabbing her finger at my arm. "Don't pretend with me. You know damn well what I'm talking about. This restaurant is mine. You think you're going to get away with stealing it from me? I'm going to get it back even if I have to kill you for it."

Whoa. As pacifying as I wanted to be, getting death threats was not something I took idly. Apparently neither did Charles. Before I had a chance to open my mouth, his eyes had narrowed and he stepped forward. "I suggest you leave right now, or I'll call the police."

"Oh, I'm leaving, all right. But this isn't the end of it. You and bitch over here are going to pay." She smiled, but it looked more like a snarl. "If I can't have it, then you sure as hell won't."

Somehow, I snapped out of my shock and concentrated on her appearance. If I had to give her description to the police I had better memorize as much of it as I could. I noted the tangled dark hair, the light blue eyes lit with an eerie brightness. Her clothes looked old and filthy. Her coat was like an oversized tent, making it impossible to gauge her size. Her hands were delicate, without an ounce of excess flesh and with long, chipped red nails. Her legs were encased in high boots, the leather worn and stained with road salt. The heels were dated but high, at least three inches. That made the woman about the same height as me—around five foot four—but thinner.

Charles took another step toward her. I suspected he was trying to look intimidating, but he looked more frightened than frightening. "If you don't leave right now, I'm warning you. I'll call the police." And to punctuate his words he pulled his cell phone from his pocket.

"Fine." She marched out, leaving Charles and me staring mutely at the door as it swung shut.

I recovered my voice. "What the hell was that?"

Charles let out a long breath. "Now there goes what I call a raving lunatic." He attempted a smile. "As scary as she was, I doubt she's dangerous, just nuts. With all the hospital budget cuts, the mentally ill have nowhere to go, so they wander the streets. Nothing to worry about."

It was easy to be brave now that she was gone.

He gave my shoulder a pat. "Why don't you go home and get some sleep? By tomorrow morning you'll have forgotten all about this."

I nodded slowly. "But the real question is, will she have forgotten about us?"

suffocating in a cloud of mac translucent powder

I ARRIVED AT Global TV promptly at seven the next morning. From the street, the industrial building didn't look any different from the others in the area. But inside was a different thing. Rows upon rows of autographed celebrity pictures covered the walls. In the center of the hotel-size foyer, a large circular reception desk held center stage. Sitting behind it was a security guard who must have been a fullback in a previous life. This was more how I'd expected a television station to look.

He peered at me. "Yes?"

"Uh, I'm here for the *Lauren Live* show."

"Talent or audience," he growled. It took a moment for me to understand this was a question.

"Oh, uh, talent I guess."

He asked for identification, checked it against a list and then directed me back outside the building and around to a side entrance. "You'll see a door that says Makeup. That'll be the one."

I thanked him and hurried back out into the freezing cold. I walked briskly to the correct entrance, rang the bell and was buzzed into a long narrow room. Two other doors were marked Greenroom and Studios. At one end of the room were wall-to-wall mirrors, sterile Formica counters and a row of bright makeup lights. Half a dozen guests were in various stages of makeup.

"Will you close the damn door before we all freeze to death?" yelled a young man with long blond hair.

"Oh, sorry." I shut it and stood there unsurely.

"Take off your coat and grab a seat," the same fellow said.

I sat in an age-crackled leatherette salon chair, feeling like an overstuffed sausage in the bodysuit I was wearing under my clothes. I'd bought the garment because it guaranteed to make the wearer look ten pounds thinner instantly—which, considering the weight I'd gained, should make me look my normal size. I'd originally planned to wear only a waist cincher but nixed that idea when, two minutes after struggling to get it on, the damn thing suddenly snap-rolled to my waist.

I pinched myself, still trying to wrap my head around the fact that I was about to sit on the famous lime-green guest chair of the one and only Lauren Long. *I*, Nicky Landry, was about to go live on national television. To what extent would it boost our restaurant business? If the dinner shift became as profitable as our noon shift, that would be amazing. On the other hand, we could barely cope with the hard work involved with one crazy-busy shift a day. Correction, *I* could barely cope. Toni had a knack for getting out of hard work.

As I waited for my turn with a makeup artist, I looked up and down the row of guests being painted and powdered. All the women looked so beautiful. I would look so plain next to them. I was getting more nervous by the second and beginning to feel awfully hot under those makeup lights. I only hoped I wouldn't sweat through my nice silk sweater. Damn Toni for getting me into this. She didn't need me. She could have done it by herself.

Speaking of whom, if this was such a great opportunity, where the hell was she? I glanced at my watch—

seven-thirty. She should have been here by now. Before my concern could turn into full-blown worry, a cadaverously thin young man with jet-black hair and dark eye makeup wandered over. My first impression was of a male punk version of Morticia Addams.

"Good morning, darling. I'm Keith, your makeup artist," he said, leaning in and studying me. "And you are?"

"Nicky. Nicky Landry," I said, slightly uncomfortable under his scrutiny.

Makeup boy lifted my chin for an even closer look. "Hmm. I'll just have to work my magic."

The way he said this made it plenty clear that he had grave doubts about the outcome.

"Not to worry. I'll have you looking gorgeous in no time." He turned away and rummaged through something that looked like a giant tackle box full of cosmetics. He selected a bottle and shook it. He leaned in conspiratorially. "You're going to want to buy some of this. It makes pores the size of Ontario disappear."

"I have large pores?" I wondered why I'd never noticed that. On the other hand, I was a chef. I worked in a hot, steamy kitchen. How could my pores not be large?

"*Gigantic*, darling. Simply *gigantic*."

Normally, any criticism about my looks would have sent me shoveling through a quart of Ben and Jerry's Cherry Garcia at the speed of a wood chipper, but I happened to like my complexion. It was the one thing about me that Toni envied. God knows there was nothing else I had over her, except maybe bigger boobs. But then, everything about me was bigger. Besides, there were worse things in life than having large pores—like makeup-artist boy's enormous nose for example. I decided to not point that out since whether I looked good or not before an audience of millions rested entirely in his hands.

"Earth to Nicky!" He abruptly brought me back to the here and now. "When was the last time you had a facial, darling?" He was seriously beginning to get on my nerves.

"Mmmph."

He proceeded to slather foundation all over my face, including my lips. "Don't try to talk."

He dropped the container of foundation and picked up a concealer stick, which he smoothed under my eyes, much the way a pastry chef would use icing to smooth out cracks in a cake.

"So what are you being interviewed about?" He pulled out some kind of strange contraption, clamped it onto my lashes and squeezed.

"Ouch, ouch!"

"Sit still. How am I supposed to make you look gorgeous when you won't stop squirming?"

"I won't be beautiful if you pull out all my lashes. What the hell is that thing?"

"This?" Keith looked stunned. "Haven't you ever seen an eyelash curler?"

I shook my head mutely and he rolled his eyes. For the next few minutes I kept quiet, praying the torture would soon end. At last Keith stepped back—not a minute too soon—and cocked a hip. "I asked you a question, darling. What are you being interviewed about?"

"Oh, er—my partner and I are the owners of Skinny's on Queen." At his blank look, I explained. "It's a new low-calorie restaurant."

Keith said nothing but I noticed his eyes traveling up and down my body.

"I just lost twenty-five pounds," I said.

"Good for you, darling. I can't imagine having to diet." He patted his ironing-board stomach and shrugged. "I have absolutely no willpower. I eat like a horse. I'm just naturally thin."

That information didn't make me like him one bit more.

He picked up a brush the size of a duster and fluffed loose powder all over my face until I was suffocating in a cloud of translucent powder. By the time I was able to breathe again, I was beet red under all the spackle.

At that moment, the door marked Studios swung open and an officious-looking brunette carrying a clipboard came charging in. "Toni Lawford? Nicky Landry?"

Shit. Where was Toni? At this point I wasn't sure whether I should be angry or worried. Possible scenarios flashed through my mind. Had she made it safely home last night? The image of a masked man pointing a gun to my girlfriend's head popped into my mind. I just as quickly dismissed it. No way. If Toni had been even five minutes late getting home, Steven would have called in a panic.

Maybe she'd had a car accident. God knows she drove that red BMW of hers way too fast. On the other hand, she was also one of the best drivers I knew. Besides, even if she had totaled her car, Toni would have climbed out of the wreckage, brushed off the debris, hailed a cab and hightailed it over here. She might show up late for work, but never for a TV appearance. Maybe she was busy doing her own makeup. Now *that* was more likely.

"Right here, darling." Keith raised his hand. "This gorgeous creature is Nicky. I'm almost done with her."

The woman hoofed it over, tapping her pen against the board. "I'm the floor director." She pointed her pen at me. "You're on in twenty." She looked up and down the row of people in various stages of makeup. "Which one is your partner?"

"She's not here yet, but I'm sure she'll…"

"She's *what?*" For a second, I thought floor-director woman would explode. Her face turned an ugly shade, but just as I expected steam to start blowing out of her ears, she stopped abruptly, took a deep breath and said tightly, in a low voice. "I will remain calm. I will remain calm." She pulled herself together and tapped her watch. "If she's not here in—"

At that moment the exit door opened, letting in a drift of snow and an unhurried Toni. She finger-combed her hair. "Sorry I'm late," she said as casually as I might say, "Would you like the dressing on the side?"

The floor director turned to face her and I steeled myself for fireworks. But the woman took one look at Toni and smiled. "Oh, you're already made up. That's great. You're on in eighteen." She turned and marched back out.

Toni shed her alpaca coat, hung it on a wall hook and turned toward me, revealing a blue shrink-wrap dress and skyscraper heels.

"Didn't you wear boots?" I was shocked. "How can you walk around only half dressed in minus-ten degree weather?"

"I hate boots." She walked languorously over, giving her blond mane a toss. "Besides, the important thing is I look good, right?" Instantly, a dozen pairs of eyes in the room zoomed over to her. I had a flash of my own appearance when I'd walked in—a down-filled coat reminiscent of the Michelin man, a wool cap pulled to my eyelids, a thick scarf wrapped around my neck and up to my nose, and boots that would have kept me warm at the South Pole. I had to hand it to Toni. She sure knew how to make an entrance.

I started getting out of the chair. Keith pushed me back in. "Not so fast. You still need eyebrows, dear." He leaned over with a sharp pencil. "Will you puh-leaze stop wiggling? I'm almost finished." He smiled sweetly to Toni. "Have a seat, darling. I'll be right with you." Toni settled in the chair on my left.

From my right, an elegant silver-haired woman smiled at me through the mirror. "First time on TV?" Her makeup artist—pleasanter-looking than mine—pulled the paper towels from around her collar.

Keith was now painting my mouth, so all I could do was convey my fear with a series of panicky blinks.

The woman chuckled. "Don't worry. All you have to remember is to follow Lauren's lead." She inspected herself in the mirror. "Think of it as a pleasant chat with a girlfriend." *Yeah, right. A chat with a girlfriend—with millions of people watching.* "And if you feel nervous, just take a deep breath."

I would have taken a deep breath right now, except that anything more than shallow breathing was impossible in my bodysuit from hell. I couldn't wait to get out of it. Any exercise more strenuous than a casual stroll would put me in danger of passing out from lack of oxygen.

The woman stepped out of her chair and headed for the door to the greenroom.

Keith stood back and gave me the once-over. "Now you are perfect." He smiled with satisfaction. "Damn, I'm good." He wiped his hands on a paper towel and moved on to Toni. "Hello, darling. You're already all done. I'll just touch you up a bit." He selected a long thin brush from his kit.

I looked in the mirror. To my surprise, I looked… amazing. On my lids, Keith had used smoky café-au-lait shadow, giving my eyes depth and bringing out the green. I leaned closer and noticed that my lashes looked extra long and super thick. That contraption was not solely an instrument of torture after all. Keith may have been a bit on the bitchy side, but he knew what he was doing. "Wow! You *are* good."

He glanced at me over his shoulder. "Told you." He rummaged through his tool kit again and pulled out a small jar. "Trust me. I'll make you gorgeous too, darling," he told Toni. In her case it would take no effort at all. At that moment, his eyes grew wide. "Oh my God. You're Toni Gordon, the supermodel." I wondered why Toni hadn't changed her name back to Gordon after her divorce. Had she subconsciously known that she and Steven would someday be back together?

Toni smiled humbly. "I haven't been a supermodel in a couple of years." The last time she'd been on the cover of a magazine was closer to ten years than two, but I wasn't about to point that out.

"I have all your *Looks* covers," Keith continued to gush as he refreshed her lipstick. "Every cover you've ever done, I've collected. If I'd known I was going to meet you today, I would have brought them for you to autograph."

Toni looked as if she'd died and gone to heaven. "Tell you what. Stop by my restaurant sometime and I'll autograph them for you." She handed him a business card and one of what I liked to call her professional smiles—a dazzling, teeth-baring smile that stretched just a bit too far and flashed just a tad too bright.

After powdering her nose, Keith pulled the tissues from around her neck and stepped back. "*Voilà*. Now, you are perfection."

Toni glanced at herself in the mirror, inspected her teeth for lipstick and nodded with satisfaction. "How's it going with you and Mitchell?"

I frowned. "I haven't heard from him in a few days. Mind you, with the schedule I keep, it's a wonder I ever see him." And then, as an afterthought, I added, "You don't think he's losing interest in me, do you?"

Toni looked at me with knowing eyes. "There you go, being insecure again—insecure and jealous."

"I am not jealous," I snapped.

"Of course not." She rolled her eyes. "I bet you have to stop yourself from following him when he leaves his house, don't you?" I must have looked guilty because she added, "Like I always say, jealousy is just another form of insanity. Better keep your insanity to yourself than to speak and remove all doubt."

Toni had this habit of reeling off an endless series of clichés. Before I could think of a snappy comeback, the floor manager showed up.

"You're on next." She waved us over to the door marked Studio. "Come with me."

She guided us through a long dark hallway littered with coils of large black cables. We emerged onto the set and sat in the famous lime-green leather armchairs next to Lauren Long.

Lauren, an attractive woman with intelligent eyes and a great smile, had been on TV for as long as I could remember. At the moment, she was busy conferring in whispers with a young man wearing very tight jeans and a very tight white T-shirt. If I had a butt like his, I would wear tight jeans too.

"Give me softer light," she was saying. "And move the floodlight a bit to the left."

Next to me, Toni leaned in and murmured, "She's got to be fifty if she's a day, and there's not a wrinkle on her. I wonder who her surgeon is." The way she was study-ing Lauren made me wonder if she was thinking of get-ting a face-lift. I wouldn't have been surprised. Toni was constantly considering some kind of cosmetic surgery.

Before I could ask, a stagehand approached. He crouched, pinning a tiny microphone to my sweater. "Move forward." He went around to my side and attached a battery pack to the back of my waistband. "Try not to touch the mike. It's extremely sensitive."

Beyond the set, three large cameras were gliding across the concrete floor as smoothly as Zambonis on ice. Behind each was a technician wearing earphones and peering through a viewfinder while handling a series of knobs, buttons and dials. Farther back, employees were running around, barking orders at each other. "Give Lauren softer light." "Where's that makeup girl? There you are, sweetheart. Go powder Lauren's nose." And even farther back was the studio audience, a hundred or so people avidly watching our every move. I felt a wave of queasiness.

The director approached, holding a black-and-white clapboard in front of Lauren. He counted backwards, "In five, four, three—" just like in the movies. He slowly backed out of camera range, "—two, one," and gave it a sharp clap.

"And we're back." Lauren smiled at the camera, speaking in a husky voice a good two tones deeper than it had been during the commercial break. "For those of you who are just joining us, today's topics are nutrition and weight loss. Our next guests are two lovely ladies, owners of Skinny's on Queen. Take note of that name, because trust me, you'll want to experience that restaurant."

On the monitor a few feet away, the screen changed to a picture of our restaurant. The old brick storefront had a wide window decorated with black-and-white striped curtains, and the name Skinny's on Queen was spelled out in curly red neon lettering at the top. It looked good, really good. My heart leaped and for a moment I almost forgot to be nervous.

Lauren was speaking. I snapped back to the present. "Please welcome Toni Lawford and Nicky Landry, chefs and co-owners of Skinny's on Queen, and creators of their wonderful Skinny menu."

Applause lights flashed on and off, and the audience clapped energetically.

When the room quieted, Lauren turned to us, still beaming. "Good morning and welcome. How did you come up with the idea of opening a low-calorie restaurant?"

From the corner of my eye I spotted one of the cameras gliding silently over, a red light flashing above it. It was focused on me. *Crap! What am I supposed to do?* I smiled—or at least tried to. But I just knew I looked like a deer caught in headlights. The right corner of my mouth began twitching, and it was a moment before I realized that Lauren was looking at me. *What did she just say?* My mind drew a blank.

"Er…" I began, lamely. Now my right eye was twitching too. I glanced helplessly at Toni.

She took one look at my panicked expression and took over. "Nicky and I recognized the need for a restaurant catering to health—and weight-conscious people." She sounded so professional. "We wanted to create a menu that offered healthy meals—delicious, but low in fat and in sugar."

Lauren nodded knowingly. "Isn't that exactly what this country needs?" She turned to the audience. "How many of you want to lose weight? Let's see a show of hands." There was an instant swell of applause. She nodded. "I'm not surprised. Lately, it seems as if every time I listen to the news or open a paper, there's an article about the obesity problem in this country. We all know that being overweight will cut years off our lives." She continued,

quoting statistics and explaining the link between obesity and diseases like cancer and diabetes. "This problem
is so serious that the next generation will be the first in
recorded history to have a shorter life expectancy than
that of their parents."

Toni nodded in agreement. "Yes, and it is Nicky's and
my belief that restaurants are partly to blame. Rather than
trying to attract customers by offering quality, most restaurants offer quantity, and portions are becoming larger
and larger. As a result, what people nowadays think of
as a normal portion, is actually twice—sometimes three
times—the healthy amount."

Toni sounded great, smart and likable. She had sort
of stretched the truth about how we'd come to adopt our
Skinny menu. The idea had come to me out of sheer desperation, not out of any sense of altruism.

Toni turned to me. "And Nicky has already lost twenty-
five pounds on our meals."

Lauren's sharp eyes focused on me. "Tell us about your
diet, Nicky."

I cleared my throat and found my voice. "The thing
is." I searched for a way to tell the truth without contra-
dicting Toni. "I didn't diet. In fact, I've never been able
to stay on a diet in my life."

Lauren's eyes lit up. "So what you're telling us is that
all you're doing differently this time is eating from your
Skinny menu?"

I avoided a direct answer. "We've created a full menu
offering three-course meals, most of which are lower than
five hundred calories."

"Unfortunately, that's not including the wine," Toni
added laughing.

"But, for those who do want a drink," I said, "they can

order white-wine spritzers. One spritzer has only forty-eight calories."

"Only forty-eight calories?" Lauren echoed, sounding impressed. "I didn't know that. I think spritzers will be my new favorite drink." The audience laughed. "You know what my weakness is? Bread. Please tell me you serve bread in your restaurant."

I nodded. "Oh, absolutely. Bread is my personal weakness too. We've come up with a few recipes for high-fiber bread, one of which is flavored with rosemary. It is so tasty you may never want to eat plain bread again."

"Rosemary-flavored bread—sounds divine." Lauren was so engaging that I found myself forgetting about the cameras. I even forgot about my twitch. "Tell us about the most popular items on your menu."

I told her about our Skinny Fettuccine Alfredo, and about one of our latest hits, a low-fat mulligatawny.

She was asking. I was answering. At one point I caught Toni's eye and she nodded imperceptibly.

Before I knew it, Lauren was thanking us for coming and then said something about being back after the break. The red lights above the cameras turned off. The floor manager took off our microphones and guided Toni and me off the stage.

"Nicky, you did great." She sounded sincere.

"I did? I can't remember a word I said."

"Yes. I loved what you said about hating to diet."

"I said that? I was scared half to death, but I have to admit, this TV thing wasn't so difficult after all."

Toni quirked an eyebrow. "Well, make sure you never get scared half to death twice, or God knows what will happen."

BACK IN THE makeup room, Toni grabbed her coat. "We'd better get to work. Hopefully we'll have the phone ringing off the hook all day."

"I have to stop by the house first. I want to check on Jackie and the puppies."

She gave me an amused smile. "You lie like a rug. You can't wait to find out if Mitchell caught your interview."

"I'm serious. I really have to check on the dogs," I protested weakly. More important, I was dying to get out of my bodysuit. "Besides, I didn't tell Mitchell about the interview."

She chuckled knowingly. "Go. Go. And if he did happen to be watching, let me know what he thought."

I didn't bother answering.

In the two and a half hours I'd been in the Global studios, a blizzard had started and the parking lot was now blanketed in white. My smart car was covered with a half foot of fluffy snow.

"Oh, hell. I hate winter," I cried, marching off toward my car with Toni on my heels. Using the sleeve of her alpaca coat, she brushed the snow off my windshield.

"What are you doing? You'll wreck your coat," I exclaimed, shocked. Taking in the fine overstitch around the collar and down the front, I said, "It looks expensive. How much did that lovely little number set you back?"

"You don't want to know." She snapped one of the wipers against the windshield. Chips of ice went flying.

She was probably right. Toni could spend more on one garment than I did on my mortgage every month. That was another thing Toni had, that I didn't—money—which was why she'd been able to bankroll our restaurant when we first opened. My contribution had been what she called sweat equity. Without her money, I would most likely be a sous-chef somewhere at best, and years away from running my own kitchen. I owed my friend a huge debt of gratitude for the opportunity she had offered me.

Toni brushed the snow off her sleeve. "See you at work." She pulled her car fob from her pocket, pressed the button, and a few yards away her BMW roared to life. She hopped into her car, turned on her wipers and waved goodbye, leaving me blowing warm air into my frozen hands. I must admit, once in a while I did envy Toni her money. Today, standing in the cold and watching her leave in her big warm car, was one of those times.

THIRTY MINUTES LATER, I pulled to a stop on the now snow-covered pad behind my house, relieved that my golf cart—as Toni referred to my car—had made it home safely on the ice-covered streets.

I sludged around the side of the house through the ankle-deep snow to let myself in by the front entrance. That way, if Mitchell happened to be looking out I could casually wave him over. I kept my fingers crossed that he might catch a glimpse of me today. It wasn't every day I was made up by a professional and looked amazing.

Having my boyfriend living right next door should have been great. At least that was what I thought when we first started dating. A smile as I came up my walk, the whiff of something delicious I was cooking, or simply a quick phone call should be all it took for him to hop over the wrought iron fence that divided our front stoops and come knocking at my door. In reality, living in such close proximity—one thin, sound-carrying common wall apart—was not always wonderful. Every time I waved at him, I was afraid he'd feel obligated to come over. Then, if I didn't wave, I worried he'd think I was ignoring him. And of course there was the uncontrollable desire to put my ear to the wall when I heard the phone ring in his house, and spy on his comings and goings when his door slammed. Whenever he left looking scrumptious, I'd wonder where he was going, who he was meeting.

Toni was right. I did have to stop myself from following him. I wondered if he felt claustrophobic, having me just next door. Would it be better for both of us if we lived farther apart? I'd been wondering a lot about that lately.

Last summer, after my ex-boyfriend's untimely death, the last thing in the world I was looking for was another relationship. But Mitchell moved in next door, and he was cute. At first, I didn't know what to make of him. Here was a mid-thirties man who spent all his time sitting by the window instead of going to work like a normal person. Until I learned that he was a writer, and that his desk sat in front of the living room window, I thought he might be a peeping Tom, or maybe under house arrest. We became friends, and then gradually the friendship ignited into a romance.

After making sure the puppies' crate was clean, that the water bowls were full and they were all comfortable, I checked the phone for messages—still nothing. I ignored my disappointment and headed back out to my car, using the front entrance again, just in case he happened to be looking out the window. I was halfway down the walk when I heard a door open and my named called out.

Mitchell. I swung around, hoping I didn't look too overjoyed. It was just my paranoia at work, but I couldn't shake the worry that showing too much enthusiasm for a man would only send him running in the opposite direction.

I gave him a casual wave. "Hey, what's up?"

"Hey, yourself. Got time for coffee?"

I glanced at my watch, my heart dancing with joy, and gave him a teasing smile. "I guess I can spare a few minutes."

He held the door open for me and took my coat, his dark eyes holding mine. No wonder I'd fallen for him. He was tall—just under six feet—and just so happened to have a really nice butt, which I eyed appreciatively as I followed him.

Considering his kitchen was a mirror copy of mine, it couldn't have looked any more different. Let me start by saying that mine wouldn't appeal to just anyone. One would need to be a lover of all things old to like it, starting with my 1927 Beach gas stove. It was butter-yellow with black trim, and sported a lid that covered the burners when not in use. I'd found the relic on eBay and had it shipped all the way from Winnipeg at a cost of over twice the purchase price. I didn't care. There was something oddly comforting about that old cast-iron cooker. Maybe because it reminded me of my grandmother's kitchen and all the hours she and I spent together baking oatmeal cookies and chocolate cakes. That stove now held center stage in mine, alongside a decades-old refrigerator I'd had refinished to match at a local body shop.

My love for everything retro didn't stop there. There were the antique high cupboards with glass panes I'd salvaged and lovingly stripped and repainted, the old wood floor I'd sanded and lacquered, and the open shelves on which I displayed all my Blue Willow dishes. I liked to think of it as French country—charming and romantic in a non-fussy sort of way.

Mitchell's kitchen was as masculine as mine was not—
charmless yellowed-oak cabinets from three decades
ago, a white fridge with faded decals, inherited no doubt
from somebody's basement or garage. The stove was har-
vest gold, which I might not have minded so much had
it worked. On the other hand, as Mitchell pointed out, he
owned a microwave. So why would he even need a stove?
And he was happy with any fridge as long as it kept his
beer cold and his frozen dinners frozen.

So what if my man wasn't exactly sophisticated. I
didn't care. In fact, that was something I rather liked about
Mitchell. Unlike his predecessor, I didn't have to do som-
ersaults to impress him. It was a refreshing change.

He brushed a lock of hair from my forehead, anchor-
ing it behind my ear, his eyes holding mine. He leaned in
and kissed me, making me almost swoon. "A few minutes to spare, you say?" He smiled wickedly. "Does that
mean you'll only have a half cup instead of a mug? And
I suppose I'll have to forget about nibbling on your neck,
and your shoulders and your—"

I put a hand to his mouth. Considering his lack of ability in the kitchen—something he more than made up for
with his talent for kissing—he could make a mean cup
of coffee. I smiled back, holding his gaze. "Well, let's not
exaggerate. Pour me a mug by all means."

I climbed onto a bar stool and planted my elbows on
the counter, wondering what he wanted to talk about. And
then I noticed the way he seemed so very concentrated on
pouring the coffee, and I guessed that whatever he wanted
to tell me was probably not good news.

He handed me the quart of milk.

"Thanks." I poured a few drops in my coffee and took
a sip. "Mmm, good."

He cleared his throat. "Sorry if I haven't had much

time for you lately, Nicky. I've been working like mad on the edits."

"And how's it going?"

He shrugged, looking miserable. "Not great. My deadline is coming up fast, and if I don't finish in time, I'll break contract." He scowled. "And if that happens, not only could they back out of it, but I'd have to reimburse them my advance." He gave me an apologetic smile. "Which is why…" Long pregnant pause. My mouth dried. "I've decided to take her suggestion," he continued, "and go to New York to work on the editing with her in person."

I managed to keep the whine from my tone. "And when are you leaving?"

"Tomorrow."

I had not once thought of wondering how old this editor was, or what she looked like. Now, I pictured her as some lithesome blonde with sultry eyes. I had a sudden vision of Mitchell dining at some dimly lit restaurant, having a whispered conversation with his sexy editor, who just so happened to be enamored with her hot new author. I swallowed hard. "How long will you be away?"

"No more than two weeks."

"Oh, two weeks isn't that long." *Hopefully not long enough for some gorgeous babe to work her magic on you.* "You can get it all done in that time?"

"If it takes longer, I'll be in deep shit."

In more ways than one, sweetheart. I jutted out my bottom lip, copying a sexy pout I'd seen Toni do very effectively on a few occasions. "I'll miss you."

It must have worked because his smile lit the room. "I promise I'll think of you all the time."

"You will?"

"Every minute of every hour." That might have

sounded more romantic without the teasing glint in his eyes. "By the way, you look amazing today."

"That's because I was on television this morning." I gave my hair a toss, à la Toni, but only succeeded in whipping a lock into my eyes. I brushed it away.

"You were on TV? Why didn't you tell me?"

"I figured you'd be too busy to watch."

"Even so, I could have recorded the show and watched it later."

I told him all about the interview over a second cup of coffee, and by the time I left for work, what little lip gloss I'd had left was gone, and his nice shirt was wearing more makeup than I was. It almost made up for the fact that he would be gone for two weeks. *Almost*.

a steady flow of fat paychecks in my future

I WALKED INTO the restaurant, fighting against the wind to close the door, and slipped out of my parka. From the back of the room where he'd been setting a table, Jake came to a full stop, giving me an appreciative stare just as Charles came out of the kitchen. "Oh. My. God. You look amazing."

"I do?" I said, hoping he'd say it again.

He strode over. "You are *hot*," he gushed, opening his arms for a hug, and squeezing until I squealed. This was an even better reaction than I'd had from Mitchell. "Hey, Jennifer, guys," he called over his shoulders. "Nicky's here." He stepped back, studying me closely. "You should always wear your makeup that way." I guess Mitchell's smooching hadn't erased *all* of it.

He and Toni were two of a kind, forever trying to convince me to glam up. Since the ad campaign, using my before and after pictures, I was making more of an effort. I now routinely wore mascara and lip gloss, but that was as far as I would go. As far as I was concerned, spending hours putting on makeup when it would only melt away in our hot and steamy kitchen was a complete waste of time.

"Enjoy it while you can because I refuse to spend half an hour painting my face every morning."

The guys came pouring out of the kitchen, staring at me as if I were some new dish they were considering for our menu. Jennifer walked over, staring closely at my makeup.

"She looks great, doesn't she?" asked Jake, nodding his approval.

"You sure do," said Jennifer. "I wish I could do my eyes that way."

I swear, I was liking that girl more all the time.

Marley and Jake gathered round. "Way to go."

"You look hot."

Toni waltzed in from the back, still wearing her shrink-wrap dress. "You won't believe the buzz from our interview. The phone has been ringing off the hook. We're booked solid for the next month."

Jake grabbed the reservations book, setting it on a table and pulling me a chair. "It's true. Look."

I sat and he flipped page after page, and indeed many of the spaces were filled. "I wouldn't call that booked solid. There are what, ten or twelve dinner reservations a day?"

"That's already twice as many dinner customers as we usually get," Toni said.

"And the calls are still coming in," added Jake. "I bet by the end of the day all the spaces will be filled. You'll see." He started toward the kitchen and stopped. "Before I forget, Edna Jamieson called."

The name sounded vaguely familiar. "Who's she?"

He shrugged. "She's a regular, comes in at least three or four times a week. I'm sure you must have noticed her. She's middle aged and tiny—under five feet tall. She has gray hair and tends to wear tweeds and jeweled brooches."

Toni's eyebrows rose. "I think Edna could use a fashion consultant."

I frowned. "What does she want?"

He shrugged. "All I know is she's nuts about our brownies. She asked me for the recipe but I wouldn't give it to her. And then she insisted on speaking to you personally. Maybe she thinks you're a softer touch and will give in to her." He handed me a piece of paper with her name and telephone number.

I groaned. Patrons often asked for our recipes. There was no way we would share them, but I should still give her a call. I stuffed it into my pocket, intending to give her a call later.

"That's not all," Charles added. "You also got a call from the *Toronto Daily*. They want you to call them back." He raised his eyebrows, announcing dramatically, "I bet they want to write an article about the restaurant."

Toni gasped. "You didn't tell me that."

He grinned. "I wanted to tell you both at the same time."

"Oh my God. We'll be rich." Toni looked as if she'd just won the lottery, which was ridiculous considering she already was rich.

I was envisioning the steady flow of fat paychecks in my future, and then, "Oh my God, we'll be so busy," I blurted, horror-stricken as I thought of all the difficulties our little business could encounter if it grew too fast.

Over the past few months, business had improved enough that we'd added four more tables to our original six, almost doubling our seating capacity. But even with all those extra customers, we were still no more than a small neighborhood restaurant. Sure, we got lineups at lunch, but our dinner clientele still lagged. In the aftermath of today's television interview and its ensuing rush, however, that just might change. I couldn't help but wonder if being more successful might not bring as many problems as advantages.

As it was, the restaurant was closed only one day a week—Mondays. And we each took a turn taking nights off. This meant I worked six days a week, five of which

I finished late, leaving me only one full day off for personal chores and errands, and one evening free for my private life. If we got any busier, when was I supposed to find time for love? The success of this restaurant was, of course, my priority. But on my list of important things, romance came in a close second. I sighed. It was a good thing Mitchell lived right next door and worked from home, otherwise we'd never find time to see each other. We'd have to start planning breakfast dates. I had a quick image of myself in a sexy peignoir, serving him eggs Benedict or omelets. I walked into the kitchen, smiling secretly.

I grabbed my chef's jacket and glanced at the daily menu board posted above the plating counter. Today the specials were butternut squash soup and a pear-and-walnut salad with gorgonzola dressing. I went to the walk-in refrigerator, picked up a crate of squash and hefted it to the counter. I set to work, chopping the squash into cubes, tossing them with nutmeg, salt, pepper and oil, and then popping them in the oven to roast. Meanwhile, I silently continued my internal debate about the whole lifestyle versus financial success question.

More business meant more money. With more money, we could hire more staff. And more staff would translate into more time off—time I could spend with Mitchell. Now, *there* was an incentive. It also meant I could pay off my bills sooner. That would be really nice too.

Suddenly, the bell above the door chimed as the first customers arrived. Jake hurried out front to greet them, and soon our kitchen became a madhouse. Pots were boiling. Pans were sizzling. Charles and Jennifer cooked and stirred over our hot and steamy stove, bumping into each other with every move. Meanwhile Marley chopped and diced as fast as he could. His dreadlocks, tied in a bun under his hairnet, were bouncing along with the rhythm of his knife. And even with Scott pitching in with the food preparation, we could still barely keep up.

I glanced around. "Where's the gorgonzola dressing I just made? It was on the plating table a minute ago."

"Oh, you mean this?" Charles pointed to a jug near the dishwashing sink. "I thought it was old gravy, ready to throw out."

I sighed deeply and raised my eyes to the ceiling. "God, give me the patience."

Charles burst into laughter. "Just kidding."

"That was about as funny as a kick in the butt," Jennifer said, pulling out quiches from the oven.

"She's right," I said. I placed a hand on my racing heart. "You nearly gave me a heart attack. Okay, enough with the funny stuff. Get back to work, everyone."

As they returned to their feverish pace I looked around, trying to imagine more workers in our already tight kitchen. I couldn't see how it was possible. Maybe we could cram in one extra helper, but we'd be really tight. *Sigh*. So much for the idea of more staff.

Suddenly, Toni grabbed me by the elbow, pulling me to the swinging door. "Take a look at this," she said, pushing it open a crack. "Have you ever seen anything so wonderful?"

Our dining room, which we'd decorated on a shoestring budget, was bright and inviting. The walls were covered with a multitude of old gold-leafed mirrors. Some were chipped, some were cracked, but the flaws only added to the charm of the place. We'd painted the ugly, eighteen-foot ceiling a velvety black, against which the crisscross of rusty old metal pipes overhead seemed to disappear. The tables and chairs were a mishmash of styles, which we'd coordinated by painting them all fuchsia, adding a welcome splash of color against the black-and-white tiled floor.

The room looked amazing. It was twelve-thirty—the peak of lunchtime rush hour—and it was filled to capacity. *Amazing.* And still more customers stood at the entrance, waiting for an available table. *Totally amazing!*

I was taking all this in when Toni nudged me with an elbow. "Imagine, just a couple of months ago we were on the verge of bankruptcy. Now, we have to start thinking about opening a second location."

"What!" I swiveled to face her. "No way—we're finally starting to make money. I haven't even caught up on my credit-card debt. I don't want to open a second restaurant and risk what little success we've already achieved."

"You know what I always say," she said. I braced myself for one of her clichés. She gave me a gleeful smile. "'You can't steal second base and keep your foot on first.'"

Just once I wished I could come up with a smart retort when I needed it, instead of hours later.

At that moment, Jake came bursting through the door, almost knocking Toni off her feet. "Oh, uh, sorry. Where's that Skinny Fettuccine for table three?" he demanded, looking harried.

"Coming right up." I rushed back to the stove, glancing at Toni over my shoulder. "It might be a good idea to take care of the restaurant we already have before you start making plans for a second one, wouldn't you say?"

She smiled knowingly. "Just think about it. You'll see I'm right." She returned to plating, humming happily.

By midafternoon, the welcome lull arrived at last. The day was not half over and we were already damp from exertion.

Toni grabbed a paper napkin and, lifting her hair, wiped the back of her neck, managing to make the gesture seem sexy. How did she do that? If I were to do the exact same thing, I'd only look sweaty and unattractive.

She glanced at her watch. "Good grief, we'll hardly have time to recover before we have to start getting ready for the dinner rush."

"So much for the joys of success," I said. Bah, who was I kidding? The busier we were, the more I loved it, even if it did mean more pressure. It was all good stress, the kind I thrived on. "By the way, Toni, I didn't tell you what happened after you left last night—a woman barged in and threatened to kill us."

"What?" Her eyes grew wide as I told her what had happened. "Do you think she meant it? Shouldn't we call the police and report her?"

"I thought about it, but what are they going to do? Take a statement and then forget about it."

"You're probably right." She shrugged and made a big show of looking at her watch yet again, this time her eyebrows giving an exaggerated jump. "Uh-oh," she said. I'd seen that fake surprised look before. And sure enough, a fake apology followed. "I hate to do this to you, sweetie. I know how busy you are, but I really have to run. You can cope without me for one evening, can't you?"

"Not so fast." I planted my hands on my hips. "Where do you think you're going? Your night off isn't until Thursday. Besides, you already took the whole day off yesterday."

She planted her hands on her hips, in a mocking imitation of me. "Tell you what—*you* can take two nights off next week. How's that?"

I groaned. "It's not a question of keeping count. It's just that we're busier than we've ever been. We need all hands on deck. You have a date, don't you? A date with Steven?"

She shook her head. "No, with Judy."

"Have you told him about her yet?"

"No," she answered abruptly.

I wrinkled my forehead. "Is everything all right between you and Steven?"

She flipped back a lock of blond hair and smiled. "All right? I'll say. That man has one thing on his mind. Sex! He wants it when he wakes up. He wants it in the middle of the day. He wants it before bedtime and even in the middle of the night."

By now, the guys were frozen on the spot, no doubt waiting for more juicy details.

Jennifer walked by with a pot of something that smelled delicious. She winked. "All I can say is I hope his right hand is getting a really good workout."

This time Toni hooted. "That's a good one."

I stifled a laugh. Toni had just met her match. I threw Jennifer a grin. She did likewise.

Without another word, Toni slipped into her coat, grabbed her bag and waltzed out. "See you tomorrow."

I stared at the door. "Well how do you like that?"

Charles joined me. "Off to play with her sister again, is she? It's like she's trying to catch up with the childhood they didn't have."

"I think you hit the nail on the head," I said, and then brought the subject back to the here and now. "So what did we decide would be the special tonight?"

"Eggplant Parmesan—remember? I just perfected a two-hundred-and-fifty-calorie version that tastes divine."

"Oh, right." We'd gradually added a number of wonderful low-cal dishes to our repertoire until we now had a different dinner special for every night of the week. We often tested our new recipes on our lunch crowd, moving them onto our dinner menu when they rated high with everyone. "Sounds yummy—is everything ready to go in the oven?"

"Not even close. Lunch was so crazy busy we didn't have a minute to start."

"Well then," I said, grabbing my chef's jacket. "Let's get this show on the road, people."

In the walk-in refrigerator I found a large cardboard box full of eggplants and preselected cheeses. And for the next hour, everybody sliced, diced, chopped and grated until we had a dozen large casserole dishes ready to pop into the oven. By the time the first batch was ready, and dinner customers were walking in, I kept expecting the crazy woman of the night before to come storming in.

Hopefully Charles had been right—nothing to worry about. But for some reason, I couldn't shake off the feeling that we hadn't heard the last from her.

i call it rabbit food

It was ten forty-five and the kitchen was clean, dishes were washed and stacked neatly on the stainless steel shelves. The floor was swept and the counters sterilized. With nothing left to clean, we waited patiently for our last customers—who were taking their own sweet time—to leave.

Jake nudged the kitchen door open a crack and sneaked a peek. "They haven't even picked up the bill yet."

Marley glanced at me. "Maybe Jake should go over and pick up the bill folder. That should give them the hint."

I turned and stared at him. "Sorry, Marley. We run a classy joint here. We don't want our customers to feel rushed." And then taking pity on them, I added, "But you, Scott, Jennifer and Charles can leave." They sighed with relief and headed for the swinging door.

"Not through the dining room," I whispered. "Use the back door."

Scott, Jennifer and Charles almost ran out—no doubt worried I might change my mind.

"You can go too, Marley," I said.

He shook his head, looking embarrassed. "I'm waiting for Jake."

Jake grinned. "We just moved in together."

I'd known about their relationship for a while now, and was happy for them. Lately it seemed that love was all around me, everybody happy. I felt a shiver run down my spine, as if thinking such a happy thought would bring bad luck. How silly of me, I thought, shrugging off the ridiculous thought.

Now, he peeked through the doorway again. "Yesss!" He pumped the air with his fist. "He just pulled out his credit card." He waited another minute and, adopting a regal bearing, entered the dining room.

A minute later I joined the couple as they rose. "I hope you enjoyed your meal," I said, escorting them to the door.

"It was delicious," the woman replied. She was an attractive middle-aged woman with caramel-colored hair and intelligent eyes. "I can't believe how good the food was, considering this is a diet place. My husband was certain he'd hate everything on the menu."

He gave me an embarrassed smile. "I don't usually go for diet food."

She chuckled. "He calls it rabbit food. I had to plead with him to come."

He went on, sounding surprised. "But everything you served tasted normal." I laughed, and he quickly explained. "I mean, who'd expect to see pasta on a low-cal menu?"

"Well, I'm glad you enjoyed your meal. And I hope we'll see you again."

"You can count on it."

I retrieved the last two coats for them from the rack behind the cash register. At last they turned to leave. I opened the door, standing aside for them. "Thank you for coming."

"You'll see us again," she said, giving a small wave.

I shut the door behind them, glowing from the compliments. Jake appeared with both our coats.

"Did you hear what they said?" I asked. "They loved the food."

He handed me my coat. "You say this like it's a surprise."

"I still have to pinch myself that we're doing well."

"Well, get used to it. If you think you're working hard now, I predict business is only going to get busier."

"Knock wood." I rapped the nearest table with my knuckles. In my experience, whenever everything went too well, something bad was bound to happen.

THE WEATHER HAD grown progressively worse all day, until now the wind howled like a wolf, and the light snow of earlier had turned into a wet drizzle. I crossed the street, holding my coat tightly against the storm and glancing around nervously for the crazy woman. There was no sign of her. I breathed a sigh of relief and made a mad dash to my car. I stopped ten feet away.

"Oh, shit." My tiny smart car was completely covered in a mound of crusty snow. Just a few days earlier I'd purchased an ice scraper and snow brush for just such an emergency, but they were now neatly and uselessly stored *inside* my car. A fat lot of good they were doing me there.

"Oh shit," I repeated, grappling through my purse for some kind of a tool. I came away with my maxed-out Visa card. It wasn't perfect, but it was better than nothing. A good ten minutes of scraping and wiping later, I had removed enough ice to reach the handle and after another ten minutes or so of struggling with it, I finally got the door open.

I climbed in and rubbed my hands together for warmth. My card was ruined. Not that it made any difference. I wouldn't have been able to use it until it was paid off in at least another few months. I turned on the motor and waited for the defrost button to kick in. Gradually, its warmth melted the ice on the windshield until I could use the wipers to push off the rest of it.

I slipped my hand in my pocket and felt a piece of paper. I pulled it out, recognizing it as the one Jake had given me, with that client's name and number. I'd been so busy all day, I'd clear forgotten to give her a call. Tomorrow, I told myself.

At last, I put the car in gear and slip-slided along the icy streets until I pulled onto the parking pad behind my house.

Only then did I realize how tense I'd been during that short drive. As much as I loved my smart car—lime green on a silver body and cheap on gas—it was not designed as a winter car. On the other hand, it was only November, for God's sake. Who the hell expected Toronto to get five inches of snow at this time of year? One of the reasons I'd moved here from Montreal six years ago was because everybody knew Toronto winters were so much shorter and milder. *Hah!*

I lumbered through the melting snow, which was now the consistency of creamed corn, and pounded my feet on the frozen outside mat. I walked into the mudroom, closed the door and was instantly assailed by the yipping and yapping of the two puppies.

"Sit," I ordered, and two little butts hit the floor at the same time. I punched in my alarm code and fished some doggie treats from the bowl on the parson's table by the door. "Good doggies, yes, you are such good doggies." I praised them, feeding them each an itty-bitty piece. "Where's your mama? How come she's not taking care of you?"

Jackie Chan was lazing on the oversized cushion in the corner.

"Come, Jackie." She looked at me blearily. "What's the matter, little girl? Are you finding it tough being a full-time mama?"

She gave me a you-don't-know-the-half-of-it look.

"Too bad, but you're getting no sympathy from me.
You wanted to go gallivanting around? Well, now you
have to pay the piper." She buried her nose under her
front paws, another attempt no doubt, to elicit sympathy. I walked right by and picked up the phone—no messages. My heart sank. The long day had left me tense, and
I would have loved to hear Mitchell's voice. I glanced at
my watch and calculated. By this time tomorrow he would
be in New York.

I hung up and returned to the mudroom, thinking
about that crazy woman again. Perhaps because last
night I'd been anxious about the upcoming television
interview, I hadn't given much thought to her threats.
But tonight I couldn't get her out of my mind. She had
sounded insane, going on and on about us stealing her
restaurant. I only hoped Charles was right about her not
being dangerous.

I turned to Jackie, who had been watching me motion-
less since I'd come in. "What do you think, Jackie? Was
that lady dangerous or just crazy?" She tilted her head,
looking puzzled.

"Want to go for a walk?" Now, this, Jackie understood.
She went into immediate hysteria, jumping and barking
for joy. If she could have done cartwheels, she would
have. "Okay, but only for two minutes. It's cold out there."

I zipped her into her winter coat and clipped on her
leash. "Honestly, Jackie, you are sorely trying my patience. If you don't stop wiggling, we won't be going anywhere."

I gave her my most serious look, but she called my
bluff. That dog knew damn well I wanted to go for that
walk even more than she did. The truth was that I wanted

to walk past Mitchell's again, even knowing all I'd see was a house bathed in darkness, and that it would only amplify my feelings of loneliness.

careening toward me at a dizzying speed

THE NEXT MORNING I woke up feeling optimistic. I hadn't slept much more than six hours but it was all I'd needed. After obsessing about that crazy woman's threats for a while, I'd finally put the whole episode behind me. It was silly to keep worrying about her. The confrontation had been two nights ago and since then, nothing.

Today was going to be a good day. It was shopping day. Twice a week I headed for St. Lawrence Market, one of my favorite places in the world. Every trip there was a treasure hunt for some interesting new ingredients to flavor our recipes.

I parked my car in the lot across the street from the cavernous old building that had been home to the market for over a century. After arming myself with half a dozen recyclable bags, I spent a leisurely hour strolling from booth to booth.

The place was a feast for the senses. There were countless stalls overflowing with a plethora of wonderful foods. And each was a jumble of colors and textures—bright reds, fresh greens, rich purples and dazzling oranges. And the blend of odors, some sharp and savory, others sweet and fruity. Each visit was a heady experience.

Nosing around a cheese counter, I uncovered a feta from France.

"Would you like to taste it?" the old man behind the stall asked. He cut off a small piece, which he offered on the end of his knife. I placed it on my tongue, waiting for the explosion of flavor on my taste buds. It was milder, the texture creamier, just perfect for a new dish I was working on. I bought a large chunk of it. A few stalls further I bought farm-fresh eggs and aromatic herbs.

There was something almost spiritual about these shopping expeditions. I always returned to work in a good mood. Soon, my bags were full and even loaded with their weight I felt reenergized.

I zipped back along Queen Street and—talk about being lucky—after circling the block only twice I found a parking spot so tiny, only my smart could fit in. And, joy of joys, it was only half a block from work. I cranked my steering wheel and backed in.

A few minutes later I was crossing the street, my arms full of groceries. I was already conjuring ways I could use the gorgeous black trumpet mushrooms I'd scored.

Suddenly somebody shouted, "Watch out!"

The woman was frantically pointing down the street. A car was careening toward me at a dizzying speed. For a split second my legs froze, my feet glued to the asphalt.

I was about to be run over.

All at once, I broke into a sprint, but on the slippery road I felt like I was running in place. The car was only a few yards away and bearing down on me fast. I glanced at the sidewalk, eyeballing the distance to safety. It was only a few feet away. I could do it. I *had* to do it. In a last burst of adrenaline, I made a desperate leap, legs stretched in midair like a pole-vaulter's. But, just as I thought I was out of danger, the car hit me. I went rolling over the hood of the car, and over its roof, and then I came crashing down on the ice-covered ground.

I lay on the icy road, numb, something warm running down my face. Oh, no. I was bleeding. I brushed a hand over my forehead. Thank God, I could move. I expected to come away with it covered in blood, but my hand was yellow—egg yolk. So maybe I wouldn't die. I glanced down at myself. I had feta crumbled all over me, crushed tomatoes, oregano, basil—hell, I was a tossed salad.

Suddenly Charles appeared over me, his eyes filled with worry. "Are you all right? I saw everything from the window."

The fall had knocked the wind out of me. I struggled to catch my breath. "I—I—"

"Don't try to move. I'll call an ambulance." He fished through his pocket, pulled out his cell and punched in a number. "I need an ambulance, corner of Queen and Niagara. Someone's just been hit by a car."

I struggled to sit up but a sharp pain tore through my ankle. "Aaarrhhhh."

"I told you not to move." He pushed me back down.

By then a crowd was beginning to form. Witnesses were recounting what they'd seen. Bits and pieces of what they were saying drifted over.

"That driver was aiming right for her."

"The car sped up just before it hit her."

"Did you get the license plate?"

"It was a big black sedan."

"It was an old beat-up car."

"No, it was brand new."

From the pitch of their voices, they could have been talking about a great movie they'd just seen.

"Charles," I muttered through my pain. "Will you call Toni? I don't think I'll be able to work today."

"How can you think about work at a time like this?" Suddenly Jennifer appeared at my side with a rolled-up tablecloth, which she gently placed under my head. Shock must have been settling in because I couldn't stop shivering. She hurried back to the store, returning again, this time with a coat that she threw over me. I was still lying there, gritting my teeth and counting the seconds until the ambulance arrived. Taking one of my hands in hers, she leaned over and whispered, "You'll be all right. Don't worry."

How could I not worry? I wanted to ask. Somebody had just tried to kill me.

ever-changing ceilings flashing by

I WAS WHISKED onto a stretcher and rushed, sirens blaring, to St. Timothy's Hospital, the same hospital where my ex-boyfriend Rob used to work. I had been there countless times during the two years he and I were together. I wondered if I might run into a nurse or a doctor I knew. I would have given anything for a familiar and sympathetic face right now.

The ambulance came to a stop and the doors flew open. I was in the grips of pain, vaguely aware of a series of ever-changing ceilings flashing by as I was wheeled from one area to another. At last a nice doctor—I would have nominated him for sainthood—gave me an injection, and the pain dulled. I became drowsily aware of people shouting orders, someone bending over me, a light being shined in my eyes, being asked dozens of questions and pronounced free from concussion. And then yet another ceiling whizzed by.

Suddenly a pleasant-looking woman was leaning over me. She had kind eyes. "Got into a bit of an accident, didn't you? Don't worry. We'll have you fixed in no time." She covered me with a heavy blanket—an X-ray shield, I realized. She swung a large machine hanging from a mechanical arm and adjusted it over me. "Try not to move your leg."

I wouldn't have moved it for anything in the world, not even cherry pie and ice cream, for which I would normally have jumped through hoops. She disappeared behind a door, and there was a loud clang accompanied by a flash of light. She repeated the process a number of times with the machine at various angles over my leg.

She reappeared and relieved me of the blanket. "All done," she said in a chirpy voice. "I'll have the pictures ready for your doctor in a few minutes." I was rolled back to the emergency room and into a cubicle surrounded by a faded blue privacy curtain.

The pain had given way to a pleasant buzz when a young man in a scrub suit looked down at me.

I met his eyes and smiled. "Hey, doc, it doesn't hurt nearly so much anymore. When can I go home?" The corner of his mouth twitched the way Toni's did when she suppressed a smile. He looked young. He couldn't have been more than a teenager. "Are you sure you're a doctor?"

This time the smile reached his eyes. "I promise you I am." He picked up my chart and rattled off a long explanation of my injuries, ending with, "In other words what you have is a pilon fracture in the distal tibia." The only words I understood were *fracture* and *tibia*, which I knew was a leg bone.

"The knee bone's connected to the leg bone. The leg bone's connected to—" I recited. "Can you say that again, but this time in English?" I knew I was being silly, but I didn't care.

"You have a broken ankle. We've secured your leg in a splint for now, where it won't move until we get you a cast."

"Can't you just put me in a cast now and send me home? I have to get back to work."

He glanced from the chart in his hands, to me, his eyebrows shifting upwards. "I'm afraid you won't be going home today. As a matter of fact you won't be going back to work for a while. Your shinbone is broken at the ankle joint. That kind of break can be challenging to manage, especially when associated with significant soft-tissue injury. That's why we'll have Dr. Goodall take a look at you. He's an orthopedic surgeon."

I swallowed hard, my warm fuzzy feeling of a minute ago quickly evaporating. "A-a surgeon? Does that mean I'll need an operation?"

Rather than answer directly he went into another long explanation, concluding with, "All those options are available to treat these fractures, but the condition of the soft tissues is crucial."

"Oh, er...so when is this surgeon going to look at my ankle?"

"He's been notified. He should be here within the next couple of hours." And before I could ask any more questions, he flipped my chart closed and clipped it back to the front of my bed. "Do you want the curtain open or closed?"

"Open, please."

He pulled it open and left. I was lying there, still reeling from the news that my leg might be cut open, when Toni peeked in.

She waved, crossing the room. Her stiletto heels clickety-clicked on the linoleum floor. Her open coat swung elegantly. "You poor thing, I can't believe what happened. The nurse told me your ankle is broken. Is the pain terrible?"

"It was, but some angel of a doctor gave me a shot of something."

She chuckled. "If you wanted drugs, there are easier ways to get them, you know. You didn't have to risk your life."

I wasn't amused. "Just my luck—when the restaurant

is crazy busy. Oh, I have a favor to ask. Until I can get out of here, would you mind making sure Jackie and the puppies are all right?"

"Don't worry about the restaurant. We'll manage fine without you."

I wasn't sure whether I was happy to hear this or not.

"As for the dogs, I'll move into your place until you get out of here."

"You don't have to do that. Just stop in four or five times a day, let Jackie out, change the wee-wee pads every few hours and maybe spend a bit of time with them. As long as they have food and plenty of water, they'll be all right. I'll probably get out of here tomorrow."

"I think you're being a bit optimistic." She raised a perfectly arched eyebrow. "Don't worry. I don't mind staying over a few days. I want those doggies to be well taken care of." She grinned. "After all, that cute little Trouble is mine."

"Thanks, Toni. I really appreciate it."

She looked down at my wrapped ankle. "I know you probably don't feel lucky at the moment, but it could have been so much worse. From what I heard, that car was going pretty fast."

My stomach did a strange little lurch the way it did whenever I pictured the car racing toward me. "The doctor says I won't be able to go into work for a few days. And when I do go back, I might not be all that efficient for a while. You and Charles will have to take over." I laughed weakly. "I think you're about to do your share of the work for a change."

She shrugged. "Don't worry about me. I can always hire one more employee until you're back on your feet."

Trust Toni to come up with a way to bow out of hard work. Truth be told, I'd known going into this business that I'd be doing most of the work. Without Toni's money financing our business, there would have been no restaurant. If we'd gone under a few months ago—as we very nearly did—*she* would have lost all the money, not me. So it was fair. She put up the cash. I put up most of the grunt work. And if she wanted to hire temporary help, that was fine too. In all honesty, I preferred it that way. I wasn't sure how confident I'd feel leaving Toni to take over my duties all by herself—not that my partner didn't know as much as I did about running a restaurant. It was just that she wouldn't do anything that put her manicure at risk, which meant there was an awful lot of jobs she wouldn't touch in the kitchen. Even washing lettuce she would only do donning a pair of opera-length marabou-trimmed rubber gloves.

I sought her eyes. "I think somebody tried to kill me." It was more a question than a statement.

Her gaze held mine. "I know, sweetie. There were half a dozen witnesses. They all said the same thing."

I thought about the implication. "But why would anybody want me dead?"

"Did you steal anybody's boyfriend lately?"

I gave her a dirty look. "Ha-ha, not funny."

She grinned. "Sorry." And then she grew serious. "What about the car? Did you get a good look at it? Or at the driver?"

"Sure. I got a flash of something big, with a lot of chrome, and from real close." I huffed. "Are you kidding? It happened so fast, I couldn't even tell you what color it was, let alone what the driver looked like."

Before I had a chance to ask her if anyone had taken down the license plate, she glanced at the door and her mouth tightened. "Uh-oh. Will you look at who's here?"

My eyes followed hers. *Oh shit.*

Police officer Crawford and his sidekick Sanders, the two cops who had turned my life into a nightmare after Rob's death, were striding toward me.

"Well, that proves it," I said. "Things can always get worse."

Crawford was wearing his characteristic expression of gleeful self-satisfaction, his beady eyes bright with anticipation. I had no idea how he would turn me into a suspect, but I figured he would find a way. As a boy, he'd probably pulled wings off of flies, and had grown up to love seeing people squirm.

"God must love stupid people," Toni said, staring at them. "He made so many of them."

Crawford smirked. "Nice to see you too." His eyes took a brief assessment of my injuries and he said, "She'll live."

In the months since I'd last seen him, the man had only grown fatter and uglier. The rosacea on his nose now extended over most of his cheeks, and his hair had receded another inch. Next to him, beanstalk Sanders looked almost handsome. On second thought, scratch that. He was just as ugly.

Crawford did not bother to pretend sympathy. "I hear somebody is out to get you." He said this as if it was good news.

Toni gave him a sardonic smile. "But with you two aces on the job, Nicky has nothing to worry about, right?"

Straight-faced, Sanders said, "We'll do our best to catch the culprit."

"Gee, that makes me feel a whole lot better," she said, wide-eyed. "Did you hear that, Nicky? They're going to do their best. Isn't that wonderful?" She punctuated this by batting her lashes a few times.

Unamused, Crawford pointed a fat index finger at her. "Why don't you get lost while we interrogate her?"

"Interrogate! You say that as if *she* was behind the wheel of that car."

"It wouldn't be the first time somebody faked an accident."

Toni's eyebrows shot up, and then she gave a resigned sigh. "Like I always say, if you argue with a fool, you become one too. I'll be back later, after these two clowns have left." She planted a kiss on my cheek, stuffed her purse under her arm and marched off, muttering something under her breath. Whatever it was, Crawford didn't like it. His eyes narrowed and followed her until she disappeared out the door. He turned to me and for the next twenty minutes I had the pleasure of being grilled by two of Toronto's finest.

Crawford's first question took me by surprise. "Do you have disability insurance?" He said this with a slight leer.

"What? I don't understand the relevance."

"How's the restaurant business these days? Are you getting a regular paycheck?"

All at once it came to me. "You think I staged this for insurance money?" I shook my head in disbelief. "For your information, the restaurant is doing very well, and, furthermore, I don't have disability insurance. And I resent the implication."

"You wouldn't be the first person to fake an injury for the insurance."

"You can't accuse me of faking this. My ankle is broken."

"Not part of the plan?"

I was feeling vulnerable, lying on a gurney in a hospital gown, and to my embarrassment my eyes welled up. "I don't need this bullshit." I looked around for a guard, a doctor, a nurse—anybody with the authority to make them leave.

Sanford moved a step closer, taking over from Crawford. "Did you see who was driving the car?"

"So you believe me."

He nodded imperceptibly and my anger dissipated.

I always did like him more—or rather, disliked him less. "It happened too fast for me to notice anything. I was crossing the street when I saw the car. It was coming toward me. I tried to get out of its way, but it sped up just as I was about to reach the sidewalk. That driver—whoever he was—he hit me on purpose."

"Do you know of anyone who might benefit from your death?"

That might have been funny if my situation wasn't so pathetic. "You've got to be kidding. All I own is a mortgaged house, a lot of credit-card debt, and half a stake in a new restaurant. So you might as well forget that theory."

"Does somebody have an ax to grind with you?"

I shook my head. "No, I'm nice. People like me."

Crawford smirked, his silence insulting.

I bit back on a nasty retort. "Actually I do know of somebody. The day before yesterday some crazy woman came by the restaurant, ranting and raving that I'd stolen her restaurant. She said she was going to get it back if she had to kill me for it." I recounted the confrontation.

Crawford put on his sarcastic smile again. "Did this person happen to leave you her name? Her number? Any way she can be reached?"

I shook my head. Crawford gave Sanders a glance. The meaning was clear.

"I am not making this up. If you don't believe me, call Skinny's and ask for Charles or Jennifer. They were there. They'll tell you exactly what I just told you."

"You say you never met this woman before?"

"I never saw her before in my life. She was somewhere in her late thirties to early forties. She had brown hair. She was about my height and looked like she hadn't bathed in a long time."

Sanders took notes, flipped his notebook closed and rolled his eyes. "She needed a bath—great description. That should make her real easy to spot."

"Next time I'll ask her to hold still while I take a picture," I snapped back.

Crawford sneered. Before leaving, he gave me one last parting shot. "You and your girlfriend better not be stupid. I don't want you to get involved with this case in any way. You hear me? Butt out. If you go out and play detective again, don't be surprised if you end up dead."

So he believed me too. But that didn't mean he gave a damn.

A minute later they were gone and I just knew they'd forgotten about this case the minute they'd stepped out of the room. If I had to depend on those two to keep me safe, I was as good as dead.

call me crazy but i like my legs to match

I WAS MOVED to a semi-private room. In the bed next to mine was a middle-aged woman who spent her time making one phone call after another. I almost felt sorry for whoever she was speaking to. When she wasn't complaining about her gallbladder operation, she was complaining about how painful her kidney stones had been. When she ran out of people to call, she turned to me. Luckily, Toni chose that moment to peek in from the doorway.

"Oh, you're awake. Good." She strode in, looking beautiful as usual. Today she wore a zebra-striped dress that hugged her figure almost indecently. Her gorgeous alpaca coat was draped over one arm.

I pushed myself up on one elbow and signaled her to close the privacy curtain around the bed. She did, and pulled a chair.

"Here's your purse by the way." She handed it to me. "Jake found it on the sidewalk after the ambulance left."

"Thanks." Until now, I hadn't even realized it was missing. I looked inside, relieved to find my wallet complete with all my overextended credit cards and, more important, my cell phone. I snatched it up and checked the battery—dead. Figured. I dropped it back in my purse. "Have you checked on Jackie and the puppies?"

"Yes, yes. I told you I would." Her face lit up. "That little Trouble is the cutest thing. I can't wait to take him home."

"He's twelve weeks old and ready to go now."

Her forehead furrowed. "Uh, is he fully trained?"

"Paper-trained only."

She wrinkled her nose. "No rush. I'll let you keep him till he is."

"Toni, even when they're fully trained, dogs sometimes have accidents. What are you going to do if your little cutie-pie pees on your white carpet?" She looked horrified for a second, and before she could answer, I continued. "You can't adopt him and just bring him back when you decide he's too much trouble. Dogs have feelings too, you know."

She shook her head vehemently. "Don't worry. I've had all the carpets removed and replaced with travertine floors."

I was shocked. "You have?" After witnessing her reaction the first time she saw the soiled wee-wee pads, I'd been convinced she would bow out of taking Trouble. "You didn't tell me that."

"I don't have to tell you everything I do." She was thoughtful for a second. "I guess that means I shouldn't have area rugs either."

I changed the subject before she launched into a full analysis of the decorating challenge owning a dog presented. I wasn't worried. I'd never known anyone to drop a bundle as readily as she did. Toni didn't think twice about redecorating, and did it regularly. Every time I visited, she had something new to show me.

I took in her fresh makeup and tight dress. "You look dressed to kill. Do you have a date tonight? Speaking of which, did you tell Steven yet?"

"Not yet." She put a finger to her mouth and threw a furtive glance toward the doorway. "Charles just stopped by the shop downstairs. He should be here any second.

Please don't say anything in front of him. I don't want anybody to know about my personal affairs."

"But things are good between you and Steven, right?"

She grinned. "Better than good. They're great."

I kept my face impassive but I was dying to know.

"Any chance you two will get married?" I whispered.

"Married? Are you crazy? Like I always say, 'Marriage is a lot like a tub of hot water.'" I waited for the punch line. She cocked a hip. "'By the time you get into it, it's not so hot.'"

I burst out laughing.

At the sound of the door opening, I turned to see Charles carrying a huge flower arrangement—hydrangea, ladies' mantle and spray roses.

"Jennifer wanted to visit too, but there was too much to do at work. She sends her best."

"Oh, Charles, they're beautiful. Thank you," I said, trying to sit up. I grimaced as a bolt of pain shot up my leg.

"Are you hurting?" Toni asked, leaning away, as if my broken ankle was suddenly contagious.

"The medicine is wearing off. I think it's time for another of those feel-good shots."

"I'll go grab a nurse." Charles shoved the flowers at Toni and took off. Some people just didn't do hospitals well and I suspected he was one of them.

She handed me the card, which read, *Get well soon, love from everyone at Skinny's on Queen.*

"Aw, that's sweet."

"It was the staff's idea," she said, placing the arrangement on my bedside table, angling it this way and that until it was just perfect. "So what's the news about your ankle?"

"The surgeon scheduled my operation for first thing tomorrow morning." I groaned. "I'm not looking forward to it." I hesitated. "Do you think you could call Mitchell for me, just—you know—to let him know I was in an accident?"

She gave me a knowing smile. "You mean, so he can come running back to you."

"Don't be silly. I wouldn't expect him to drop everything. It's just that he's my boyfriend and should be notified."

"Okay, give me his number."

I wrote his cell phone number on the back of the card envelope and handed it to her, wishing she'd call him right this second.

"I'll let you know when I reach him," she said, putting an end to that thought.

"How come you two aren't at the restaurant? Is it totally quiet at work today?"

"Are you kidding? After yesterday's television interview, we're stars. The place is hopping. Thank goodness we have Jennifer now, otherwise we'd never make it. I was thinking of trying to find a temp to pitch in until you're back on your feet."

"It's an idea," I said.

She looked at her watch. "We can't stay more than a few minutes, but I had to come in and tell you the good news in person." She waited until she had my full attention and continued. "I spoke to the editor of the lifestyles section at the *Toronto Daily*, and she wants to do an article about us."

"So Charles was right," I said, trying to focus on something other than the throbbing that was rapidly taking over my ankle. "But I don't get it. Why would a newspaper want to interview us?"

She threw up her hands in a "who knows" or "who cares" gesture. "The important thing is that we're interesting enough to warrant an article. I'm telling you, since our TV interview, we're famous. And guess what else?"

The pain seemed to be increasing by the second, and I was not in a guessing mood. "Just tell me."

"She mentioned possibly giving us a regular column where we could publish a skinny recipe of the week."

"Are you serious?" I was already imagining all the publicity, not to mention the credibility, a column like that would bring us. We couldn't pay for that kind of advertising. "She's offering it to us for free? I hope you said yes."

Her eyes widened. "What are you talking about, for free? People get paid to write columns. I don't think it would have been a lot of money—probably no more than a token amount. But we're so busy we can barely come up with one new recipe a week for our restaurant menu. If we took on the responsibility of a column, we'd have to come up with two, maybe three." She planted a hand on one hip. "Unless you think we should just give away our menu recipes, so people can make them at home themselves. Then they won't even have to come to us anymore."

"Are you serious? People would kill for this kind of opportunity. This will be as good for us as the TV interview has been. We can't pass it up. We'll just have to come up with different recipes for the column. We'll hire more staff if we have to." Anticipating her next objection, I continued. "And if there's not enough working space in the restaurant, we can use the kitchen in my house, and if that isn't enough, we'll use your condo too. If you turned them down, I swear I'll…I'll…I don't know what I'll do but I'll think of something."

She gave me a wide smile. "Don't be ridiculous. Of course I didn't turn it down." I looked her straight in the eye. "I wouldn't turn down an offer without running it by you."

I didn't believe her for a second. "Tell me the truth, Toni. You said no, didn't you?"

She opened her mouth, then closed it. Looking down at her nails, she smoothed the tip of a perfectly manicured finger with her thumb. "Well…maybe I did sort of mention that we were so busy I doubted we could take on such a time-consuming project. But it's not like, final, or anything. She told me to think about it." Grinning, she added, "It won't hurt to make them wait. It will only make them feel lucky to have us."

I bolted upright, only to collapse on the bed from the pain. "Toni," I said through gritted teeth. "If you don't call them back this minute, I swear I'll never speak to you again."

"Promises, promises." Then seeing that I was still in pain, she added, "Okay. I'll call them back the minute I get back. In the meantime, try to rest."

"Not when you get to back to work. Now."

"Okay, okay."

As if on cue, the nurse—a gray-haired woman built like a refrigerator—marched in, brandishing a hypodermic needle. Behind her, I glimpsed Charles peeking in from behind the doorframe, looking a bit greenish.

The nurse turned to Toni. "Sorry, love, our patient needs her privacy right now." She closed the door firmly. "Time for your injection," she singsonged.

I'd never been so happy to get a needle in my life. I turned on my side and offered up my butt. I felt a quick pinprick, and then, "There, that should make you feel better in no time." She opened the door and gestured my friends back in.

Whatever that medication was, it was magical. Five minutes later, the pain was almost entirely gone. But along with the relief came an almost overwhelmingly pleasant grogginess. My mind floated in a fog.

After a few minutes of struggling to keep my end of the conversation, Toni took notice. "You look exhausted. Charles and I should get back to work and let you sleep." They said goodbye, and left.

I must have fallen asleep instantly because the next thing I knew, another nurse—this one tall and sinewy—was leaning over me. "I have to start your IV. You'll be going into surgery in about an hour."

Could it be morning already? I looked out the window, confused. Outside was dim—either early evening or very early morning. I thought of Mitchell, wondering what he was doing right now. Had Toni even called him? "What time is it?"

"Five-thirty. I'm here to prep you. Your surgery is scheduled for seven."

"I slept almost thirteen hours?"

"Uh-huh." She nodded. "It's not unusual after an accident. Shock is a wonderful soporific, better than any sleeping pill." She attached a saline bag to an IV pole, inserted a needle in the crook of my elbow—*ouch*—unwrapped my ankle—*ouch ouch*—and shaved my leg from my knee to my toes.

"While you're at it, could you shave my other leg too? Call me crazy but I like my legs to match."

She looked surprised for a second, and then, realizing I was just teasing, she chuckled, picked up the discarded bandages and left. Soon, she reappeared followed by a beefy attendant.

"One, two three, up," he said, and together they lifted me to a gurney and rolled me into a hallway at the end of a long lineup of beds.

A nice-looking man—fiftyish—appeared at my side.

"Hi, I'm Dr. Marlow, your anesthetist." He plunged a needle into the catheter. "You'll feel a bit groggy, but you won't be fully anesthetized until just before the surgery."

Soon, I became vaguely aware of being wheeled into a bright room, and of lights shining down on me. Somebody in a surgical gown appeared over me. "Can you count backwards from one hundred for me?" It was Dr. Marlow. I hadn't recognized him behind the mask.

"One hundred, ninety-nine, ninety-eight…ninety…"

The next thing I knew, a nurse was leaning over me. "Take a deep breath." I did. "And another."

I blinked. "Am I going into surgery now?"

She patted my hand. "Your surgery is over, and everything went very well. We'll have you back in your room in a little while." I raised myself onto my elbows, looking down at my ankle. It was encased in something that looked like thick gauze.

"I'm afraid your leg is still in a splint. Your ankle is pretty swollen right now, so you'll be getting a proper cast when it goes down. We'll keep it raised, and that should help with the swelling."

I couldn't help asking, even though I already knew what she would say. "Will I be able to walk once I get the cast?"

"The doctor will answer all your questions. He'll be by to see you in a few minutes."

She no sooner said this than the surgeon, a tall thin man with graying hair and kind eyes, appeared at her side. "So," he said jovially. "How are we doing here?"

"I don't know about you, but I'm feeling a bit queasy."

He chuckled. "Normal after anesthesia. You'll feel better in about an hour." He grew serious. "You have nothing to worry about. The surgery went very well. Your soft tissues were in excellent condition. You'll have to wear a cast for six to eight weeks. During this time you'll have to stay off that foot entirely. But the good news is that you'll be like new when it's healed." He grinned. "Pardon the pun." At my lack of response, he added, "Okay, so I'm not very good at comedy. But I'm an excellent surgeon."

This did elicit a smile from me. "When can I go back to work?"

"You'll be discharged tomorrow. We'll put you in a cast, give you a pair of crutches, and as long as you don't put any weight on that foot, you can go back to work whenever you feel up to it. What kind of work do you do?"

I told him.

He grimaced. "So you're on your feet all day." He thought for a second. "If you got yourself a stool and promised to never, ever put so much as your foot on the floor. But before you run off to buy a stool, I suggest you take a couple of days off. You might want to get comfortable walking around with crutches. We wouldn't want you stumbling and coming down on the wrong foot, now would we?"

I shuddered. The very idea was painful.

A FEW HOURS later I was back in my room, my leg held high on a stack of pillows. The whining woman in the next bed had been replaced by an old woman. Judging by her almost skeletal appearance and her shrunken-apple of a face, she must have been ancient. She snored with her mouth open and let out loud farts every few seconds. But even that was preferable to the ongoing litany of complaints from my previous neighbor.

By midafternoon, I was feeling better. The queasiness and grogginess had passed, and I was famished and dying to hear Mitchell's voice.

"Good morning, sunshine." Toni sauntered in, bearing—joy of joys—a restaurant doggie bag. "I figured you'd have had enough of hospital food by now." She noticed my wrapped-up ankle and her eyebrows jumped. "Well, that should keep me safe from bears."

"What in the world are you talking about?"

"If I ever come across a bear, I don't have to outrun it. As long as I can outrun you, I'll be safe."

Trust Toni to turn even the worst of times into a joke. I chuckled. "Gee, thanks. I'll remember never to go hiking with you."

She stopped and took a whiff. "Oh phe-ew, it stinks in here." She waved in a vain attempt to shoo the odor away.

I put a finger to my mouth and pointed at the curtain behind which was my elderly roommate. "She's an old woman," I whispered. As if on cue, the old woman let out a ripper.

Toni rolled her eyes. "Can't you ask the nurse to cork her?"

"Toni, shhh. She might hear you."

"I wish she would. If I ever get so old I can't even hold back from farting in public, just shoot me." She threw her coat on the nearby chair, tossed her hair and perched herself on the edge of the bed. She dangled the doggie bag before me. "Did you have lunch yet?"

"They brought me soggy vegetables, some kind of grayish meat and a bowl of green gelatin. Yuck." I struggled to sit up. "Can you hand me that gadget?"

She placed the bag on the bedside table, picked up the control button and pressed it until the bed squeaked to a sitting position. "There, is that better?"

"Much. Thanks." And then I asked her what was really on my mind. "Did you call Mitchell?"

She squirmed, avoiding my eyes. "I tried to reach him

but the call went straight to voice mail. I thought it better to speak directly to him rather than leave him a message."

"Oh." I wasn't convinced she'd even tried. I'd seen that guilty look on her face.

"But I promise I'll try again later. Why don't you look in the bag?"

I stared at it, famished. "What did you bring me?"

"Ah, so you're hungry. Well, that's a good sign."

"I'm not sick, Toni. I broke an ankle. Besides when have you ever seen me not be hungry?"

"You've been doing a good job of sticking to your diet."

Ha, little did she know.

She opened the bag, pulled out a plastic container and tore off the cover. She handed it to me along with a knife and fork, and the delicious aroma of tomato sauce and garlic filled the air.

My salivary glands went into instant overdrive. "It smells divine."

"You're going to love it—another one of Charles's wonderful creations, chicken Parmesan and only two hundred and ninety calories per serving."

She tucked a napkin under my chin, bib style, and I dug in. "Heavens, this is so good." I took another bite. "Did you call the editor at *The Toronto Daily?*"

"I told you I would. And it's all set up. As it turns out, she's decided to hold the article back a couple of weeks. That'll give us time to come up with a few good recipes, and then we can start the column at the same time the article comes out. Anyhow, that was her suggestion."

"Great idea," I said through another mouthful. "In a few weeks the rush from the TV interview might have slowed down. We'll probably need another plug by then. How are the dogs?"

"They're fine. I stayed overnight and then on my way

here from the restaurant I stopped by again. I let Jackie out back, filled the bowls and changed the wee-wee pads." She wrinkled her nose. "Boy, they sure poop a lot for such tiny little things."

"Dogs do poop, you know, which is why you have to take them out regularly. Are you sure you're ready to commit to the responsibility of a dog? You'd have to take Trouble out at least three times a day. You'd better let me know now if I have to start looking for another home for him."

She put up her hand, swearing on an invisible Bible. "I promise Trouble is coming home with me, and I will take excellent care of him."

"Good, I don't know what I would do if you suddenly announced you'd changed your mind. I can handle Jackie and one pup, but no more." After falling in love with all three newborn puppies, I'd decided to keep one, the little female I'd already named Sugar. I just knew she'd wear her name well. I gestured toward my ankle. "You'd be a real friend if you took him as soon as possible." I returned to my meal, expecting her to put up some objection.

She quietly watched me eat for a few minutes, looking preoccupied. She cleared her throat. "Are you ready for the bad news?"

I looked up at her and put down my fork. "Give it to me."

Her mouth tightened. "It turns out that Jake hasn't been entirely forthcoming. He's been keeping a secret from us."

What was she talking about—cooking the books, embezzling? I dismissed each thought just as quickly as it popped into my mind. I couldn't imagine Jake doing anything illegal. "Keeping what exactly?"

She gave me a concerned look. "I don't want you to get excited now."

"Toni! When somebody tells me to not get excited, it only makes me worry more. Cut to the chase, will you."

"It turns out he got a phone call from some woman during our television interview." She stared at me, watching for my reaction.

I shrugged. "So?"

"He said she sounded hysterical, screaming something about us stealing what was rightfully hers, and she was going to see us all dead."

I gaped at her. "Why didn't he tell us earlier?"

"Don't be upset with him. I would have done the same thing. We'd just given a great interview. Reservations were coming in faster than we could take them. He didn't want to put a damper on our day. Besides, he figured it was just the same mental patient who made those wild accusations to you and Charles and that she wasn't dangerous."

"Was he sure she was the same woman?"

She quirked an eyebrow. "Gee, I don't know. I mean— how many lunatics would you say are running around out there, imagining we somehow stole their restaurant?"

"I know. I know." I suddenly clicked on what she'd just said. "And now she wants *all* of us dead. That means you're in danger too—maybe even the guys. Did Jake check the call display? Maybe we can locate her."

She gave me a sardonic smile. "Of course he checked. But it seems our lunatic was smart enough to call from a confidential number."

"Figures." I must have grimaced because she leaned over, and put on her solicitous voice.

"How are you feeling, sweetie?"

"Okay, I guess."

"Make sure they give you lots of Demerol. That's the only positive thing that can come out of this."

"I may be nice and high on painkillers right now, but I'm really low on morale. So it's pretty much a wash." And then, with a catch in my throat I said, "Oh, Toni, what are we going to do? Do you think her threats are serious? That she's really coming after us?"

She tilted her head, looking serious but surprisingly calm under the circumstances. "It sure sounds that way."

"Why don't you look more scared?"

"Hey, like I always say, being alive is a lot more dangerous than being dead."

"You are so full of it, Toni Lawford," I said, chuckling. "If you thought for one minute that you were in danger, you'd be the first to scream bloody murder. What gives?"

She put a finger to her mouth, opened her purse and angled it so I could see inside.

I gasped. "You've got a gun?"

"I told you to be quiet," she said, glancing furtively around. "I don't want the whole world to know."

"Are you crazy?" I whispered. "You don't even know how to use a gun—or do you?" I realized there were still a few things I didn't know about my friend. Maybe she did know how to shoot. *Toni aiming a gun—now there is a scary thought.*

She snapped her purse shut. "It's not as if we can count on the cops to protect us, is it?"

I grimaced at the truth of that statement. "I told Crawford and Sanders about that woman's threats. I described her as well as I could, but I doubt they'll even try to find her. But back to the gun—you don't know how to use it, do you?"

She looked at me as if I had rocks in my head. "Of course I do. Don't you remember me telling you about that movie where I played the detective? Well, I had to take shooting lessons—you know—so I'd look like I knew what I was doing."

I let my head drop back on the pillow and stared at the ceiling. "Have I ever told you, you drive me crazy?"

She gave me a crooked smile. "Oh yeah? Well it's a short drive."

"Ha-ha. Very funny."

"You don't believe I can shoot, do you?" She was already fumbling with the latch on her purse. Oh God. The last thing I needed was a demonstration.

"I believe you. I believe you."

She studied me, trying—no doubt—to determine whether I meant it.

"Really," I added, and this seemed to convince her.

She gave me a little self-satisfied smile. "I don't believe in gun control. I believe in *idiot* control." She leaned over and patted my hand. "Just so you know, I called Steven and told him everything that happened—about that woman and her threats."

Steven was one of the best defense attorneys in Toronto. He had once been very kind to me, helping me with invaluable legal advice, which I had followed—at least for the most part. Without him, I might have gone to jail and, for all I knew, could still be there. It was during that time that he and Toni began seeing each other again. As far as I was concerned, that meant their reconciliation was entirely because of me. Toni *owed* me.

"Getting back to the hit-and-run," I said, "did anybody take down the license plate?"

She shook her head solemnly.

"What about the driver? Was it a man or a woman?"

Again, she shook her head.

"Did anybody at least recognize the make and model?"

She gave a one-shoulder shrug. "Sure, at least half a

dozen people did. One person was sure it was a Lexus. Another swore it was an Infiniti. His wife disagreed, said it was a Volvo. And for what it's worth, Jake is convinced it was an Audi."

"Some help."

"The only thing everyone did agree on was that it was big and dark—either navy, dark green or black."

"Well, at least we know it was some kind of big expensive car. That's not much, but it's better than nothing."

"Eh, I don't think that will help. There are probably a hundred thousand luxury sedans in Forest Hill alone," she said, naming one of Toronto's most affluent neighborhoods.

This subject was starting to give me a headache. It was time to change it. "I have another problem. You know me. I'll go crazy if I stay home by myself. I want to go back to work, but how am I supposed to get around with a broken ankle?"

"Give yourself a break, will you? It wouldn't kill you to take a few days off, you know. The restaurant won't go under if the guys and I take over while you recover." Her eyes lit with sudden understanding. "That's it, isn't it? The reason you want to get back isn't because you're bored. It's because you don't trust anybody else to run the business."

She was more right than I cared to admit. I had a brief vision of the kitchen looking like a cafeteria food fight and almost groaned out loud.

"It's not the restaurant I'm worried about. It's my sanity."

"Oh, well, in that case don't worry. It's already too late."

I tried to keep a straight face but I could feel a smile

peeking out from the corners of my mouth. I gave in and laughed.

"I can't stay too long. I took off as soon as the worst of the lunch rush was over. I told the guys to put up a sign that we'd reopen at five. And Jennifer is such a help."

I nodded. "She is, isn't she?"

"So there's nothing to worry about. Everything's fine." She checked her watch. "Oops, I think it's time I got back." She hopped to her feet, gave me a peck on the cheek and took off, blonde hair bouncing on her shoulders and high heels clicking. "See you later, sweetie."

"Don't forget to call Mitchell," I called after her, but the door was already closed.

For the rest of the day, I couldn't stop thinking about the threats the woman had made. Was she the hit-and-run driver? And if so, what else was she planning? I was probably safe as long as I was in the hospital. But it was just a question of time before I'd be released. I had a quick vision of myself with a bull's-eye painted on my back, and cringed. Did that mean Toni was now in danger too? There had to be something I could do to keep us all safe.

some things are just not meant to go together

AT SIX O'CLOCK the next morning, I was considering the bowl of cold and glutinous porridge when Dr. Goodall stopped by. "How are we doing today?" He picked up my chart from the foot of the bed and scanned it briefly. "Are you still in very much pain?"

I looked at the spoonful of unappetizing oatmeal before me and let it dribble back into the bowl. "My one complaint around here is the food." I beamed him a smile. "Good thing those painkillers more than make up for it. They are magical."

He chuckled. "All I can say is don't get used to them. I can't prescribe them for more than a few days." He moved closer. "Let's take a look at that ankle now." He gently unwrapped the gauze around the splint. It wasn't as bad as I'd feared but I still gritted my teeth against the pain. He looked at it from one angle and then another, testing the swelling and pressing down lightly with an index finger much the way I might test cookies for doneness.

He nodded. "There's still considerable swelling, but I think we can give you an air cast. They're light, comfortable and adjustable, and you can tighten it as the swelling continues to go down. I'll show you how before you're discharged."

"Does that mean I can go home?"

"Yes—just as soon as we get you that cast."

A short time later, I signed myself out and hobbled on

my new crutches all the way to the main entrance of the hospital. My purse was slung over one shoulder. I had a winter boot on one foot and some newfangled thing that looked more like a ski boot than a cast on the other. By the time I got to the front door, I felt as if I'd run a marathon. My underarms had taken a beating, and I suspected the palms of my hands would soon begin to blister. And I was supposed to do this for six to eight weeks? My arms would either give up and I'd spend all my time in bed. Or maybe I'd end up with a toned upper body. *Hmm, maybe not a bad trade-off.*

A cute intern hurried over to hold the door open for me, and I stepped into a gorgeous fall day. The sun was shining and the streets were dry—thank God. I gathered my strength and trudged over to the taxi at the front of the line.

Twenty minutes later the driver pulled up in front of my house. He ran around to the passenger side and helped me out.

"There you go," he said, and before I knew it, he'd jumped back into the driver's seat, calling out, "Have a nice day," before slamming the door shut.

"Hey, wait. I can't—"

To my horror he drove off, leaving me staring at the expanse of slippery sidewalk to my front door. The streets in the city were dry but my sidewalk still looked like an ice rink. *Great.* It might as well have been a mile long.

Some things were just not meant to go together—for example, icy paths and crutches. I threw a quick look at Mitchell's house. He had once joked that I sure knew how to make a man feel needed, because he seemed to be forever coming to my rescue. Where was my prince charming now? *Sigh.*

I measured the distance to my front door, wondering

whether I should just abandon my crutches and crawl, when the door opened and Toni flew out, wearing a sheer negligee, the peignoir billowing behind her.

"What in the world do you think you're doing? Are you crazy, trying to walk this icy patch on crutches? Here, hold onto me."

I grasped onto her shoulder with one arm, dropping one of the crutches.

She picked it up. "I'll hold it. Are you ready?"

I nodded. She took one careful step forward. I followed, half shuffling, half hopping. So far so good.

"You know," she said, taking another careful step, "if Jackie hadn't sounded the alarm, I would never have known you were out here."

"What do you mean?"

"It was the weirdest thing. A few minutes before you got here, she hopped on top of me and then onto the back of the sofa, barking like mad out the living room window. I looked out to see what that ruckus was all about, but there was nothing. And then, the very next second, a cab drives up, and who comes out but you?" She moved another foot forward and I followed. "It was almost as if she knew you were about to come home. I tell you, it gave me goose bumps."

I chuckled, spotting Jackie still on the back of the sofa, still barking madly. "I'm not surprised. She does that all the time. I can't decide whether she's telepathic or just has such a great sense of smell that she can tell when I'm blocks away."

"I hope it's the former," she said, snickering. "I wouldn't want to think any creature could smell you from so far away."

A few steps more and we were inside. Toni closed the

door behind us and Jackie came galloping over, throwing herself at me.

"No, Jackie, no. Jackie, down, girl." I wasn't sure enough on my crutches yet to handle even a three-pound dog. The next thing I knew, I was falling. I put out my arms and saw the floor coming at me as if in slow motion. Then I was on my stomach, with Jackie doing cartwheels on my back, while licking one of my ears with enthusiasm. I'd made it safely all the way down the icy walk, only to end up sprawled on my stomach within two seconds of reaching the safety of my hallway.

"I love you too, Jackie. Now, would please let me get up?"

She hopped off, marching away in disgust and giving me a reproachful look, as if to say, "That's what I get for demonstrating my love?"

Toni helped me back up to my one good foot, handing me my crutches. "Are you okay?"

I nodded, shakily. But just the jar of the fall had sent shock waves throbbing up and down my leg.

"Thank God. How about I make some coffee? Like I always say, there's nothing a good cup of coffee won't fix."

"Maybe you should make a cup of coffee for that lunatic who wants us dead, and throw a little arsenic in it while you're at it. That might be a more effective fix." Suddenly I noticed her feet were blue with cold. "You ran outside in your bare feet?"

She shrugged. "Of course. I couldn't risk you hurting yourself. What are friends for?"

Once in a while Toni did something so incredibly selfless, it left me speechless.

a much highlighted self-help book

WHILE TONI RAN upstairs and changed into four-inch heels and yet another clingy dress, this one turquoise with a plunging neckline, I popped a painkiller and checked my phone messages—three, one of which was from Mitchell. My heart skipped a beat.

"Hi, sweetheart. I made it safely to New York. Bunny and I are working like mad." *His editor's name is Bunny?* I immediately pictured a blonde *Playboy* centerfold in my mind, hating her instantly. "I tried reaching you a few times but I kept getting your voice mail. Anyhow, we'll speak soon—love you." I was listening to the message for the third time when Toni came back down. I put down the phone and settled myself at the kitchen table, while she busied herself making coffee. Soon it began to drip, its aroma filling the air.

She rummaged through my cupboards for mugs, set them on the table and then opened the fridge. "Did you hear from Mitchell?" she asked casually. "I tried to call him but never got through."

I grinned. "There was a message from him on my voice mail. He's fine, working hard."

She set cream and mugs on my blue checkered place-mats. "That's good." She seemed about to add something, but just then the coffee machine beeped and she turned away. She brought the pot to the table and poured.

I took a long gulp, almost swooning with satisfaction. "I needed this. I'm already beginning to feel better."

"I bet being home doesn't hurt either. By the way," she said, giving me the eyebrow. "I came across one of your books, *How to Keep Your Man From Straying.*"

I felt my face heat up. "What do you mean you came across it? That book was in my underwear drawer. Were you going through my drawers?"

"Sweetheart, you should hide it better than that. Your underwear drawer is the first place where a curious boyfriend will peek."

"That's ridiculous. Mitchell would never. Besides, you're the one who looked, not him."

"And lucky for you. I found it by accident, looking for fresh towels. If I came across it that easily, anybody could. And you know what I always say."

Uh-oh. I readied myself.

"The only thing worse than your boyfriend finding you diary is your boyfriend finding your much-highlighted self-help book."

I shuddered at the thought. Toni chatted on about how comfortable my bed was, how much fun she had with the puppies, but behind her light banter, I sensed she had something serious on her mind. She kept jumping up, wiping the counter, refilling the cups, all the time avoiding my eyes.

I took another sip of coffee and set my cup down. "So, moving on to business—do you know if the police found out anything about that lunatic who ran me down?"

She pulled herself a chair and sat, staying put for a change. "No, and I don't expect we will. Steven says that she's probably just some poor schizophrenic off her meds. It's sad, but since the hospital budget cutbacks, there are thousands of people just like her, wandering around with nowhere to go."

"That's what Charles says."

She nodded. "And he's probably right. Those poor souls may look scary, but most of them are perfectly harmless."

"Whoa. I don't know that I'd call someone who ran me down *harmless*."

She took a deep breath as if readying for a battle. "Well, here's the thing. The woman who came into the restaurant ranting and raving looked like a homeless person, right? Or at least, that's the way Charles and Jennifer described her."

I remembered the matted hair, the crazed eyes and the filthy coat. "That's true."

Toni quirked an eyebrow. "So how do you figure a homeless person could not only come up with a car, but a luxury car at that?"

She had a point. And it shocked the hell out of me. I was the one who usually made the points—not Toni. "You're right. That never occurred to me."

The corners of her mouth curled into a triumphant smile. "So the way I see it, that poor soul probably had nothing to do with your accident."

"Oh, so now it was just an *accident?*"

"As a matter of fact, yes, in all probability that's exactly what it was. And if you thought about it logically, you'd agree with me."

"You think I'm being illogical? That car was aiming right for me, Toni, and it sped up instead of slowed down. It had to have been on purpose."

Her smile was full of patience—irritating as hell. "I'm sure it seemed that way. But Steven says it was probably just some teenage boy with more testosterone than brains. He lost control, got scared and hit the gas instead of the brakes." She shrugged. "The truth is, our little restaurant is not important enough for anyone to want to kill for it. And for that matter, neither is either one of us."

Toni saying she wasn't important? I didn't believe it. Sure enough in the next breath she took it back.

"Well, maybe some people might think of me as important." She flipped a lock of hair off her shoulder. I let that one pass, knowing that under that veneer of self-confidence Toni was really a mass of insecurity. According to her, she was too old, too fat and not attractive enough— all fears stemming from her modeling career. I'd once asked her if she'd ever been happy with her weight. Her reply was that she must have been just right at one point, but since she always woke up too fat or too thin, it had to have been in the middle of the night. She'd said this as a joke, but it was a sad reflection of how she really felt.

I returned to the subject at hand. "So you *really* think it was just an accident."

She contemplated this for a moment. "Well, it certainly makes more sense than somebody being out to get us."

I very much wanted to believe that car had hit me by accident—much less frightening that the thought of someone wanting me dead—but I wasn't convinced. Somehow that explanation just seemed too easy.

a man is a man is a man

TALKING ABOUT THE hit-and-run had made me forget about food, but my appetite came raging back when she offered to make breakfast.

"I'm going to make you something delicious," Toni said, grabbing one of my aprons from the hook behind the door and getting to work.

"Are you sure you don't mind?"

"Mind? Why would I mind? I love to cook. Just because at work I choose to do the plating instead of the cooking doesn't mean I don't enjoy it."

Toni had spent the same two years in chef's school as I had, but what she really excelled at was making food look like edible art. I, on the other hand, was a great chef, but lacked the patience to make each plate look beautiful. This made us perfect partners in the kitchen.

Toni paused, waving a spatula at me. "You'll see. You're going to love it."

I watched with fascination as she whipped up a batch of what she called her secret recipe French toast, which she used to make back when she was a model. Toni looked so domestic wearing my apron and with a large bowl tucked under her arm, as she whisked the eggs and milk. Soon she had slices of bread sizzling in a pan. When they became perfectly golden, she scooped them onto plates.

"I serve them with strawberry syrup instead of maple syrup, a dollop of vanilla yogurt instead of English cream, and top it all with fresh berries. Here you go." She set one in front of me and poured me a fresh cup of coffee.

I stared at the food. It looked good. I took a bite, and then another. It was every bit as delicious as Toni had promised. I was so hungry I gobbled it down and pushed away my empty plate, sighing with satisfaction.

"That sure beats hospital food. If we ever decide to open for breakfast, this has to be on the menu. Where did you learn to make these?"

"It's nothing really," she said, waving my compliment away. "Back when I was modeling, I came up with a whole bunch of ways to treat myself by making low-cal versions of my favorite dishes."

I looked at her in wonder. "And it never occurred to you to share those recipes, or to even mention them?"

She wrinkled her nose. "They're just ordinary recipes—nothing fancy about them."

"Who cares whether they're fancy or not. Not every dish has to be gourmet. If they're delicious, that's all that counts." I took a sip of coffee and put my cup back down. "Too bad we don't serve breakfast at Skinny's." I snapped my fingers. "Hey. I have an idea. Why don't we use recipes like this one for our column?"

She nodded slowly. The thought appealed to her. "Not a bad idea. Maybe I could write down all my old recipes. They're all so easy anybody could whip them up in a flash."

I clapped my hands in delight. "That's exactly what we'll do—develop easy recipes for the column, recipes anybody can prepare."

"There you go." She got up from the table and carried the dishes to the sink. "I told you we'd come up with a solution, didn't I?"

I raised an eyebrow at her. "*You* told me?" That wasn't

exactly how I remembered it, but it wasn't worth arguing about. Besides, for all her outwardly good mood, I still sensed something was up with Toni, and whatever it was, was clearly not good. "Toni, talk to me. I know something's wrong. I wish you'd tell me what it is."

There was a long silence, and just when I'd decided she wasn't ready to talk about it, she cleared her throat. "There is something I think you should know."

Here it came. I readied myself. "Go on."

She took a deep breath. "I don't know quite how to tell you this."

"Out with it."

"Last night…" She paused and for a second I thought she'd changed her mind about telling me. And then she blurted it out so fast that for a moment I thought I hadn't heard right. "I saw a woman go into Mitchell's house."

"What are you talking about?"

"I saw a woman go into Mitchell's house." She paused, and then added. "I never saw her come back out. I think she stayed the night."

Whatever I had expected, this was not it. I laughed. "Mitchell is out of town, Toni. He's in New York. I told you he had to go out of town to work on his manuscript with his editor."

She frowned. "Oh, right." Long pause. "But that doesn't explain the girl."

She had a point. "For all we know, it could be a cleaning woman, or maybe just a friend using his house while he's away."

"Oh."

I could see the gears clicking in her head. And truth be told, they were clicking in my head too, but I wasn't about to let her know that. The thing about my friend was that since catching her husband in an affair with his young secretary—prompting their divorce—Toni trusted no man. That was one more reason I'd been so shocked to find out that she and Steven had reconciled.

"He's with his editor? A girl?"

"Yes, with his editor. And yes, this editor is a she. And before you say any more, Mitchell isn't the kind of man who would cheat on his girlfriend."

She smiled knowingly. "Sweetheart, I know you don't see men the way I do. I may be just a couple of years older than you are, but I have a lot more experience."

I stopped myself from laughing. Toni had months ago admitted she was close to forty, and I suspected she might even have passed the fourth decade mark rather than be approaching it.

"Let me give you a little piece of advice," she continued. "Before you start hoping to marry the guy, just stop and think. Is he the man you want your children to spend their weekends with?"

I knew she hadn't meant it as a joke, but I couldn't help myself. I laughed until I cried. When I finally caught my breath again, I said, "So, tell me the truth, did you even try to call Mitchell?"

"I did try…once. Like I told you, when I got his voice mail I decided to call again later. But after seeing…" She waved a hand vaguely, looking embarrassed, and then she raised her chin defiantly. "I know you love him, and I hope you're right about him. But be careful, because in the end, a man is a man is a man."

There was no point in arguing with her. The best thing to do when she was in this frame of mind was change the subject. "Tell me about the girl. What did she look like?"

"She was blonde, but nothing special," she said, avoiding my eyes. That told me everything I needed to know. Not only was the woman beautiful, but Toni still believed

Mitchell was somehow involved with her. I felt sorry for my friend. "She sure didn't look like any cleaning woman I'd want Steven to be using," she continued.

"You and he are still not living together?"

"He spends most nights at my place, but still goes back to his apartment once in a while—mostly to pick up fresh clothes." She glanced at her watch. "I have to get to work." She stood, and hesitated. "Are you going to be all right by yourself?"

I nodded. "I'll be fine."

She wiped her hands on a dish towel. "Mind if I don't do the dishwashing right away? I'll leave it in the sink, but I'll come back and do it later. I promise."

"You go. I'll clean up. It'll give me something to do."

"Don't you dare! You just take it easy for today. Promise?"

I nodded. "Fine."

She petted the puppies, gave me a quick peck on the cheek and took off. All at once the house felt almost unbearably empty. Jackie came over, scratching at my leg to be picked up. I wrapped her in my arms and held on tight. "I love you, little girl," I said, feeling vulnerable. Even when I knew they were complete nonsense, Toni's comments about men always left me feeling insecure. And now I couldn't get the thought out of my mind. Who was that blonde Toni had seen going into Mitchell's house, and what was she to my boyfriend?

Jackie squirmed out of my arms and hopped down, giving me a look as if saying, "Don't just sit there, you have some cleaning to do. Get to it."

"You're absolutely right. Why should I sit around feeling insecure? I haven't a problem in the world, right?" Not a problem, except I had a broken ankle, and my best friend was convinced the man I loved was cheating on me. Assuming Toni's theory about the hit-and-run being no more than an accident was correct, at least I didn't have a homicidal maniac after me.

I leaned on my crutches and set to work. I washed the dishes, wiped the counters and the table. By the time I was finished, I knew I was in even worse shape than I'd thought. I'd barely been able to get from the table to the sink on my crutches a couple of times without huffing and puffing like a steam engine. I was damp with sweat and my face beet red from the effort. I scooped my crutches back under my arms and headed for the living room. I paused for a second halfway down the hall, debating whether I should call Mitchell.

It was strange that, apart from that one short message, I hadn't heard from him. He'd left four days ago. Actually, it was more than strange. It was worrisome. I shuffled back to the kitchen table, where I'd set down my purse, and pulled out my cell phone. Was I worrying over nothing? When Mitchell was in his writing mode, he could sit at his computer for eighteen hours a day and forget everything else—even eating. If he was in that frame of mind, three days was nothing. Also, my cell phone battery had been dead. He couldn't have reached me if he tried.

Speaking of which, I headed to the living room, where I kept my charger, and plugged in my cell. And then I went to the window, angling for a better view of Mitchell's front walk. There was no fresh snow. What was left from the storm a few days ago was now packed and icy, making it impossible to see tracks. For all I knew, that blonde woman could still be there.

I studied the items on the stoop—a cast-iron planter, a mat and a boot scraper in the shape of a porcupine. I was looking for evidence, any indication that somebody was there. But there was absolutely nothing. It left me feeling uneasy.

BY FIVE O'CLOCK, I had been by myself for the better part of a day and was bored out of my mind. I turned on my reading lamp and parked myself in my favorite living room chair with a recipe book in my lap. If I was to start working on a Skinny Recipes column, I would need some inspiration. I flipped pages, pausing now and then on something that sounded especially delicious. Whenever my thoughts wandered, I looked out the window.

About an hour later I happened to glance up as a cab pulled to the curb. I put down my book and watched a woman step out. She was the kind of blonde beauty one usually sees on television commercials—lovely model running in slow motion through meadows of wildflowers, her long blond hair floating in the wind. She wore a short white trench coat and thigh-high black boots, and carried a duffel bag and a red—was that a Vuitton purse? *Nice.* I squinted for a better look. There was something familiar about her. But whoever she was, she wasn't anybody I'd ever met. She looked up and down the street and then dashed across to Mitchell's front door. She pulled a key out of her bag and disappeared inside.

I leaned back against my chair, wondering who she was and what she was doing in Mitchell's house. More important, why hadn't he told me about her? There had to be a rational explanation. Mitchell was a good guy, I reminded myself, and I wasn't going to let myself get swept away in a whirlpool of doubts and insecurities.

I returned to my book, turning the pages blindly. I was soon interrupted by a shrill sound coming from the wall separating Mitchell's and my house. Some kind of power tool? And then it came to me—an electric drill. The noise continued on and off for a few minutes and then stopped. There was some light scratching noise, then silence. I was still sitting in the same spot some time later when the woman left. She marched down Mitchell's walk and turned toward Queen Street. Toni's paranoia had rubbed off on me, because long after the woman had disappeared from view, I was left with a strange sense of foreboding.

I'D BEEN ON pins and needles all day hoping to get a call from Mitchell. By the time I was ready for bed I still hadn't heard from him and my worry was slowly but surely turning to anger. I picked up my phone and dialed his number, going straight into voice mail. I hung up without leaving a message. The next morning, I was just finishing a late breakfast when the phone rang at last. I snatched it up, convinced it was Mitchell.

"Oh, Toni, hi," I said, trying to hide my disappointment.

"Aww, were you hoping it was Mitchell?"

"No," I said unconvincingly.

"Well, sorry it's just me. I was just wondering what your plans are for today. Do you feel up to stopping by the restaurant for a bit? I know you're dying to make sure everything is fine."

"That's a good idea. I feel great this morning." In fact, I hadn't slept very well, waking up every time I turned. Sleeping with a cast was not exactly comfortable. Every movement had sent waves of pain reverberating throughout my leg. "So great, in fact, that my crutches and I are ready to come in to work."

"What did the doctor say about going to work? Aren't you supposed to stay off your feet?" She sounded amused. "I was proposing to stop by for a few minutes—not to work."

"Well, Dr. Goodall had a good idea. All I need is a bar stool or something high enough that I can park myself at the counter. If I have to, I'll use a phone book on top of a chair. As long as I stay off my feet, I'll be fine. I've had enough of staying here by myself all day. There are tons of things I can to do make myself useful. I can peel, and chop, and dice and—"

She chuckled. "I suppose anything is better than staying at home all by your lonesome and obsessing about Mitchell." One thing about Toni, she knew me too well. "Be ready in half an hour and I'll pick you up."

To my amazement Toni showed up on time, gorgeous in a form-fitting red coat. She sauntered up my walk, threw me a happy hello and helped me to her BMW.

"You're in a good mood today," I said as she slid into the driver's seat.

She closed the door, checked her lipstick in the rear-view mirror and turned on the motor. "That's because I am." She threw me a radiant smile. "I can't tell you how nice it is to have a sister."

"You sure are spending an awful lot of time with her."

She laughed but didn't deny it. She put the car into gear and took off.

Half a dozen blocks later, we pulled up to the restaurant and parked. "If a cop tries to give me a ticket for stopping here, I swear I'll shoot him," she said, tapping her purse.

"Are you crazy? You can't walk around with a gun in your purse. Isn't carrying a concealed weapon illegal?"

She threw her hands up, looking innocent. "Somebody threatens our lives, I say, shoot first and beg forgiveness later."

I bobbed my eyebrows. "I don't think that's quite the way that saying goes."

"I like it better the way I put it," she said, climbing out of the car. I struggled out and onto my one good foot as she retrieved my crutches from the back seat. I was clop-clopping across the sidewalk to the entrance, when, to my surprise, a nice-looking man ran ahead of me and opened the door.

"Allow me," he said, standing aside as I went through. I turned to look, almost disbelieving what had just happened.

Toni threw him a beaming smile. "Thank you. So kind of you," she said—somehow managing to make those benign words sound suggestive—and proceeded to sashay by him like a sultry siren from a 1930s movie.

How did she do that? If I tried to walk that way, even without my cast I'd probably just look as if I was holding back gas.

"This is great," she said, glancing back at him as he walked away. She gave me an admiring look. "You've got it made, sweetie."

"What are you talking about?"

"Look at how much attention you're getting. Don't tell me you didn't notice."

"Yeah, right—attention—everyone is staring at the girl on crutches."

She shook her head in exasperation. "While you trekked those ten steps between my car and the front door, there must have been a dozen men practically falling over each other to open the door for you. That cast can be a real advantage."

I quirked an eyebrow. "I've never heard such nonsense in my life. If they were falling over themselves, which I seriously doubt, it would have been for the sexy blonde— you—not the girl on crutches."

She tossed her hair. "Don't be silly. You know what I always say. Opportunity comes in all sorts of disguises. This time it came dressed in a cast, you lucky girl."

If I'd been a bit more proficient with my crutches, I

think I'd have used one to clobber her over the head right about then.

At that moment, Jake appeared from the kitchen. He took one look at me and called over his shoulder, "Hey, guys, Nicky is here."

Toni patted me on the shoulder. "I'll go park the car. Be right back." And she took off.

Scott, Marley, Charles and Jennifer came spilling out of the kitchen. Everyone started talking at the same time. "We were all so worried when we heard."

"How are you?"

"How's your ankle?"

"Does it hurt much?"

"Are you sure you shouldn't be home in bed?"

I help up one hand in the international signal for stop. "Don't worry. I'm fine. I'll have to wear this ski boot for the next six to eight weeks, but I can do anything I like as long as I don't put any weight on that foot. So here's how it's going to work." I explained my plan and the doctor's suggestion. "Charles, you have a car, don't you?" He nodded. "Can you go shopping for stool, or a chair—anything as long as it's bar height?"

"Sure," he said. "I bet I can find one for next to nothing at one of the used-furniture shops down the street."

"That way, I can still supervise and even do some of the prep work." I looked at Jennifer. "How would you feel becoming sous-chef until I'm back on my feet."

She gave me an engaging smile. "I'd love it."

I turned to Charles again. "And that means you'd be head chef."

He grinned. "Great. Don't recover too soon, please. I've always wanted to be head chef."

"You're going to have to do the shopping, create the menus."

"I know the drill, don't worry." He grabbed his coat from the rack. "I'll go get that seat right now, and be back in no time." He ran out the door.

"Did you call that customer?" Jake asked. I looked at him, unsure what he was talking about. "Edna Jamieson, you know, that woman who keeps leaving messages for you. I gave you her number the other day. She called again."

Gesturing toward my leg, I said, "I hope you explained I've been sort of busy."

"I did, but she insisted that she had to speak to you as soon as possible. Please give her a call. She's driving me nuts. She won't tell me what she wants." He flapped a tablecloth over a table, adding, "Promise me you'll call her soon. I know her type. She'll keep bugging me until you do." He moved on to the next table and the others headed back to the kitchen.

Toni brought over the reservations book. "Wait till you see all the bookings we've been getting," she said, setting it on the corner table.

I shuffled over. "Thanks." I flipped the pages back to the past three nights, running my finger down the long list of entries. From what I could see, every table had been booked an average of twice during every shift, in some cases, three times.

"Not too shabby is it?" asked Toni, watching my reaction.

"Not bad at all." I was impressed and continued flipping pages until the entries tapered off. By then I was well into the next month, a good three weeks away. "I can barely believe it. One television interview and suddenly our dinner shifts are jam-packed."

"I hate to be the bearer of bad news, but business has been great." She gave me a victorious smile. "I told you so."

"Why would that be bad news?"

She gave a one-shoulder shrug. "It proves we can get along fine without you." Luckily she winked as she said this, otherwise I might have felt a tiny bit hurt. "I'm just joking. You know this restaurant wouldn't be the same without you. We held our own for a few days, but if you'd been gone any longer, there might not have been a business to come back to."

"That would have made at least one person happy," I said, thinking of the crazy woman.

HALF AN HOUR later the door blew open and Charles came stumbling in carrying a stool—and not one minute too soon. Until his return I'd had no choice but to sit in the dining room and wait, not something I did well.

"I got you one with a telescopic seat," he said. "You can bring it up or down to whatever height you like. Tell me where you want it. It weighs a ton."

"It's perfect. How about at the meat counter?" I said, hobbling to the kitchen after him. I looked around. I'd only been gone three days but it felt more like a month. I was amazed at how good it was to be back. "I really missed this place."

"All kidding aside, we really missed you too," Toni said from the doorway.

Jennifer paused from chopping onions, blinking away the burning in her eyes. "By the way, Nicky, Charles started working on that burger you asked for. We've been eating burgers until it's coming out our ears," she added laughing.

"How's it coming along?"

Charles answered. "Good. We've tested a couple of versions and I think we'll almost there. I have a secret ingredient that cuts the calories by one third." Before I could ask him what was the secret ingredient, he raised a hand and said, "I'm not telling you. You'll have to guess when you taste it."

"Okay," I said, climbing onto the bar chair. I glanced around again. I could hardly believe how smoothly everything seemed to going.

Everybody was working calmly and efficiently. The giant stainless steel bowl by the sink held the usual stack of fresh vegetables waiting to be peeled and chopped. Rows of individual crustless quiches sat on the counter by the oven. Toni had been telling the truth. They *could* run the restaurant without me. I wasn't disappointed in the least. This was good news. It took loads of pressure off. "Do we have all the ingredients we need for the lunch menu?"

Charles nodded. "We're fine. I made sure we were fully stocked." He walked by Jennifer and patted her back, his hand lingering there an extra minute. Those two were so clearly in love. I was happy for Charles. He was a good guy and deserved happiness.

I nodded my satisfaction. On the chopping block, leaves of freshly washed romaine were stacked, and on the stove soup simmered. "What's the soup of the day?"

"*Crème de poivron rouge*," replied Jennifer. "It sounds fancier in French. Cream of red pepper soup. I made it."

Yum, one of my favorites. "All right, first things first— how are we on supplies for the rest of the week?"

Marley hurried over, his dreadlocks bouncing as he handed me a notepad. "I took inventory. We're good on meat and poultry, potatoes and root vegetables, but we're getting low on cheeses."

I scanned the list. "It looks like we're about to run out of eggs too. And how are we on fresh herbs and salad fixings?"

"You're right. I didn't have it on the list, but we are low on all of those, and also, Charles, weren't you hoping to make risotto tomorrow? We'll need mushrooms—morels and chanterelles."

"You'll have a big shopping to do tomorrow." I threw Toni a glance. "Can you make sure he has enough money for the shopping?"

She nodded. "Not a problem."

I settled at the counter in front of the mound of vegetables and began to peel and chop. I felt particularly clumsy and unattractive with one foot in a cast and the other in a sneaker. My strawberry blond hair was in a net, my queen-size body in a chef's jacket, which did nothing for my five-foot-four frame. Toni, of course, was garbed in a black cashmere sweater, a miniskirt and her usual four-inch heels, making her over six feet tall. She wasn't scoring any points by standing there looking like a fashion model. Strangely, I didn't feel as envious of Jennifer, yet she was just as lovely. Maybe it was because she was self-effacing whereas Toni was so not.

Soon the lunch crowd began drifting in, and before I knew it, the kitchen was a tornado of activity. I sliced and diced as fast as I could. Meanwhile Charles was calling out the orders to "Stir," "Whisk," or "Get that frying pan off the stove before it burns." Pots boiled, kettles whistled, and pans sizzled. And all around the wonderful aromas of savory foods and sauces filled the air. The rush of activity left me energized. There was nowhere in the world I would rather have been.

I got through lunch and then dinner, surprisingly pleased at how much I had been able to accomplish. Granted, I hadn't been anywhere near my usual performance, but considering my handicap I hadn't done badly. I grabbed my crutches and made my way to the door for a peek. The dining room was empty. I breathed a sigh of relief.

"Okay, everybody. We can call it a day." My words were followed by a general exit, leaving only Toni and me. "I don't know about you but I'm dead tired," I said. "All I want right now is to crawl into bed." And hopefully hear from Mitchell.

As if she could read my mind, Toni said, "Will you give him a call if you don't hear from him tonight?"

There was no point in playing dumb. "I haven't really thought about it."

"Liar. I bet you will."

"What about you?" I retorted. "Are you going to tell Steven about Judy?"

She shrugged, suddenly looking miserable. "I don't know. He's been in a real mood these last few days. He's still harping about my not telling him about my money when we were married."

She disappeared into the kitchen for a moment, reappearing with her purse in one hand and a wallet in the other. "Somebody forgot their wallet." She rummaged through, pulling out a driver's license. "It's Jennifer's. I guess there's no point in calling her tonight. She can pick it up in the morning." She returned to the kitchen.

"Toni," I called after her. "Have you considered that maybe Steven's upset about the lie and not about the will? I wouldn't be surprised if he didn't care at all about your money. He's probably just hurt that you never trusted him enough to tell him."

She appeared in the doorway, hand on hip. "Yeah, right."

"Just out of curiosity," I asked. "Who became your beneficiary after you got divorced?"

"You did," she said, watching for my reaction.

My mouth suddenly went dry. "M-me?" I swallowed hard. "Wow." For one brief instant, I thought about all that money and how wonderful it would be to be rich, to never have to worry about another bill ever again. What would I even do with millions of dollars? Would I sell my house? Buy a bigger, fancier one? Have a maid? Drive an expensive car?

All at once it struck me that I was actually drooling over the prospect of being rich. I had momentarily forgotten that for me to inherit would necessarily mean my best friend would be dead. If the thought of that kind of wealth could put *me* in a near trance, there was no telling what it might do to other people. Maybe Toni was right about Steven. Maybe he did care about the money more than about the lie. It was a disconcerting thought.

Toni looked amused. "Yes, you. Lucky for you that driver hit *you* and not *me*, otherwise the cops would be all over you for attempted murder."

as practical as an unloaded gun

TONI OPENED THE passenger door, handing me my crutches. I stumbled out of the car.

"Tell me you at least got one call from him since he left," she said, seeing me looking at Mitchell's house.

I shrugged, or rather tried to, only to realize shrugging was just one more thing I couldn't do while holding myself up on crutches. "Just that one voice mail."

"You haven't spoken to him at all since he left? Not once?"

"It doesn't surprise me," I answered defensively. "When he's writing, nothing else exists. It isn't as if he doing anything wrong. He's just working hard."

She mumbled something under her breath. All I could make out was, "*Blah, blah, blah,* while the cat's away. *Blah, blah, blah,* he'd be so dead."

"I *trust* him," I said, perhaps a bit too forcefully.

"Suuure you do." She chuckled. "Just promise me you'll let me know when he comes back. I want to be there for the fireworks. I would hate to miss all the fun."

I didn't bother arguing. Truth was I *was* irritated with Mitchell for his lack of attention. Why the heck did I even need a boyfriend if he was going to ignore me all the time?

She helped me safely to the door and stood by while I let myself in.

"Do you want to come in?" I asked.

"Maybe if you offer me a glass of wine." She followed

me into the kitchen and poured herself some white wine from the fridge.

"Don't you think you're drinking a bit much these days?"

She shrugged. "No more than usual." Suddenly, she slapped her forehead. "Damn. I'll have to go back to the restaurant."

"Why? What did you forget?"

"I left my gun in the drawer behind the cash register."

I looked at her, horrified. "You what?"

"Don't get your panties in a knot. I figured it was safer there than in my purse. I keep my purse in the kitchen, but with everyone going in and out all the time, I figured it might not be the best place to leave a loaded gun."

"It's loaded!" I shrieked. "You keep your gun loaded?"

She gave me incredulous look. "What good is a gun if it's not loaded? By the time I found the bullets and got them inside the chamber, I'd already be dead."

"That is *so* not funny. First of all, statistics show that gun owners are more likely to get shot than people who don't own weapons. And by the way, you'd better make sure you keep it somewhere safe at home. Imagine what could happen if Celia came to visit and found it?"

Toni took a gulp of wine. Looking contrite, she said, "You're right. I never even thought of that. From now on, I'll have to keep it somewhere high up, where she can't reach it."

"Are you kidding? Kids are resourceful. They can get into the damnedest places. You have to keep it locked up, maybe in a safety deposit box."

"Fat lot of good that'll do me the day I really need it. I'll just tell the robbers to hold on while I run to the bank and get my gun."

I groaned with frustration. "Are you sure you want to

go back to the restaurant tonight? It's late. Can't it wait until tomorrow?"

"I'll just finish my wine before I go." She marched off to the kitchen and I heard the fridge door open and close. She reappeared a moment later with a second glass—for me.

We settled in the living room. Toni was quiet, thinking about Steven maybe? That worked for me, I was too exhausted to talk. Fifteen minutes later she pulled herself off the sofa. "I'd better get going. I won't sleep knowing my gun is still there."

As well as I knew her, I had no idea whether a gun was something she always carried, or if this was a new thing.

"Honestly, Toni, what's the point? It's late."

"It'll only take me a minute." She blew me a kiss and left, calling over her shoulder, "See you in the morning. I'll pick you up at the same time."

I closed the door behind her and went to the mudroom to let the dogs out. While they ran around in the backyard, I got rid of the soiled wee-wee pads and set out clean ones. The minute they were all back in, safe and sound, I picked up my house phone and checked my messages.

"Hey, sweetheart." It was Mitchell. My heart did a somersault. "Just calling to let you know I'm thinking of you. Bunny and I have been working since seven o'clock this morning and we're just going out to grab a bite. If you try to call me, you'll probably get my voice mail. I'll be turning off my phone while we're in the restaurant. I'll call you back soon. Love you."

Bunny. I pictured the two of them sitting across from each other in some cozy little restaurant. I imagined them leaning close, feeding each other morsels from their plates, while playing footsies under the table. The vision left me feeling sick. I put the phone down, scowling. And then on the spur of the moment, I picked it up and punched in his number—hard.

I waited for the beep, and using a light easy tone I said, "Hey, Mitchell. I'm happy the writing is going well. Sorry I haven't been around when you called. I just got out of the hospital." There, that should make him feel guilty. "I was in a bit of an accident a few days ago. I got hit by a car. By a hit-and-run driver, actually. My left ankle got pretty badly broken. But the orthopedic surgeon operated on me and now I'm getting around on crutches." Maybe I was pouring it on a bit thick. But hey, every word was true. "So, all's well. Ciao for now." I hung up, wondering how long it would be until I heard from him. It had better be soon, otherwise Toni would turn out to be right. There would be fireworks.

"Ready for bed, doggies?" I locked the doggie door and hobbled up the stairs, followed by a parade of Yorkies. They climbed, every step a challenging height for their tiny legs. When they reached the landing, they scurried by madly to their night kennel.

I slipped on a nightgown and picked up a piece of paper I noticed on my night table. It contained a phone number. It took me a second to decipher the handwriting, and then could only make out the first name, Edna. *Damn*. This was the number of that client Jake had asked me to call. I'd forgotten all about her—again. This time, I copied down her name and number on a larger piece of paper, which I set on my bedside table. It would be the first thing I saw tomorrow morning.

By the time I collapsed into bed, it was midnight. I was out like a light. It felt like just a few minutes later that the phone rang. I groped around in the dark and picked it up on the third ring. This time it *had* to be Mitchell.

"Hello?" I answered groggily.

"Is this Nicole Landry, owner of Skinny's on Queen?" asked a male voice I didn't recognize.

"Who is this?" I asked, looking at my alarm clock. Four-thirty in the morning—what the heck?

"This is Inspector McCartney of the fire department. We have your name as the contact person for your business."

I bolted upright, biting back a shriek as a flash of pain ran through my ankle. "The fire department? Why? What happened?"

"I'm sorry I have some bad news, ma'am. There's been a fire at your place of business."

An image of flames leaping from our restaurant flashed through my mind. Oh, no. My Wolf stove, all the lovely old dishes and cutlery that Toni and I had spent months of Saturdays hunting for at flea markets and garage sales, the fuchsia tables and chairs we'd painted ourselves—would they all be reduced to ashes? I squeezed my eyes against the nightmarish picture. "How bad is it?"

"I'm afraid it's pretty bad."

"I'll be right over." I slammed down the phone and picked it up again, dialing Toni's number. I let it ring four times and then her message came on. "This is you know who," it said, sounding suggestive. "At the sound of the you know what, you know what to do." *Beep.*

Of course, Toni would have chosen tonight, of all nights, to sleep at Steven's. I was about to dial her cell phone when it occurred to me that there was no point in waking her with the horrible news. Why should both of us have to get up at such an ungodly hour? I would take care of the problem myself and give her a full report in the morning. I hung up and picked up again immediately, punching in the number of a cab company.

"This is an emergency. How fast can you get a car here?"

"We'll have somebody there in a few minutes, ma'am," the dispatcher answered.

I hopped around on one foot, pulling on any clothes that fell under my hands, until, fifteen minutes later I was dressed. My hair was a mess and my eyes were still puffy from sleep when the taxi drove up, but at least I was ready. I hurried out as fast as I could.

The driver—bless him—took one look at my stricken face and put the pedal to the floor, getting me to within three blocks of the restaurant in record time. But from there he had to inch along in the stalled traffic. About twenty feet farther we came to a complete stop, half a dozen emergency vehicles blocking the road.

"Sorry, lady, this is as far as I can take you."

"Please, can't you do something? I have to get there. That's my restaurant on fire. There must some way you can get me closer."

He studied me through the rearview mirror and took pity on me. "Hold on. I'll be right back." He turned off the motor and got out of the car, jogging over to the nearest cop. He said something, pointing insistently in my direction.

The cop followed him back and opened the back door. "Are you the owner of that restaurant?"

"Yes, I am. The fire inspector called and asked me to come down. But I can't walk. I have a broken ankle."

"Okay." He closed the door and spoke to the driver, who hopped back into the driver's seat and turned the key in the ignition. We crept on another fifty feet or so, snaking our way between one emergency vehicle after another. Meanwhile the police officer ran on ahead, waving us through.

The closer we got, the more I could see of the devastation. The fire seemed to be out, but the front of the restaurant was dark with soot. The window was smashed into a giant gaping mouth with glass shards shaped like teeth. Through this wide-open jaw bellowed clouds of thick smoke. I squinted, trying to see farther inside, and caught a glimpse of even more destruction—black walls, burned and smashed furniture and, everywhere, dripping water. My entire future was gone.

Tears trembled on my lashes. We had worked so hard to create this restaurant. I had pinned so much hope on it. "It's ruined. The whole place is destroyed."

The driver's eyes met mine in the rearview mirror. "I can't get any closer. Maybe I can find someone to help you. I'll be right back." He jumped out of the cab again, returning a few minutes later accompanied by two firemen.

I pushed open the car door. "I'm the owner of the restaurant. Can you tell me where Fire Inspector McCartney is? He wants to talk to me."

The taller of the two—a muscular young man who could have performed in a Chippendale's show—began to say something, and then noticed my cast. "Oh." He scratched his head. "Hold on to my neck." In one easy movement he swept me off the seat and into his arms.

"Wait, my crutches," I said.

The driver pulled them out and handed them over to the fireman, who carried me as if I weighed no more than a feather, all the way to a small emergency vehicle a short distance from all the commotion. "That's the fire inspector." He nodded toward a middle-aged man with a handlebar mustache and flinty eyes. "Hey, chief, I've got the owner here," he called out to him.

"Nicky Landry?" the man asked. "After we talk, the police will want to have a moment with you too." He marched off toward a police car, said a few words to someone inside and returned. "Come with me."

The young fireman had been standing by. Now, he scooped me up again and carried me to the fire inspector's car. Soon, I found myself sitting in the back seat with a cup of takeout coffee, while I tried to make sense of everything the inspector was telling me.

"We'll have to do a full investigation and get a pathologist's report before we call it murder, but I have to tell you, so far it looks pretty suspi—"

My mind snapped to attention. "Did you just say *murder?*"

He stared at me, hard. "That's what I said, ma'am."

My mouth went dry. "Somebody is dead? How do you know it was murder?"

He pointed to a man in fireman's garb. "He's the coroner's investigator, and he's found evidence of a bullet wound."

My pulse went into overdrive. Even as I asked, I wasn't sure I wanted to hear the answer. "Do you know who it is?"

"We haven't identified her yet." At that moment, a group of firemen walked out of the building carrying a gurney. On it was what I assumed was the body of the victim. I wasn't certain since it was covered with a fireman's blanket. I couldn't tear my eyes away. I hoped, I prayed that it wasn't—

At that moment the blanket slipped, and one of the men quickly pulled it back in place, but not before I caught a glimpse of a human head covered with something that looked like a tangle of string.

I swallowed hard. "You said *her?* You mean it's a woman?"

The inspector nodded. "Any idea who she might be?"

My breath was coming in short little gasps. "My girlfriend…partner…she—"

"Is your girlfriend a blonde?" he asked, and all at once I realized the tangle had been a lock of wet blond hair. Toni's? Black spots suddenly appeared before my eyes. They grew bigger until everything went black.

The next thing I knew, I was lying on the back seat of the cop car, and the good-looking young fireman was holding up my head.

"Here, drink this. Ah, here we go," he said, as I choked back a gulp of water, and then over his shoulder he called out, "She's coming around now, sir."

A police officer came jogging over and together he and the young fireman helped me to a sitting position, as the inspector stood by, studying me coldly. My coat was dripping wet from the coffee I'd spilled all over myself. All I could think was that it couldn't be Toni. *Please God make it not be Toni.*

The policeman, a tall bald man who exuded authority, gave me a sympathetic smile. He handed me a paper napkin from the coffee shop. I wiped my eyes, blew my nose.

"I know this is hard for you," he said, "but any information you can give us at this point will be of great help."

Unable to utter a sound through my tight throat, I nodded.

He turned to the inspector. "I'll take it from here, if you don't mind." He climbed into the back seat, sitting next to me. "I'm Officer Duncan," he said, handing me a card. "Do you have any idea who the victim might be?"

I tried to speak again but nothing came out.

"Take a deep breath," he said.

I did, and found my voice. "It could be my partner, Toni Lawford." Speaking the words made it seem all the more real, and tears welled in my eyes.

"Is your partner tall and slender and has blond hair?"

It took all I had to just nod.

"What makes you believe it could be her?"

"She dropped me off at home after work, and she was going back to pick up something she'd left behind." I purposely avoided mentioning this *something* just so happened to be a gun.

"At what time was this?"

"I think it was somewhere around eleven-thirty."

As he wrote this down, a horrible thought occurred to me. The inspector had used the word *murder*. Toni did not just die. Somebody had killed her. I began hyperventilating.

This confirmed it. What had happened to me a few days ago was no accident. That woman was out to kill Toni and me. And she had already accomplished half her goal. And then another thought occurred to me. Toni hadn't yet changed her will. I stood to inherit millions. I would be rich—filthy rich. But I had just lost my best friend. A lump settled in my stomach. I didn't want her money. I wanted Toni.

"Why would anybody want to kill her?" I asked, tears trembling on my lashes.

"It could be just a case of being at the wrong place at the wrong time. Or—" He studied me for a second and then added, "Any idea who might benefit from seeing your partner dead?"

Knowing the way cops think, I was sure to become their number-one suspect. I decided to play dumb. "I have no idea."

it doesn't mean we have to lie down and take it

THE QUESTIONING WENT on for a long time. I gave him the name of all the restaurant employees and their contact information. He asked for the name of the business's insurance company, and I had to admit that being new and since we'd only recently started covering our operating costs, we hadn't gotten around to getting coverage.

His eyes studied me. "That's too bad. You probably invested a lot of money in this, didn't you?"

"Everything I had," I said. As terrible as that was, it was nothing compared to losing Toni.

"Any idea who could have done this?" he asked, and I told them about the threats the crazy woman had made. And then I spent the next hour going over every detail of the confrontation, describing her in detail. I answered questions until I couldn't think straight. Meanwhile, I wanted to point out that, if the police had taken my hit-and-run seriously, they might have found who did it. And then Toni would still be alive.

At last he called over one of the younger officers milling around and told him to take me home. By then it was six o'clock in the morning. Most of the emergency vehicles had left. Two fire trucks remained, and a few police cars. The policeman jogged over to one of them, hopped in and drove over. He helped me into the passenger seat and I gave him my home address. It was still dark out, but not for long. It was almost time to get up.

"You're sure you'll be all right by yourself?" he asked, pulling up in front of my house. He handed me his card.

I slipped it into my pocket, adding it to the others I'd collected.

"If you like, I could drive you to the hospital," he continued. "You've had a bad shock."

"I'll be fine." I glanced at Mitchell's house, which was bathed in darkness. My throat clenched. I so, so needed to hear his voice, feel his arms around me. I pushed the door open and struggled to get out.

"Wait. Let me help." The officer hopped out of the car and hurried around to the passenger side. He handed me my crutches from the backseat and saw me to the door. "Are you sure you don't want me to call someone for you? I don't think it's a good idea for you to be alone right now."

"I'll be fine," I said, putting my key in the lock. To my surprise, the door swung open. In my rush to get to the restaurant I must have forgotten to lock it. I glanced over my shoulder at him shuffling, unsurely.

"We've already put out an APB with a full description of this woman," he said. "I'm sure we'll pick her up in no time. In the meantime, keep your door locked, stay close to home and call me if you think of anything else we should know."

I nodded. "I will. Thank you." And before he could give me any more advice, I stepped inside and closed the door. I needed to be alone. From the window I watched as he hesitated another second or two. And then he turned and strode down the walk back to his car.

At that moment Jackie came tearing down the stairs, barking at full volume. I tottered over, dropped my crutches and plopped myself down on the bottom step, gathering her in my arms. I buried my nose in her neck and the tears burst forth. They came in heaving, racking sobs, leaving me gasping for breath.

"Oh, Jackie, what am I going to do? She's dead, Jackie. She's dead."

"Who's dead?" The voice took me by such surprise I nearly jumped out of my skin. I screamed. When I looked up, Toni was standing before me in living flesh and blood. She looked disheveled but perfectly healthy.

I gasped, clutching my heart. "Oh my God, you're alive!"

She looked at me as if I'd lost my mind. "And why, exactly, does this surprise you?"

"I thought you—" Before I could complete my thought, I burst into tears again. And before I knew it, I was laughing and crying, tears mingling with my runny nose. I had completely lost it, and I couldn't have cared less.

Toni came over, sitting next to me on the stair. She wrapped an arm around me and sniffed my hair. "You smell like smoke. Unless you've picked up smoking, I'm guessing you were just at the restaurant." I hiccupped and more tears came streaming down my cheeks. She patted my arm. "There, there—don't worry. It was just a small business, no big loss. We can start over."

I wiped my eyes and looked at her. "You—you know about the fire?" I hiccupped.

"That's why I'm here." She rummaged through her pocket and pulled out the copy of the house key I'd given her months earlier in case of emergency. She brandished it. "I hope you don't mind that I just let myself in." She slipped it back in her pocket and continued, "I was watching television when a report of the fire came on. I was going to call you but decided to let you sleep. I raced over, but I couldn't get anywhere near. There were emergency vehicles everywhere. So I came over here. When

I found you gone, I guessed you heard about the fire too. I decided to wait."

I looked over to the living room and noticed the pillow and blankets on the sofa. She offered me her hand and helped me up, handing me my crutches. "Come on, I'll make us some coffee."

I followed her to the kitchen, and she pulled up a chair for me.

"So you saw the damage?"

I nodded, grimacing.

"How bad is it?"

"Bad, Toni, really bad. It's gone. It's all gone."

"Thank goodness we're insured. We can always rebuild if we want to."

The problem was that we *didn't* have insurance, a small detail I couldn't bring myself to mention at that moment. "What do you mean *if* we want to rebuild?"

She scowled. "Seeing as we were working ourselves haggard and barely making any money, why would we want to go through all that again? Before I forget—" she opened the cupboard and pulled out the coffee grinder, and then turned to face me, "—will you please explain why exactly you thought I was dead?"

"They found a body in the restaurant," I said, the full horror of it hitting me again. "Oh God, Toni, I was so sure it was you. They said it was a woman's body."

The answer hit us both at the same time, and we blurted it out together. "Jennifer!"

"It must have been her," Toni continued slowly. "She probably discovered she'd left her wallet there and went back for it. She and Charles are living together. She must have borrowed the key from him."

I'd had no idea Jennifer and Charles were living together. It made the tragedy seem even worse. Charles was such a nice person, and losing a loved one was one of the most painful experiences in the world.

Jennifer was tall and thin, and had shoulder-length blond hair. From the description the fire chief had given me, no wonder I'd automatically concluded the victim was Toni.

I cleared my throat. "Uh, Toni, did you know that the fire was deliberately set?"

She looked at me, her eyes wide with shock. "It wasn't an accident?"

"No, and the fire inspector said that the victim was probably murdered." I stared hard at her. "Toni, listen to me. First I get hit by a car, then the restaurant burns down, and now Jennifer is dead—murdered. I don't know about you, but I'm finding it harder and harder to believe that this is all just some gigantic series of coincidences."

The color drained from her. "Somebody is willing to kill, just to see us out of business? Oh, my God. It has to be that crazy woman. What do you think we should do?"

I furrowed my forehead, thinking furiously. "I don't know." And then I made up my mind. "Just because somebody is trying to force us to close shop—damn it—doesn't mean we have to lie down and take it. You and I have to fight."

She dropped into the chair across from me. "That's exactly what I was afraid you'd say."

everybody thinks you're dead

Toni was making coffee—the last thing in the world I wanted. All I felt was an overwhelming need to figure out who was responsible for what was going on, and find a way to stop them. Was it the bedraggled woman? Could someone who appeared to be a homeless person or mentally ill, if not both, somehow get hold of a car and run me down, and then find a gun, shoot Jennifer and burn down our restaurant? As unlikely as that scenario seemed, I couldn't come up with a better one. I limped over to the living room, collapsed on the sofa and stared at the ceiling, as thoughts whirled inside my head.

"I almost forgot," I shouted to Toni in the kitchen. "I have to call the inspector. Everybody still thinks you're dead." I reached over for the house phone on the coffee table, pulled out the bunch of business cards from my pocket and sorted through them until I found the one I was looking for. I punched in the number.

She came racing back. "Tell me you're not calling Crawford and Sanders. I don't think I could stomach having to deal with those two right now."

I covered the mouthpiece and whispered. "No, I'm calling the fire inspector. And there's another police detective in charge, thank goodness."

On the third ring the inspector picked up, sounding surprisingly concerned considering how cold he had been earlier. "Ms. Landry, what's up? Did something happen? Are you all right?"

"I'm fine. I have good news. My friend Toni is alive. It was somebody else's body you found." I tried to explain but realized that I wasn't making much sense. "Here, you can speak to her yourself. She's right here." I passed the phone to Toni.

She answered his questions, told him who we thought victim might be, and after looking up Charles's number on her iPhone and giving it to him, she hung up. "He's going to let the police know. He said they'd want to talk to him."

I couldn't imagine a worse way of receiving such tragic news than by a policeman showing up at your door. I looked at Toni earnestly. "Don't you think we should go to Charles before the police get there? He shouldn't have to be alone."

She hesitated. "We're really sure about this, aren't we?—about the victim being Jennifer, I mean."

I nodded grimly. "It certainly looks that way."

"I guess we should." She pulled out her iPhone and touched the screen. "I have his address." She named a trendy area of the city.

This took me by surprise. I hadn't expected Charles to be living in one of Toronto's pricier neighborhoods. Toni rechecked the address. "That's the address he gave me."

I let the dogs out, refilled their water bowl, and then we took off.

We headed east of downtown, toward Cabbagetown, so named for the Irish immigrants who first came to live there in the eighteen-fifties. The area had been gentrified—much like my own neighborhood of Queen West—until its real estate had risen to astronomical prices.

We turned from Winchester onto Sumac, pulling up in front of a lovely old Victorian house across from a small park. Again I asked, "Are you *sure* this is where he lives?"

I couldn't imagine that my sous-chef, whom we were paying a pittance, could afford to live in a near mansion.

She pulled her cell from her pocket and rechecked the address. "No mistake—this is it."

I stared at the house, taking in the three-floor brick structure, its richly carved wood door, the detailed stained-glass windows and meticulous landscaping. This place had to be worth well into the seven figures. "How the hell can Charles afford to live here?"

"It's certainly not from the money we pay him." Toni was staring at it in awe. "This place is gorgeous. I wouldn't mind living here myself."

I gawked at it for a minute longer, as much in procrastination as in admiration. "Well, we can't stay out here forever." I pushed open the door and hopped out on one foot, grabbing my crutches from between the front seats and pulling them under my arms. Another week and I'd be getting around almost as comfortably with them as without.

Just as Toni reached for the bell, the door flew open and Charles appeared in his terry bathrobe. The deep circles under his eyes hinted at a sleepless night. "Jennifer?" he blurted, looking faint with relief until, seeing it was only Toni and me, his face fell. "Oh, hi." He frowned, puzzled. "What are you two doing here?"

"Uh, Charles, I'm afraid we have some bad news. There's been a fire at the restaurant."

"Oh?" he answered, glancing over my shoulder, still looking for Jennifer no doubt.

My heart sank for him. "The restaurant is pretty much gutted," I added.

This seemed to get through to him. "The restaurant is gone?"

"Burned to the ground, Charles—it's gone."

He took a step back, tightened the belt around his robe

and gestured for us to come in. "That's unreal. That means we're all out of a job?"

Nodding, I took a deep breath. "There's more. The fire inspector thinks it was probably arson."

"Are you serious?" He frowned. "Was it that lunatic who threatened you?" Pausing between the foyer and the living room, he shook his head in disbelief. At last he gathered himself and pointed toward the sofa. "Have a seat. Can I get you anything?"

I shuffled further in. "No thank you." I turned and almost gasped out loud. The living room was magnificent—large yet inviting, with dark hardwood floors, robin's-egg walls and creamy white high ceilings. I looked around, admiring the light taupe sofa and armchairs. An arched doorway separated this room from the dining area—a long dark-wood table, upholstered chairs, a sparkling chandelier and what looked like hand-painted wallpaper with an oriental motif. The decor was magnificent, elegant yet comfortable with tasteful furnishings and walls covered in art. It could have been featured in a decorating magazine.

"Are you sure? Coffee? Tea?"

"No, thank you," I said again, letting myself sink into one of the down-filled armchairs. I cleared my throat. "Er, Charles, I need to ask you, did you give anybody a copy of the restaurant key by any chance?"

He looked taken aback. "Of course not—I've only got one copy, and I have it right here." He rose and went to an antique desk near the entrance, picking up a key ring and going through it. He paused, his forehead furrowing. "I know I had it yesterday." Understanding flashed through his eyes. "Jennifer must have borrowed it. We had an argument last night and she took off in a huff. But why would she have wanted—" He froze, blood draining from his face. "The fire—did anybody—?"

My mouth dried. But just as I was about to tell him, I was saved by the doorbell. Charles looked too shocked to move.

"I'll get it." Toni strode to the door. "Hello, Officer, I'm Toni Lawford," I heard her say in a low voice.

And then I heard a male voice I recognized as Police Officer Duncan's. He walked in, and nodded to Toni and me. "Are you Charles Bateman?"

Charles paled and nodded.

The officer turned to me. "If you don't mind, I'd like to speak with him in private."

"Of course." I turned to Charles. "We'll be waiting in the car in case you need us."

I wasn't sure he'd heard me, but we pulled on our coats and left. Soon we were sitting in Toni's car, shivering. She turned on the motor and put the heat on full blast. Hot air instantly streamed in. "Poor guy," she whispered, breathing in her hands for warmth. "I can't imagine what he must be going through. He's probably feeling a hundred times worse because his last memory of Jennifer will be of them arguing."

I was trying to picture the timeline according to what Charles had just told us. "Jennifer didn't tell him she was going to the restaurant." I thought for a second. "If she was storming out after an argument, she was probably planning on checking into a hotel, but since she'd forgotten her wallet at work, she must have swiped the restaurant key from Charles's ring as she left."

I was quiet for a few minutes as I pictured the scenario unfolding in Charles's house as we spoke.

"Poor guy," I said, echoing Toni's words.

We sat in silence, our shivering quickly fading as the

interior warmed. Ten minutes or so later, long after the temperature had reached toasty warm, the front door opened and the inspector stuck his head out. He glanced up and down the street until he spotted us and waved us over.

I followed Toni into the eerily silent living room. Officer Duncan nodded a greeting. Charles was sitting in the same spot, now with his elbows on his knees and his head in his hands. His grief was almost palpable. I paused, uncertain what I should do or say.

Toni didn't hesitate. She strode over and sat next to him, rubbing his back. "I'm so sorry, Charles."

He raised his head and looked at her through red-rimmed eyes. "I have to go identify the body. I don't think I can do that by myself."

Toni squeezed his hand. "Would you like me to go with you?" He nodded silently.

"All right then," Duncan said. "We might as well get this over with. It shouldn't take very long."

Charles seemed to gather his courage. He pulled himself out of his chair.

Toni turned to me. "Why don't you stay here? Maybe you can call the guys in the meantime."

A minute later the three of them were gone. I took out my cell phone, staring at it as I drummed up my nerve. For all I knew they could have already heard. But if they hadn't, and I didn't call them, they would leave for work. I punched in Jake and Marley's home number.

This time the words poured out of me. The restaurant had burned down during the night. The police suspected arson. A body was found in the debris and Charles was on his way to identify the remains as Jennifer's.

"Jennifer is dead?" he said in disbelief.

"Her identity hasn't been confirmed yet. But it looks that way."

"But—" He struggled for words. "What happened?" In the background I could hear Marley asking, "What's wrong?"

I tried to give him some answers, but I still had as many questions as he did. To my great relief he offered to call Scott. I hung up and breathed a sigh of relief.

There was nothing I could do but wait. I put my aching ankle up on a footstool as I contemplated the possibilities. There were only three I could think of.

The first was that one single person was responsible for everything that had happened; the hit-and-run, the burning down of the restaurant and Jennifer's murder. Whether this person was the woman who had uttered the threats was a different matter. Much as I would have liked to believe that theory, if I did, I would also have to believe that this woman, who appeared insane and possibly homeless, had access to a luxury car and to guns, and as crazy as she was, that she had formulated some kind of plan to get rid of us and or the restaurant.

Another theory was that not all of those incidents were committed by the same person. Maybe Steven was right and that the hit-and-run really was no more than an accident. I liked this theory. But it still left unanswered questions. Even supposing that crazy woman had burned down the restaurant, how did she get her hands on a gun?

My last theory was that the hit-and-run, the burning of the restaurant and Jennifer's murder were all related, but that somebody other than the crazy woman was responsible. This idea scared the bejesus out of me, but I had to consider it nonetheless. It implied someone sane was behind it all. There were countless questions with that one. What did Toni and I have in common other than the restaurant? Nothing.

I had to be missing something, but what? I was still puzzling over this when my cell phone rang.

It was Toni. "We're on our way back—should be there in ten minutes or so. Why don't you make a pot of coffee in the meantime? I have a feeling Charles will need a cup."

I bit back the countless questions I had. Now was not the time, not with Charles in the car and hearing every word. I'd wait for a moment alone with her. I hung up and made my way down the hall toward the back, where I found the kitchen. I searched the cabinets until I found the coffee. I was grinding the beans when in occurred to me that Charles had probably not eaten since last night. He could do with some food too.

By the time I heard the front door open and close, the coffee was ready and I had the eggs whipped and ready to pour into the skillet. I returned to the living room, praying Toni would tell me the victim was somebody else— not Jennifer. But one look at Charles's stricken expression was all the answer I needed.

I caught Toni's eyes and she nodded grimly.

I clomped back to the kitchen where I set the coffee on a platter, dropped a spoonful of butter into a pan and poured in the beaten eggs. "Toni, could you come out here and give me a hand?" She hurried over and I pointed to the coffeepot, whispering, "Do they know how she died?"

"So far, all they know is that she was shot in the back. But they have no idea if she died of the gunshot or from smoke inhalation. They'll know more after the autopsy," she said in a low voice. "The news of Jennifer's death was already on the radio when we came back. Poor Charles. I thought he was going to pass out when he heard it."

She picked up the pot and a cup and carried them out

to the living room. I followed. "Here you go," she said to Charles. "And Nicky made you something to eat."

He sat crumpled over, staring vacantly at the floor. He shook his head. "Thanks, but I'm not hungry."

"I won't give you too much, just a little bit. You have to keep up your strength," she insisted. She set the cup down and disappeared to the kitchen, returning with a plate of scrambled eggs and toast. She handed it to him. He picked up the fork and took a halfhearted bite.

I sat across from him and cleared my throat. "Is there anything I can do for you? Is there anybody you want me to call?"

"No thanks, I'll call Jennifer's family myself," he said flatly. "Before they hear it on the news."

At that moment, the overture for *Sex and the City* began to play—Toni's cell phone. She pulled it from her pocket and disappeared down the hall, holding a whispered conversation.

She reappeared a moment later. "That was Jake. He wanted to know if Charles needed company. I told him to come over."

Toni was in the kitchen refilling Charles's cup when the doorbell rang. I shuffled over to the door and peeked through the peephole. It was Jake. I opened the door and he walked in looking distressed, Marley in tow. They both appeared to have just tumbled out of bed, with day-old beard and bed hair. They gave me the same questioning look I had given Toni. I nodded, just as she had to me.

"How is he?" Jake whispered. He slipped out of his coat, glancing at Charles over my shoulder.

I shook my head. "Pretty upset as you can imagine."

He and Marley stepped into the living room. I stayed in the entrance hall, giving them a moment of privacy.

At that moment the doorbell rang again. This time it was a stranger.

He stepped inside. "I'm Jennifer's brother. I just heard—" He turned and spotted Charles. He hurried over.

The doorbell rang again. I opened the door to another stranger. "I'm Bret Atwood, Jennifer's husband," a muscular and sullen-looking man said, and without any further ado he went storming over to Charles.

I hovered by the entrance. *Jennifer's husband? What the hell?*

A heated argument was going on in the living room. I might have been tempted to join in and stand by Charles, who seemed at the receiving end of the second man's fury. But Jake and Marley stepped in protectively. Meanwhile, the brother was playing ping-pong with his eyes, from Charles to Jennifer's husband. Why wasn't he standing up for Charles too?

Toni appeared. "Scott is on his way over too. There's enough going on in here, I think we should leave." She handed me my parka and pulled on her coat. We said goodbye, not that anybody noticed, and left. I followed her to her car and we rode back to my house.

"Who the hell were those two bozos?" Toni asked.

"Jennifer's brother," I said. "And, it seems, her husband."

She swung her head around. "Her *what?*"

I took a deep breath. "You heard me. The second guy who came in, that's how he introduced himself, as Jennifer's husband."

As we turned onto Shaw, I glanced at Toni, who looked lost in thought.

"You know, I was just thinking," she said. "When I die,

I want to go like my grandfather, peacefully in my sleep—
not screaming like the passengers in his car."

It might have been the stress, but I burst out laughing and kept laughing until tears rolled down my cheeks.

you're forgetting something, Sherlock

WE WALKED IN, and Toni offered to make a fresh pot of coffee while I checked on Jackie and the puppies. As soon as her back was turned I checked my voice mail again. There was a new message from Mitchell.

"Hey, honey—" oh, so now that I had a broken ankle, I was *honey*, "—I got your message last night. I hardly slept, I was so worried. Please call me the minute you get this."

I definitely had a mean streak in me, because I was pleased as punch that he was worried.

From the kitchen Toni called out, "Are you good for one cup or two cups?"

I put down the phone and joined her in the kitchen. "You have got to be kidding. I've been guzzling coffee nonstop since I got the call in the middle of the night. If I have any more I'll start shaking like a wet dog."

She turned to face me, jar of coffee beans in hand. "We've both been up for hours. I don't know about you, but unless I keep slugging it down, I'm likely to fall asleep on my feet." She turned on the grinder and the rest of what she was saying was drowned out.

I took care of the dogs and when the coffee was ready I joined her in the living room. I dropped down into the overstuffed cushions of my sofa. It felt good to relax.

She poured me a cup. "If we're going to brainstorm, we might as well be alert."

I took a few sips and looked up to find Toni staring

into her coffee, her brow furrowed with worry. "What are you thinking about?"

"Jennifer. I can't believe she's dead. So full of life one minute, and then—"

"I know." She paused. "What I can't figure out is who's behind all this and why. Because, honestly, that crazy lunatic can't be responsible for all that's happened. First of all, her claims were outrageous. Nobody stole her restaurant. And what did she think we'd do? Hand her the keys and walk away? That's completely illogical. And I just don't see her driving some luxury car, or for that matter torching the restaurant."

"Except for the bit about it being illogical, you just voiced my thoughts exactly."

"What do you mean?"

"You can't expect a lunatic to be logical. To be insane *is* to be illogical."

"Good point."

"I can't imagine she was involved with the hit-and-run either. But she could have started the fire."

"But what about Jennifer? Why?"

I nodded. "I know. That's the problem with that theory. Last I heard, mental patients were not allowed to buy guns."

"Who says she got it legally?" Toni said, putting down her cup. "It's probably easier to get a gun illegally than it is to get a permit." With that, she patted her purse, which had been resting next to her.

I gasped. "You don't even have a permit?" And then quickly, "Don't tell me. I don't want to know." I went back to our conversation. "Let's go over everything again. We've got to be missing something."

She looked at me expectantly.

I drummed my fingers on my cup. "What did Jake tell you about that phone call he got while we were being interviewed?"

"He said the call came in a few minutes after our segment. He answered the phone, expecting it to be another reservation. Instead he got an earful of screaming from some crazy woman about how we stole her restaurant. She was rambling and threatening, he said. When he told Charles, he was convinced it was the same woman." She pursed her mouth. "All I can say is it's damn lucky she didn't show up in the middle of the dinner rush that night."

I had a brief image of a roomful of shocked patrons. "What a disaster that would have been. Can you imagine? Those clients would have never come back."

"I mean lucky for *her*. With a restaurant full of people, at least one person would have called 911. She'd have been picked up and brought straight to jail." She shrugged. "Or to the loony bin."

I stared at her, stunned at her comment. "Wasn't—that—convenient," I said slowly.

Her eyes lit up. "What are you suggesting?"

"As you pointed out—" I was still connecting the dots in my mind, "—it was very fortunate. I wonder if she could have planned it."

Toni leaned in, setting her cup on the coffee table. "You think she was faking that whole Looney-Tunes business?"

We were both silent for a moment as we contemplated this new possibility. Toni picked up her cup again and leaned back, absently rubbing its rim with a perfectly manicured finger. My eyes followed the movement almost hypnotically.

"That's it!" I exclaimed, as the idea flashed through my mind. "If I'm right, this could explain everything."

"What?"

"I don't know why I didn't think of this before. How much do you want to bet that woman was wearing a disguise?"

Toni looked stunned. "You think she wasn't a bag lady at all?"

I shrugged. "I don't know for certain, but if she was, then she could well have done everything else—the hit-and-run, the fire, even Jennifer's murder. As far as her motive, your guess is as good as mine."

Toni fixed her stare on me. "This puts a whole different spin on everything."

Toni was right. But the new spin was a whole lot more scary. Somebody was going to great trouble to throw us off course. I cleared my throat. "If somebody is hiding their identity, Toni, I can think of only two possible reasons."

Toni stared at me, worried. "What?"

"She was either worried about being identified later, or that we might recognize her, in which case it would mean she's someone we know."

"That's ridiculous. We don't know anybody who would want to kill us." Her response had been so quick I couldn't help wondering if she was afraid I might be right. "All this theorizing is stupid. We should just let the cops solve it."

"You know me. I don't trust them to get things right. Just give us a little more time, and we'll get to the bottom of it."

Toni bobbed her eyebrows. "I think you're forgetting something, Sherlock. Considering somebody wants us dead, time is one luxury you and I might not have."

The TENSION OF a moment ago had dissipated, when suddenly the doorbell rang. Toni got to her feet wearily. "I'll get it." She hurried down the hall, her high heels clicking on the hardwood floor. A moment later the door opened and I heard the unmistakable voice of Inspector Crawford. I cringed.

"Good, you're here too," he was saying. "I have some questions for both of you."

Crawford and Sanders—ugh. I should have known not having to deal with them was just too good to be true. A moment later, the gruesome twosome strode into the living room. Crawford wore his usual leer. If he'd been dressed in suspenders, he would have been snapping them with self-importance.

I forced myself to sound civil. "What can I do for you, inspectors?"

Crawford smirked. "Why is it that every time I turn around, you're in trouble again?"

"I guess I'm just unlucky."

He gave me a mocking smile. "From where I'm standing, I'd say your friend is unluckier than you are. She's the one who's dead." Without waiting for an answer, he plopped himself down on the sofa, and for a moment I had a mental picture of him sitting in the middle of a pile of sofa debris. My sofa held. Sanders sat next to him and pulled out a notebook.

"If you really believe that," Toni said, looking down at

Crawford from her skyscraper heels, "maybe you should keep your distance from her—or better yet, from both of us."

She came over and perched herself on the arm of my chair. She was as tense as a spring ready to pop. I prayed she'd keep her cool. Having her and Crawford at each other's throats was the last thing I wanted to do. It would only make him dig in his teeth deeper.

The stream of questions began.

"At what time did you last see the victim?"

The question was for both of us, but Toni answered. "Must have been around ten-thirty, or maybe closer to eleven." She looked to me for confirmation.

I nodded. "That sounds about right."

"Which one of you left last?"

This time I answered. "We left at the same time. Toni locked up behind us and then drove me home." I gestured to my cast. "I'm not driving these days."

"And I only went back for a minute," Toni added.

Crawford glanced up at her, suddenly alert. "You went back to the restaurant? Why?"

Toni squinted, looking defiant. "I forgot something. I just went back to pick it up. I was in and out in less than a minute."

"What did you forget?"

"Oh, I forgot my purse." The hesitation had been so brief he might not have noticed. But his eyes shifted over to me, and I just knew he'd seen the surprise in mine. I put on a blank expression and stared at the wall.

"Your purse," Crawford repeated slowly.

"That's right," she said. Silence descended.

At last he spoke again. "Did you happen to see the victim when you returned for your purse?"

"No, as I said, I was in and out in less than a minute."

Crawford continued with the interrogation. During all of this, Sanders kept taking notes, his face impassive.

At last Crawford paused and, looking at Toni, he said, "The fire inspector is under the impression you might have been the intended victim. If you don't mind my asking, Mrs. Lawford, if something happened to you, who would benefit?"

"That's none of anybody's business. Even if somebody had been trying to kill me, it couldn't have been anyone I know."

He leaned back wearily. "Whenever somebody gets murdered, the first thing I do is look for the motive. And unless we're dealing with a psychopath, the two first reasons are usually love or greed."

I happened to glance at Toni at that moment and saw the flash of an idea go through her eyes. She'd just thought of something. I tried to think what Crawford had just said that might have ignited that spark, but drew a blank.

Crawford continued. "Knowing your situation will help me establish possible motives. So, for the record, ma'am, who stands to benefit from your death?"

"Actually, I'm in the process of having my will changed. So it's irrelevant. But since you insist, Nicky has been my heir for the last few years, but I have an appointment with my estate lawyer in a few days. And then I'll be making my sister and my niece my primary beneficiaries."

Crawford's eyebrows almost jumped off his forehead. "Really," he said, his gaze sliding from her to me. He studied me measuringly. "Really," he repeated. "Isn't that interesting?" And then he asked the question I just knew would be my undoing. "And how much would Miss Landry inherit if you were to die before then?"

Sanders picked up his pad again, ready to jot down the answer.

Toni looked at the ceiling as she counted silently. "Somewhere around seventeen mil," she said at last. "Give or take."

For a moment I thought the two men would have heart attacks. Sanders blanched. Crawford coughed and the blood flooded into his face until it was the same deep red as his blood-orange nose. He stared at Toni in disbelief. Slowly his eyes swung back to me. "Seventeen million bucks." He whistled. "The way I see it, that's seventeen awfully good reasons for somebody wanting you dead." Again, his eyes shifted over to me.

All at once I had the uncomfortable feeling that I now had a new bull's-eye on my back, and that Inspector Crawford was taking careful aim. I'd escaped prosecution once, but I suspected he had no intention of letting me escape him again. If he had his way, this time he'd put me away for life.

I exploded. "I told you about the woman who threatened us days ago—when I was in the hospital. If you'd gone looking for her instead of dismissing everything I told you, then maybe I'd still have a business to run and, more important, Jennifer would still be alive."

TONI SLAMMED THE door shut and strode back to the living room, looking livid. "Can you believe that man? I don't know *what* makes him so stupid, but whatever it is, it really works. How exactly does he imagine you got to the restaurant? Maybe you called a cab and asked the driver to wait while you went inside and shot Jennifer. And then you coolly took the cab back to your place? Or, maybe you jogged over on one foot." She picked up our cold cups of coffee and carried them to the kitchen.

"At least he didn't arrest me," I called after her. I had almost expected he would, especially after my outburst. "I don't know why Crawford dislikes me so much."

"You made mincemeat of all his theories when Rob was murdered, and then you caught the murderer," Toni shouted back.

Could a cop really hold a grudge against a person just because they went looking for the truth? Wasn't that exactly what the police want in the first place? The truth? I thought of all the trouble Crawford could cause me, and an anvil settled in my stomach. "Knowing the way that man operates, he's mounting a case against me as we speak."

"He's a moron—a dangerous moron, but a moron nonetheless."

"By the way, seventeen million? Is that how much you're worth?" I'd always known Toni had tons of money, but seventeen million was an insane amount. "And I'm your sole beneficiary—for another few days," I added, grinning.

She smiled right back. "Actually, I'd say my net worth is closer to double that amount, but I didn't want those two bozos to know how much I really have."

I was speechless.

Toni continued as if nothing. "They'd be crazy to try and pin this on you. If Jennifer really was mistaken for me, all it proves is that you're innocent."

I found my voice. "How do you figure that?"

She smirked. "You would never have mistaken Jennifer for me."

"You're right. But Crawford will probably argue that it was dark, and that I was expecting you to be there, so I didn't take the time to look before I shot."

"He's an idiot."

"In this case I think he might have a point," I said, and

seeing the surprise in her eyes I explained. "*I* wouldn't have made that mistake, but somebody else could have easily mistaken her for you, especially in the dim light."

"Do you really think someone was after *me?*"

"It's possible. But then, I suppose there are other possibilities."

She groaned. "Why can't it be that somebody was after you?"

I laughed outright. "That's one advantage of having no money. Nobody can profit from my death. All I have to leave are debts. Besides. Look at me. I'm a redhead, and about five inches too short and a couple of pounds too heavy for anyone to have mistaken Jennifer for me."

She gave me a bleary look. "I need a drink." She hopped off the sofa and strode over to the kitchen, calling over her shoulder, "Where do you keep your liquor?"

It wasn't even noon yet, but all I said was, "In the cupboard by the window."

Some banging followed, and then the clinking of glasses. A moment later she was back, carrying a bottle of whiskey. "Hey, don't look at me like that. I'm only having coffee—Irish coffee."

I raised an eyebrow. "On an empty stomach?"

"I was starving until those two morons showed up. Now, all I want is to drown my worries away." She took the spot where the two morons had been sitting a minute earlier. She leaned forward to pour. "One shot or two?" she asked herself. "Aw hell, when in doubt make it both— one shot *plus* two."

"Er, Toni. I just thought of something. When you went back to the restaurant, you said you were only there for a second. Do you think Jennifer might already have been there?"

She paled. Her brow furrowed as she thought furiously

for a few seconds. She spoke at last, sounding very un-convincing. "No, absolutely not. We'd only been gone a few minutes when I went back. She couldn't possibly have come in during that short time…could she?"

"We should find out what time Jennifer left Charles's house." I had another thought, this one even worse. "There's something else we have to consider. What if Jennifer was shot with your gun?"

A dozen emotions played over her face. She set the bottle of whisky down and snatched her purse. She fished out her gun, opened the barrel and looked inside. And then she sniffed it. "No," she said, weak with relief. "This gun hasn't been fired in a long time. And all the bullets are still inside."

"What makes you think it wasn't fired?"

She put her gun away, placing her bag on the floor. She turned to me with a knowing look. "It would still smell of cordite."

"I hate to tell you this, Toni, but cordite hasn't been used in ammunition since the Second World War. Where'd you come up with that idea?"

"Oh, er, I saw that on a TV show." She looked down at her purse. "You're telling me I can't tell by the smell whether it was recently fired or not?"

I shook my head. "Only in the movies, sweetheart."

She looked worried for a second, and then brightened up. "It couldn't have been my gun because all the bullets are still inside, unless you're suggesting that someone reloaded it, which would mean they just happened to be carrying the right caliber bullets for my gun."

"You're right. That's not likely." I puzzled over it for a moment. "I have a feeling we might be looking at this the wrong way."

"I can't argue that. At this point we're not sure of

anything." She stirred her coffee reflectively. "What's on your mind?"

"There is one possibility we didn't consider. What if Jennifer was the intended victim all along?"

This took her by surprise. "Why would anybody want Jennifer dead?" And then she answered her own question. "It's true that we hardly know anything about her. She could be a drug dealer. She could be a…a…" She groped for other possibilities.

"We know she was Charles's girlfriend and that they lived together. I think that if Charles was in love with her, she must have been nice. Also, she's been working with us now for nearly two weeks, and she was absolutely lovely." My throat tightened. "Such a tragedy."

She nodded. "You're right. But, much as I hate to remind you, she was a lovely *married* person. And, I've been thinking about Charles, too."

"What *about* Charles?"

She looked down into her nearly empty cup, reached for the pot and refilled it, adding a generous splash of whisky. She leaned back. "Don't you think he's living in an awfully expensive house for someone earning barely more than minimum wage?"

I knew exactly where she was going with this, and I didn't like it. "What do you mean?" I asked, pretending confusion.

She rolled her eyes. "Sometimes, I swear, you're more of a blonde than a redhead. Don't you want to know who that house belongs to? Is it Charles's or Jennifer's? Don't forget, they had an argument the night Jennifer was killed. I wonder how solid their relationship was. For all we know they could have been on the verge of breaking up. Maybe she wanted to go back to her husband."

I almost gasped. "You're implying that Charles might

have killed Jennifer…out of jealousy…or for the house? That's ridiculous."

"No more ridiculous than somebody wanting to kill *me* for my money. Think about it. Everybody seems to think that somebody tried to kill me for my estate, but, hey, I'm not the one who died. Jennifer did."

"Not Charles. I refuse to believe that."

She sighed. "Okay, so maybe it wasn't Charles, but if that house belonged to Jennifer, it would suggest the woman had money—maybe a lot of money. I can't help but wonder who inherits her estate."

I preferred her theory that Jennifer had been the intended victim. I felt an immediate stab of guilt. Poor Jennifer. She didn't deserve what happened, so unfair. It was just too scary to think somebody was after Toni—or me—or both. What bothered me was her suggestion that Charles might have been involved.

I shook my head again. "There are too many things wrong with that idea. First of all, Jennifer was killed in our restaurant. That is one coincidence too many. I'm not buying it."

She leaned forward, speaking excitedly. "What I'm saying is, if Jennifer was the intended victim, what better cover than making it look as if her death was a case of mistaken identity?"

I turned this over in my mind. Somebody could make an argument for that.

She continued. "And who knows, maybe the threats and the hit-and-run were all part of the same plot. They might have wanted to turn the attention off the real motive by staging that crazy-lady confrontation and the hit-and-run. Don't forget, it was Charles who suggested I hire Jennifer to help in the kitchen."

I stared her in the eyes. "You're talking about Charles,

Toni. *Our Charles.* Do you really think he's capable of murder?"

She lost her earnestness and became serious. "One thing I've learned is that no matter how much we think we know another person, we only ever see what they allow us to see. The truth is we have no idea what really goes on in other people's minds. How often have you heard people say, even after years of marriage, that their spouses turned out to be complete strangers?" She was talking about herself and Steven again.

I put up my hand. "Stop it. You were there when Charles got the news. The man was devastated. Do you really believe his grief was all an act?"

Her certainty of a moment ago wavered, leaving her looking frightened and confused. She crossed her arms sullenly. "I just want the case to be solved. I want the whole thing to go away. I don't want to walk around wondering who wants me dead."

I gave her my best reassuring look. "Don't worry. We'll figure it out. But coming up with absurd theories is not going to help."

She jutted out her chin. "It is not an absurd theory." I waited. At last she scowled, sighing. "Okay, I admit, I don't want to believe that somebody is trying to kill me. If that were true, it would mean it's somebody I know and love." She counted on her fingers. "That leaves only three people, you, Steven and Judy—unless you suspect my five-year-old niece." When she put it that way, it did sound ridiculous. It sure as hell wasn't me. And I would be shocked if it turned out to be Steven or Judy.

She looked at me pleadingly. "Can't we talk about something else for a while?"

I'd had all I could take of the subject myself. There

were a few other things I wanted to discuss, starting with how we'd go about resuscitating our business.

No matter what she'd said earlier, I refused to believe she'd willingly walk away from Skinny's. But getting her to agree wholeheartedly with a plan to rebuild would demand some finesse. I made a quick list of possible arguments in favor of starting over.

We had so many exciting things to look forward to—the newspaper column for one. What I should not mention was that we didn't have insurance and that all costs would have to come out of her pocket—not that I planned to keep that from her. But choosing just the right moment to drop that bomb would be crucial.

When it came to money, Toni had her own unique way of deciding what made an investment worthwhile. Once, during those early months when the business kept getting deeper in the red, I had asked if she would mind lending the company a bit more money. She had bluntly refused, giving me a good lesson in the way the rich handled money.

"I didn't mind contributing the start-up money," she'd said. "I calculated just how much I was willing to gamble, hoping it would pay off. But the business isn't taking off the way we'd hoped. And one thing I never, ever do is throw good money after bad."

I'd been shocked. The amount was small—not to me, but it was less than what she spent monthly on her wardrobe, as I'd pointed out. But she just shook her head, saying that spending on her wardrobe was a good investment, one that brought very nice dividends. The dividends to which she was referring was the plethora of men she was dating at the time.

"Toni," I said now, deciding the direct approach was best. "We have to come up with a plan to start over again."

Toni snorted. "And why exactly would we want to do that?" From her tone, I knew this discussion had a very real danger of turning into an argument.

I pulled myself off the sofa and hobbled over to the kitchen. "If I remember correctly, just a few days ago, you were talking about opening a second location. And just around that same time, you were giving me a speech about opportunity coming in different disguises." I expected a sharp retort but to my surprise, Toni was silent. Was she considering it? I dared hope.

I'd been in the kitchen about ten minutes and during all that time I hadn't heard a peep out of my friend—stewing, no doubt. While I busied myself, I debated how hard I should push. Toni was notoriously obstinate. She was more likely to turn down a suggestion than to accept it—unless she believed the idea was hers.

When at last Toni appeared in the doorway, I had butter sizzling in the pan and my ingredients measured and lined up on the counter.

She held a cup of coffee in each hand. "You left it in the living room." She stepped closer. "What's with all the racket?"

I had been opening and closing cupboard doors and drawers, gathering my cooking utensils and ingredients, and I was already beginning to feel calmer. Whenever I felt most stressed, cooking was my cure of choice. Toni used to joke that she always knew when I was most upset by the amount of baking I did.

"I'm making us something to eat." I cracked another egg into the bowl and whipped them with milk and a tiny amount of walnut oil. "I liked your Skinny French toast and I'm trying my hand at Skinny pancakes. I don't know about you but my mind is sharper when my stomach is full."

"Good idea." She opened the cupboard and took out two plates. "Come to think of it, I am a bit hungry."

Funny, I didn't have to think to know I was hungry. As long as I was breathing, I could eat.

TONI SET THE TABLE. "So, getting back to the restaurant, how, exactly, do you propose we start over again? Are you talking about waiting for our building to be repaired and setting up in the same location, or finding an entirely new place?"

"Waiting for the building to be fixed could take months. I suggest we find a new location." This was met with a long silence. I finished mixing and measured quarter cups of batter onto the hot griddle, making half a dozen perfect silver-dollar-size pancakes.

At last she said, "So much work. I don't know if I have the energy."

"That's normal. I wouldn't expect you to feel any other way after all that's happened. But a few days from now you'll be seeing things differently."

"Hey, that's my speech."

I flipped over the pancakes. "For one thing, this time around we can do it faster and cheaper. We learned a lot getting ready for our Queen location. Also we'd cover the overhead in no time. We already have an established reputation and clients who will follow us."

She waved away my arguments. "Speaking of customers, did you call back that lady?"

I picked up the spatula and scooped up the pancakes. "Damn. I completely forgot about her. What's her name again?"

"Edna Jamieson."

I put down my spatula. "I still don't understand why she wants to speak to me. Might as well get it over with. What did I do with her number?"

"Tell me where it is. I'll get it for you." She jumped up and disappeared up the stairs, returning a moment later with the piece of paper in hand.

I wiped my hands on a dish towel, and grabbed my home phone from its cradle. I punched in the woman's number, waited three rings and got a voice message.

"Leave your name and number, and the reason for your call. Thank you."

I left a brief message and hung up. "At least she'll know I tried." I hurried back to the stove and flipped over the second batch of pancakes. "Getting back to business, the first thing we should do is find a new location. Unless you think we should wait and reopen in the same place? The problem with that is that it will take months. All the goodwill we've earned will be gone by then."

"We don't even know that the owner will want to re-build—at least not the same commercial-type building. Remember? When we signed the lease he was talking about how he didn't want to give us a long lease because he was considering tearing it down and putting up con-dos?"

I did remember vaguely. "All the more reason to start looking. Once we have a place we like, we can send out flyers announcing our new restaurant and the date of our reopening. Then we work like mad to get everything ready on time."

She smiled at me the way I might at a four-year-old talking about wanting to become an astronaut. "You're making it sound as if all we have to do is show up for work as usual, the only difference being the location."

I turned off the burner and wiped my pan clean. "I'm

not saying it will be easy, but it wouldn't be nearly as difficult as it was when we prepared for Skinny's opening."

"For your information, finding a new location is the least of our problems. Once we found it, we'd have to fix it up." Toni carried the food to the table.

We sat down to eat, and I continued my argument. "Don't forget we have a staff with nothing but time on their hands at the moment."

Toni dropped a dollop of vanilla yogurt on her pancakes and covered it with blueberries.

"We can keep the guys on payroll and split up the work," I said. "Give everyone a list of chores to accomplish. With five of us working, we can probably get everything done in a month or so." I paused. "Make that four of us. I doubt Charles will be up to working for a while."

Toni took a bite of the pancakes.

"What do you say?" I asked.

"They're delicious."

"I was talking about my idea."

"Oh—good idea," she said, sounding more bored than interested. "You're probably right about Charles not being ready to get back to work. Aren't you afraid to reopen? What if Jennifer's death really does have to do with the restaurant? We just might make that lunatic even crazier."

Here it was again, her greatest objection. "Just a minute ago you were saying you thought the whole thing about us stealing the restaurant was just a diversion." I put on a mocking tone. "We're too small. We're too unimportant, except for you of course."

She rolled her eyes and went right on eating.

I waited a beat and then said, "Right now we don't know if anybody is after us or not. So, what are we supposed to do? Sit on our asses and wait? Or just give up?" I forked another few pancakes onto my plate and ate in silence for a few minutes. At last I said, "Maybe you're right. It's not as if our restaurant was worth very much. All we really had was some old secondhand furniture and a bunch of recipes."

Surprise registered in her eyes. "You agree with me?"

"Maybe we should just walk away. Saving our business would mean a lot of work—much easier to do nothing. For all we know that crazy woman wasn't faking and really is behind the whole thing. And if we reopen she might come after us with a vengeance. To hell with Skinny's on Queen." I paused for a moment, and then added, "I think I'll go into catering." I wondered if I had overdone it.

Her eyes widened. "Catering! Are you crazy?" She hesitated. "I suppose it wouldn't hurt to look for a location…just in case. I mean, there's no point in deciding one way or another until we at least know what's going on."

"If that's what you want to do," I said unenthusiastically. I grabbed my crutches and left the table to hide my smile.

a whole other perspective on it

TONI CLEANED THE table and took the dogs for a short walk, while I used the opportunity to call Jake.

He answered on the second ring.

"Are you still at Charles's?" I asked.

"That's right," he said, in a tone that told me Charles was within hearing distance.

"What about Jennifer's brother and husband? Are they still there?"

"They're gone." He sounded relieved.

"By any chance, did Charles happen to mention at what time Jennifer left the house last night?"

"No, why?"

"It's just something I need to check. Would you mind asking him? It's important," I added when he hesitated.

He covered the mouthpiece for a moment and I heard some muffled conversation. "He said it was around twelve."

"Thank you, Jake. Tell Charles I'm sorry I had to ask."

I hung up, and still having a few minutes before Toni returned, I considered calling Mitchell. He had asked that I get back to him as soon as I could, but after waiting so long for a call from him, I was reluctant to give in so easily. For a while I'd wondered if Mitchell had completely forgotten about me. Absence was supposed to let the heart grow fonder but for all I knew, he and Bunny were getting along like a house on fire—no pun intended. An image of him kissing a gorgeous blonde popped into my mind again, making me slightly nauseated. I picked up the phone, still hesitating.

The front door opened and closed, killing any hopes of a private conversation. I put the receiver down.

Toni walked in, followed by the pitter-patter of tiny paws. "I am so in love with that little Trouble," she said, picking him up and planting a kiss on top of his head.

Trouble did not seem to return the sentiment. He struggled to get out of her grasp. At last she returned him to his pen, along with Sugar. She gave them all liver treats and returned to the kitchen.

"By the way, I forgot to mention that Judy heard about the fire on the news. She was so worried, I told her to come over." She glanced at her watch. "I thought she'd be here by now."

"No problem," I said, and told her about my call to Jake. "If you had any more doubt about it, this proves it. Your gun was not the murder weapon. You had already picked it up before Jennifer had even left the house."

Even though we'd already concluded that it was highly unlikely that her gun had killed Jennifer, she looked as if a load had just been lifted from her shoulders.

We washed the dishes and cleaned the kitchen and, just as we finished, the doorbell rang. "That must be her." Toni hurried to answer and reappeared a moment later, followed by Judy.

"I am so sorry about the restaurant," Judy said, looking heartbroken. "The news report said someone was killed in the fire, but I didn't catch the name. I can't tell you how scared I was it might be one of you. Thank goodness—" And then, looking mortified, she added, "It's still tragic of course."

"It is," Toni agreed. She poured Judy a cup of coffee and we all settled in the living room.

Judy looked from Toni to me and back again. "Do you think it has anything to do with that crazy woman who made all those threats?"

"At this point we have no idea who's behind it," I said. "We don't even know if the hit-and-run and the fire are related. At the risk of sounding like a conspiracy nut, I think that woman might have been wearing a disguise. And if I'm right about that, it puts a whole other perspective on what's going on."

Judy's eyes widened. "Oh my God." She seemed to digest this for a few seconds and then said, "That makes it even scarier."

"Our thoughts exactly," Toni said. "And you don't know the worst of it." She waited a beat for drama. "Jennifer was shot."

Judy's mouth dropped. "She didn't die in the fire?"

Toni shook her head. "Her body was found in the rubble, but she'd been shot. And—" she paused for dramatic effect, "—the police think I was the intended victim."

Judy's eyes grew wider. "Was the fire set to try and hide the murder?"

"That's one possibility," I said.

"What are you going to do?" Judy asked.

Toni shrugged. "It isn't as if there's a lot I can do, short of standing in the street, waiting for whoever it is to come and get me."

If I didn't know her better, I might have thought Toni was enjoying this. I gave her the eyebrow. To Judy I said, "Don't worry. The police are investigating. It's just a question of time before they catch the killer." And then I changed the subject. "Before I forget, Toni, one of us should call *The Toronto Daily*. Whether we reopen or not, we have to make sure we don't lose that column. It'll be worth a fortune in free advertising no matter what we end up doing."

She looked at me as if I had rocks in my head. "I don't see how it could be worth a dime if we decide not to reopen."

"The food industry is huge," I said. "Restaurants are only a small percentage of it. There's catering—"

She grimaced. "Oh for God's sake, will you forget that idea? Can you imagine me at some function walking around dressed in a little French maid's outfit?" She glanced from Judy to me. "Don't answer that."

I tried to keep a straight face, but it crumpled into a grin. Judy laughed out loud. Even Toni was suppressing giggles. It was a welcome moment of lightheartedness.

Toni regained her composure. "Come on, be serious. Catering is the last thing I'd want to do—long days and even longer nights. We'd be on our feet eighteen hours a day."

"Sometimes it feels like that already," I said, still chuckling, "but I happen to agree with you. I'm just giving catering as one example. Then there's also the gourmet-meal pick-up or delivery service."

Judy said, "Oh, I love those. There's one place in Ottawa where I go all the time."

Toni nodded unenthusiastically. "I like that idea better."

"Or, we could give skinny-cooking classes—teach people what kind of ingredients they can use to replace the high fat and sugar in their regular recipes."

"That's a great idea," Judy said. "I'd sign up for something like that."

Toni shook her head. "There's no money in teaching. What else?"

"We could…" I snapped my fingers. "We could start a line of frozen diet meals. Or write diet cookbooks."

Toni got a dreamy look in her eyes. "Written by Toni Lawford and Nicky Landry," she said, underlining the imaginary line with her hands. "I'd be an author."

"Don't go shopping for your book-tour wardrobe until we've at least written the first page," I said, stifling a laugh. "Those are just off the top of my head. There are countless other things we could do."

"You're right," she said, showing some interest at last. "There are lots of opportunities. You know, maybe re-opening wouldn't be the best thing to do. We could think of something so much more exciting that operating a res-taurant."

Uh-oh. I'd gone a bit too far with my sales pitch. I had to do some backtracking, and fast. "I still think our best bet is to reopen our restaurant. Even if we did eventually decide to expand into other areas, Skinny's could remain the parent company. I think your idea of finding a decent location before making a decision is a good one."

Toni hesitated and looked at Judy, but her sister kept silent, leaving the discussion to us.

At least Toni hadn't given me an outright no. But if I wanted her cooperation, I would have to let her choose the location—or at least make her believe it was her choice, otherwise my friend was likely to dig in her four-inch heels.

"It wouldn't hurt to look," Judy said. I could have kissed her.

Toni shrugged. "I suppose you're right." She retrieved my laptop from my bedroom and set it on the dining room table. I sat, and Judy drew up a chair and settled next to me, sharing the laptop.

Toni pulled out her iPhone. "Looking for a new loca-tion when we still don't know who's behind the hit-and-run and Jennifer's death makes me nervous."

"It would make me nervous too," Judy said. "But you can't put your life on hold until the police figure out what's going on." I was liking this woman more and more. "Let's make a list of what you're looking for, everything the space absolutely must have."

"Good idea," I said. We both turned to Toni, waiting until, after a long pause, she nodded.

We threw around some ideas and decided the most important was to find a commercial space that was already set up as a restaurant. Not having too many renovations would save us a bundle. The next "must" on the list was that the location be as close to downtown as possible. Last, the square footage should be larger than what we had on Queen, but still be small enough to feel cozy. Anything more would be a bonus.

"Why don't you do the real estate listings, while I do the online classifieds?" I said.

"Good idea," Toni said.

After a few more cups of coffee, we had a list of a dozen places that answered our criteria.

"Why don't we go over what we have so far and eliminate all the listings we don't like."

We reviewed them, discarding some spaces as too big, another as small and too out of the way, and a couple as too expensive. By midafternoon we had narrowed the possibilities down to eight. We split the list down the middle. While I went to check on the dogs again, Judy and Toni started making calls, contacting the leasing agents for the more information. In the end we had a total of three commercial spaces worth seeing.

I looked over the printout. "If none of these works out, we'll make a new list tomorrow."

Judy looked from me to Toni. "Are you going to look at those places right now?"

Toni nodded. "We might as well drive by before we book appointments."

I was about to plead fatigue and ask to postpone this until the morning, when Judy said, "I'd love to come along, but I'd better get back before Richard goes stir crazy."

Toni threw me a look that said, "See what I mean?" To Judy she said, "Too bad. I'd like your input."

"Why don't we reconvene tomorrow morning?" I suggested. "That way Judy can join us."

"You wouldn't mind waiting until I can go with you?" Judy asked.

"Sure," she said.

"What time?"

"Let's make it early…say…ten?" Toni said.

"Ten?" Judy looked startled. "I was afraid you'd say seven. Sure, ten is fine."

I laughed. "Ten is the crack of dawn for Toni."

Judy went to the front, returning with her coat. "By the way, I know we said we'd have dinner tonight but after what you've been through, I think we should reschedule."

I could tell from the look on Toni's face that she'd completely forgotten about her dinner date.

"Tomorrow works for me," she said.

"Great. I can't wait for you to meet Richard. He's going to love you," Judy said. She looked at me. "Why don't you join us? I'd love you to meet Richard too."

"I'd be happy to," I said.

Toni jumped to her feet. "Hold off a second. I'm leaving too, so I might as well give you a lift back to the hotel."

Soon they were both gone and, except for the dogs, I had the house to myself. I made myself a quick sandwich, eyeing a cherry pie in the freezer. I let the dogs out

and then climbed up the stairs and curled up on my bed
for a nap.

I'd intended on no more than a half hour snooze, just
enough to keep myself going until bedtime, but when I
next opened my eyes, it was dark. I glanced at my bedside clock—eight o'clock. I threw off the covers. Damn.
I'd been sleeping for nearly four hours. Now I'd probably
toss and turn all night and I'd feel like hell again all day
tomorrow.

I went downstairs and pulled out the cherry pie I'd sali-
vated over earlier. I popped it in the oven. Forty minutes
later I'd just finished my second piece and was squash-
ing major guilt when the phone rang. I glanced at the call
display—Mitchell. My heart did a happy dance.

"Thank God I finally got you," he said. "I was going
crazy trying to reach you."

"You were worried?"

"Yes. Didn't you get my message? I called you back
this morning. I must have tried your cell a dozen times,
but it kept going to voice mail. And then when I finally
hear from you, I find out you were in the hospital, hit by
a car. What happened? Are you all right?"

All the insecurity I'd been suffering over the past few
days faded away. "I'm okay, don't worry."

"Why didn't you call me?"

"Sorry about that. I thought Toni was going to call
you, but after everything that happened it just slipped
my mind." I wasn't trying to sound distant, but I wouldn't
mind him getting just a little bit jealous. "But, as Toni
pointed out, there is a bright side to all this."

"I can't imagine what that would be."

"Men are swarming around me, trying to be helpful.
They're opening doors, helping me in and out of cabs,
carrying my parcels. I've never had so much attention in

my life." Okay, I was exaggerating, but I wasn't about to admit that the only time a man had rushed to my help was when Toni happened to be standing next to me.

I heard his smile in his next words. "As long as nobody is helping you out of your clothes. I'd have to come back and shoot them."

I laughed. "Oh, lots of them are trying, but I'm saving myself for this hot young author I know."

He laughed, and his voice grew husky. "I miss you."

My heart skipped a beat. "I miss you too."

"Are you sure you're all right? If you need me, I'll hop on the next plane and come back."

"You would do that?"

"Just say the word."

That was all the reassurance I needed. "Don't be silly. You have a book to edit. How's it going, by the way?"

"Good. Bunny is amazing. I'm learning so much from her." That was not what I wanted to hear. "Crutches, huh?" he continued.

I gave a little laugh. "You should see me. I'm getting good. Although, I suspect it might put a crimp in the bedroom acrobatics."

"Don't worry. Where there's a will, there's a way." There was a pause, and then as if he guessed that I was suddenly blushing, he changed the subject. "Well, I hope you're taking it easy. You shouldn't be going to work with a broken ankle."

"Er, actually there is no more work to go to."

I imagined his eyes growing dark and sexy the way they did when he furrowed his eyebrows. "What do you mean there's no more work?"

"The restaurant is gone—burned down to the ground." I told him what had happened, starting with the threats and ending with Jennifer's death. He listened quietly.

And then he suddenly made the link between the threats and the hit-and-run. "Are you telling me that was not just an accident? Somebody was actually trying to kill you? And now they've destroyed the restaurant?"

I decided to make light of it. "That's what I thought at first, but Steven is convinced the threats had nothing to do with the hit-and-run, that it was just some teenager who lost control of his car, panicked and sped away."

"What about the fire? That's a bit much for a coincidence. It sounds to me like somebody is out to get you. What are the cops doing?"

I hadn't even told him about Jennifer being killed, and he was already freaking out—which I sort of liked. Still, I didn't want him worrying too much. "You know the police. They have a million other cases to solve. Anyhow, I'm sure one had nothing to do with the other. Toni and I have been looking for another location."

"You mean you're planning to reopen? Are you crazy? You'd only be giving this lunatic another reason to come after you."

"Actually, we think the arsonist was after somebody else." I told him about Jennifer.

"You're telling me one of your employees was murdered?" His voice had risen a full octave. "Are you sure you're not in any danger?"

"That's what Toni and Steven seem to think. Although I kind of like you worrying about me."

The smile was back in his voice. "Well in that case, I'll keep worrying. And I'll hurry back and protect you as soon as I can."

"Hmm, good idea." I cleared my throat. "By the way, who's that sexy blonde I keep seeing going into your house?" I was aiming for a light tone, but I didn't quite achieve it.

"Blonde?" He chuckled. "That would probably be the location scout who rented my place for two weeks."

"Location scout? What are you talking about?"

He laughed. "I didn't have a chance to tell you. The day before my flight, just a few minutes after you left my place actually, a location scout stopped by. She was looking for an old Victorian house to use for a scene in a movie. She said my house was perfect."

"Somebody wants to shoot a movie in your house? What kind of movie are they making?"

"Not an entire movie—just one scene. Probably some kind of horror flick about a serial killer." He had his teasing voice on again. "Whatever it is, it's obviously not a big budget production."

I was stunned almost speechless. Of all the places a company might want to rent, Mitchell's was the last I'd expect.

"Unless the blonde in question is one of the actors," he continued.

"I doubt it. It doesn't look like anything is going on. How long did the production house tell you they'd be filming?"

"They only said they'd need the place for ten days. I tried calling them, but there's no more service at the number they gave me. It's weird."

I would have said that was more than weird. It was downright worrisome. "I hope they paid you in advance."

"They gave me a deposit, and the balance is due at the end of the shoot. They said they'd email me the money."

That did not fill me with confidence. Could this have been some kind of a scam? But if so, what for? To raid Mitchell's house? I might have been worried if the thought wasn't so ludicrous. The most valuable thing in Mitchell's house was probably the tight designer jeans he liked to wear. Not exactly the kind of valuables anybody would go after—unless he happened to be wearing them.

"How much was the deposit?"

"Three hundred bucks."

"A check, I suppose?" I hoped it wouldn't bounce.

"No, she gave me cash. I was surprised, but she said deposits were always paid in cash." He sounded unworried.

He changed the subject and we chatted on flirtatiously. By the time we hung up, I was feeling silly for all my doubts and insecurities. Bunny might be working with him day in and day out, but I was the one who had his heart. If not for my air cast I would have danced for joy.

THE NEXT MORNING I woke up feeling much better. After Mitchell's phone call, I'd had my first good night's sleep in nearly a week. Now if that case could only get solved, maybe I could actually go on with my life.

"How are you feeling this morning, Jackie Chan?" I said as I filled the doggie bowls. "Do you miss Mitchell too?"

She gave me a bleary look, as if to say, "One phone call and you're all gaga over him again?"

"You would be too, Jackie, if you'd had a few of his kisses."

She marched off disgusted.

I ground enough fresh beans for a pot of coffee and made myself a poached egg served on half an English muffin. I grated a bit of aged cheddar on top, added freshly ground pepper and some chopped fresh chives. Hopefully, my low-calorie breakfast would balance out the two large pieces of cherry pie I'd wolfed down last night. I consulted my calorie counter. Half a muffin—55 calories, one egg—65 calories, half ounce of cheese—67, for a total of 187 calories. How great was that? Feeling holierthan-thou, I poured myself a cup of coffee, adding real cream, and sat down to eat. I had just finished when the bell rang. I grabbed my crutches and hurried to the door.

"Jake," I said, stepping aside. "Come on in. I just made a pot of coffee." He followed me to the kitchen. I pointed him to the coffeepot. "Help yourself."

He shook his head and joined me at the table, looking serious. "The police showed up at my place yesterday. They seem to think Jennifer's murder was a case of mistaken identity—that Toni was the intended victim."

I nodded. "They told us the same thing. They also seem to think I might have done it."

"That's just plain stupid," he said. "I think they're wrong. I think Jennifer might have been murdered on purpose."

"What makes you say that?"

"According to Charles, Jennifer was having trouble with her ex. They'd only been separated about a year and the guy was being a jerk. He was stalking her, for one thing."

"Did she report him to the police?"

He shrugged. "She was afraid it would only make things worse. But he was escalating. Whenever she went shopping, there he'd be, running into her in the vegetable aisle or something. And then when she'd leave the store, she'd find him waiting by her car. He called her constantly, begging one minute, threatening the next. She was spooked. She finally warned him that if he didn't leave her alone, she'd get a restraining order."

"When was that?"

"About a week ago."

I calculated quickly. That would have been just a few days before I was hit by that car.

"And there's something else," he continued. "It turns out that her ex is a fireman."

This floored me. "Well, that settles it. He must have started that fire. I can't think of anyone who would know better how to start one than a fireman." My head was spinning. "Did you tell the police?" With any luck, he would be apprehended, if he hadn't already been, and all suspicion would be off me. Toni and I would no longer feel like walking targets. We could reopen our restaurant without worrying.

"I did, but I have no idea if they questioned him or not." He still looked troubled and I realized there was more to come. "I'm worried about Charles. I suspect he's going to take matters into his own hands. I'm pretty sure he's on his way to confront Jennifer's ex right now."

"What makes you think that?"

"He was on his laptop for a long time this morning. He looked so focused that I got suspicious. At one point he went to the washroom and I got a peek at his screen. It was just as I thought. He was searching through the on-line phone listings for every Atwood in Toronto. He came back and continued working at the computer for a while, and then he wrote something down on a piece of paper and took off in a rush. When I asked him where he was going, he said he had a doctor's appointment."

"Maybe it wasn't an excuse. Maybe he really did have a doctor's appointment."

He looked me straight in the eye. "People don't bring guns when they go to the doctor."

"Oh my God!" My first thought was *Call the police.* But what if they arrested him for carrying a gun? "Why didn't you tell me sooner?" I blurted. "Do you have any idea where he was going?"

"I copied down the last address he had on his computer. Here it is," he said, pulling out a folded piece of paper from his shirt pocket.

"Let's go," I said, already making my way over to grab my coat.

"My car's out front," Jake said, "and I have a GPS."

I got my purse, threw in my cell phone, and we took off. In the car, I punched in Toni's number. It was still early by Toni standards but to my surprise she answered sounding out of breath.

"This isn't a good time," she said, languorously. "I'm fucking busy." She sighed. "I wish it were the other way around."

At any other time I might have been amused, but today I didn't have time for any of her smart-alecky remarks. "We'll have to postpone those drive-bys until two-thirty," I said briskly, and repeated what Jake had just told me. "Can you call Judy?"

I hung up without waiting for her reply, and held onto the grab bar for dear life. Jake was driving like a maniac, zigging and zagging through traffic at neck-breaking speed. I squeezed my eyes shut as he swerved between two huge trucks. *Dear God, let us make it there alive.*

My cell phone rang. "Nicky? Are you there?" It was Toni. "Judy agreed to meet at your place at two."

"That works for me too, as long as I survive this car ride." I hung up and looked out. We were on the Gardiner Expressway heading west. "How far away does he live?" I asked, hoping we'd take the next exit. Even if I didn't get killed in a car crash, I might still die of a heart attack.

"Near Bloor West Village. We're almost there. I don't know whether he's home or at work right now. With any luck, he'll be at work and Charles will be outside ringing his doorbell when we get there."

A few minutes later we came to a tire-screeching stop

in front of a pretty barn-style house, just steps from High Park. After seeing the house where she lived with Charles, I was surprised at the modesty of this one. It answered one question. If the house in Cabbagetown belonged to Jennifer, it was unlikely her wealth came from her ex-husband—unless she'd cleaned him out in a separation agreement. That, in itself, could give an ex a good reason to be mad as hell. Or, for all I knew the house belonged to Charles, and if it did, I wondered how he could afford a place like that.

"There he is." As he said this, I spotted Charles creeping stealthily around the corner of the house. Jake jumped out of the car, slamming the door shut. I fumbled with the door and my crutches, and followed.

"Charles," Jake called out.

Charles swung around and his face grew fierce. "You had no business following me. Get out of here."

"Charles Bateman," I said, with as much authority as I could muster. "What do you think you're doing?" As I got closer, I could see something metallic in his hand— a gun. He stuffed it back in his pocket, looking guilty.

For a second I couldn't help wondering whether this might be the gun that had killed Jennifer.

"You had no business following me," he repeated more mildly.

I stopped a few steps from him. He looked so vulnerable that I dropped the stern tone. "You know I care about you, Charles. And you know I cared for Jennifer too. Believe me, I know how you feel. I've been there, remember?" Charles had witnessed my own grief when Rob was killed.

His eyes watered suddenly. "It—it's just so hard. I loved her so much," he said, in a choked voice.

I wrapped an arm around his shoulders. "I know,

Charles, I know. But please don't do anything you'll regret later. Why don't you come back with us and let the police take care of this?"

At that moment the front door flew open and Bret Atwood stepped out. Jennifer's muscular husband looked ready to fight, hands tightly fisted at his side. He stared at Charles. "What the hell are you doing here?"

No wonder Jennifer had been afraid of him. Some men's features looked particularly fierce when they were angry. Bret Atwood was one of them.

He continued, his face a mask of rage, "Haven't you done enough already? Jennifer and I were happy until you came around."

I suddenly remembered the gun Charles was carrying, and stepped between him and Atwood. "There's no reason to get upset, Mr. Atwood. Nothing happened. We're leaving right now."

"No reason to get upset? How am I supposed to feel? Three days ago Jennifer and I agreed to give our marriage a second chance. And twenty-four hours later she's dead." Atwood glared at Charles. "You killed her, you son of a bitch."

And before I realized what he was doing, he'd sidestepped me and was lunging at Charles. Fists flew and, seconds later, Charles lay on the sidewalk, blood oozing from his nose.

He looked up at Atwood, his face ashen. "She was leaving me?" He looked so stunned that I just knew he wasn't pretending. "That's a lie," he said, sounding uncertain.

All at once, the fight seemed to leave Atwood. "She didn't tell you?"

Charles struggled back to his feet and wiped his nose with the sleeve of his coat. "She was leaving me? I don't believe you." He stared at Atwood. "You're only trying to throw suspicion on me because you killed her. You murdered her, you son of a bitch."

"Me?" Atwood said, outraged. "That's ridiculous. If anybody had a reason to kill her, it wasn't me. It was you."

Charles paled. "I didn't kill her. I loved her," he said, his fury rising again. "And I don't believe for one minute that she was going to leave me. I'd just asked her to marry me. And for your information, she said yes."

Atwood looked dumbfounded. "Fuck you," he said at last, lurching forward.

Both Jake and I jumped in front of him before things got out of control again. Which might not have been a good idea, because seconds later I was lying on the hard sidewalk, my crutches strewn yards away. This put an immediate end to the brawl. Atwood took a step back, embarrassed. Charles and Jake scrambled to help me back to my feet.

"Are you okay?" Jake asked, his eyes scanning me for injuries.

"I'm all right," I said, although the fall had jolted my ankle and now it throbbed painfully.

"You don't look all right," Charles said.

"It's just my ankle. Oh, God it hurts."

He spun around to Atwood. "See what you did, you moron."

Atwood stormed back inside his house and slammed the door shut.

I gritted my teeth against the pain and after a few moments it dissolved. "Let's get out of here before he calls the police." We made our way to Jake's car.

"Charles," I said, sliding into the back seat as he held the door open for me. "You shouldn't be carrying a gun. What if Atwood called the police? You could get arrested."

He reddened and snatched it out of his pocket, handing it to me.

"I don't want it," I said, pulling my hand away. The gun dropped to the sidewalk and, for one split second, I saw my life flash before my eyes. I imagined the gun firing, a bullet ricocheting and hitting me.

Seeing the look of panic on my face, Charles gave me a jaundiced smile. "You don't have to be afraid. It's not loaded. In fact," he said, stooping to pick it up, "it's not even a real gun. It's a lighter." And to demonstrate, he pulled the trigger and a flame came out of the barrel. "I only wanted to scare him—make him admit that he killed her."

"Of all the cockamamie plans," I muttered, as he closed the door and climbed into the front. "You're just lucky nobody got seriously hurt."

half a dozen buff young men in tow

AT TWO-THIRTY Judy arrived, eager to get going, and soon after Toni showed up. "So, what are you waiting for?" she said. "Let's get this show on the road."

I threw on my coat, locked up, and we piled into Toni's car. I filled them in as we got into her car.

"So if it wasn't Jennifer's ex and it wasn't Charles," Judy said, "who's left?"

"Not so fast," I said. "I'm not convinced her ex is as innocent as he claims. For one thing, he was stalking Jennifer. And stalkers often become violent when their victim doesn't do what they want."

Toni paused, key in the ignition. "Do you really think it could be him?" She looked relieved. "That would mean it wasn't a case of mistaken identity."

"I would very much like it to be him. It would make both of us feel a lot safer."

"What do you mean, both of us? I didn't see anyone suggesting you were at risk." Toni put her car into drive and we took off.

"If you were the intended victim, that would make me the most likely suspect—at least in the eyes of the cops," I said tightly from the backseat. "The police always start by looking at whoever has the most to gain financially. So, guess who they'd go after?"

Judy looked at me, bewildered.

Toni caught my eyes in the rearview mirror. "Perhaps, but I'd still rather be a suspect than a victim."

"So far, I'd say I'm more of a victim than you are. I'm the one wearing a cast."

She ignored my comment. "Her ex might turn out to be innocent, just as Charles could turn out to be guilty. Remember, you can't tell a liar any more than you can tell a killer." For once, Toni's quote was a serious one. She grimaced. "Enough talk about murder. I don't want to spend the rest of the day worrying that somebody wants me dead. All I want, at least for a little while, is to go look at real estate, so not a word about murder out of either one of you. Is that too much to ask?"

"No problem." I'd had enough of the subject too.

"I thought we should start with the place on King," Toni said, as she turned left onto Queen, a route that would take us by Skinny's. My heart constricted.

A few blocks later traffic came to a crawl as looky-loos slowed for a look at the charred remains of our restaurant. We drove at the speed of a funeral procession, inching by and staring mutely. If anything, the devastation looked worse by daylight—the charred remains of my life's dream. I took in the gaping hole where the front window had been, and the frayed, burned fabric of the curtain, swaying in the breeze. The ceiling had caved from the weight of the water. Soggy plasters and broken ceiling pipes now joined the rubble on the floor. It was a heartbreaking sight.

"Let's get out of here," Toni said mournfully. She sped up.

"One good thing about the place on King," I said, trying to inject some optimism in our excursion, "is how close it is to this location—only half a dozen blocks."

"Good point," Judy said.

"You see that as an advantage?" Toni said. "I look at it as a drawback. Once all the repairs are done on Queen, and we reopen, our two locations will be too close to each other."

I was dumbfounded. "I can't figure you out. One minute you don't want to reopen at all. And the next, you're talking about operating *two* restaurants." With any luck, after all the work of getting the first one going, Toni would be less enthusiastic about opening a second one.

"Well, I've been thinking about it, and I'll be damned before I let some homicidal maniac control my life. If I have to hire some bodyguards for protection, then that's what I'll do."

I nearly burst out laughing at the image of Toni with half a dozen buff young men in tow. I wouldn't put it past her to hire them for the eye candy alone. Now that was the Toni I knew and loved.

"Good for you, Toni. You have such a great attitude," Judy said.

As we drove along, I found myself glancing back after every intersection. Toni watched me from the rearview mirror.

"What are you looking at?" she asked after a few blocks.

"Call me paranoid, but I'm just making sure nobody is following us."

Judy swiveled around in her seat. "Do you see anybody?"

I looked again. "There are so many cars it's difficult to tell." A number of them had been behind us for the past few blocks, but as we drove through the next intersection, two of the three turned right. A few hundred yards later the last one sped up and passed us.

"It looks like we're good," I said. Toni's eyes lost their fear and her hands relaxed their grip on the wheel.

She pointed to a storefront. "There it is." The space

was at the street level of an old brownstone. She slowed to a crawl and swerved into a parking lot across the street.

"Not here," Judy said. "You and I might not mind crossing the street on foot, but I think Nicky would rather we park a bit closer."

I nodded toward my crutches. "If a car decides to hit me, I wouldn't stand a chance in hell of getting out the way with these things."

"I doubt anybody's out to mow you down, but I'll park closer all the same," Toni said. She pulled out of the parking lot and circled the block, until after going around twice she scored a spot a few feet from the entrance. "Is this close enough?" she asked, grinning at me from the mirror. "Or do you need to take a cab from here?"

We left the car and soon were peering through a dirty window at an empty and very dusty interior.

"This place looks awful. Must have been a fast-food restaurant," Toni said. "I didn't think anything could look worse than the way our Queen location did when we took it over, but this one beats it hands down."

"It's not that bad," Judy said. "At least it still has booths and a food counter. Maybe after a good scrubbing—"

Toni shook her head, already walking away. "That might work if we were running a cafeteria, but we need an upscale location for our restaurant. We'd have to gut this place entirely. And did you see the grease on the ceiling? It's practically coming down in stalactites. Ugh. Forget this one."

"I don't think it's that bad," I said, even though I was secretly glad she hated it. "The next one on the list might be better."

"It can't be worse," she retorted.

This time we headed north to an address on Avenue Road. Again, I kept checking behind, and again nobody seemed to be following us. Judy asked about various sights along the way.

"That's the ROM," Toni said, answering one of her questions. "The Royal Ontario Museum." And a few blocks later, "That's Hazelton Lanes—the first few floors are a shopping center, the rest are all condos. That's where I live."

Toni's condo was on the top floor, a gorgeous, four-thousand-square-foot condo. We drove on. This time, Toni found a parking spot just a few doors down from where we were going. I struggled out of the car and joined Judy, who was already staring through the store window.

"This place is wonderful," she said, excitedly. "Come and look, Toni. I just know you'll love it."

Toni was standing a few feet away, arms crossed as she studied the building. "It looks all right from the street. The location is good, between two dress shops."

I looked inside. Judy was right. It was a beautiful space. I only hoped my friend liked it too. She stepped closer and peered inside. I held my breath.

She walked over, peering through the glass with her hands like blinders around her eyes. "Ohhh, I *love* this one." She turned to Judy, smiling. "You're right. This place is great. What do you think, Nicky? It looks good, don't you think?"

Knowing Toni, agreeing too fast might have the completely opposite effect. I squinted and peered inside again. The interior was about twice as big as our present location and, from what I could see, it wouldn't need much work. The ceilings were a disappointing nine feet high instead of the eighteen feet we now had. But they were free of the crisscross of old metal pipes we'd struggled to disguise.

"It reminds me of Skinny's on Queen, but bigger. Aren't you afraid it might be too big?"

"What are you talking about? We decided bigger was what we wanted. It'll give us room to expand." She went back to examining the inside like a child looking through the window of a candy store. "Look at that floor. It's industrial vinyl flooring—the latest thing—worth a fortune."

I hadn't noticed the floor. Granted, it did look impressive, solid black with textured silver-dollar-size rondelles.

Toni spoke to herself rather than to Judy and me. "We could do something really gorgeous with this place."

I continued playing my role of devil's advocate and pulled away from the window. "I don't know. The next one could be even better. That's the one that went bankrupt just a couple of months ago. And the area is a lot cheaper than Avenue Road." It wasn't exactly in the best neighborhood, but I would let Toni point that out.

Toni regarded me dubiously and strode back to her car. "If it went belly-up, chances are it won't be in great shape."

"*We* almost went belly-up, and our place looks great," I argued, trying to keep pace with her long legs.

She bobbed her head from side to side, noncommittally.

"Are you suggesting you don't think your restaurant is gorgeous?" Judy asked.

"Gorgeous?" she repeated, pausing with her hand on the car-door handle. "I wouldn't exactly use those words. Cool? Yes. Quirky? Definitely. I might even say it's attractive. But gorgeous, most certainly not." She opened the doors for Judy and me, and walked around to the driver's side. She turned the key in the ignition and the motor roared to life.

Judy looked stunned. "I can't believe you didn't love Skinny's decor. From what you told me, you and Nicky worked so hard to create it. Everybody I talk to agrees that it was beautiful."

It felt odd hearing it referred to in the past tense.

Toni glanced into the side mirror. "That's not what I said. All I'm saying is, this time we could do even better." She checked the traffic from the rear and moved into the flow of cars.

"Okay, if you could do anything you want with the new location, what would you do differently?" Judy asked.

Toni brightened with enthusiasm. "I'd probably keep the decor similar to Skinny's on Queen. I liked the black-and-white harlequin floor. I just wish we'd used stone, or at least tile, instead of linoleum."

I felt defensive of the nice decor I'd come up with. "Linoleum is making a comeback. And it's ecologically friendly."

"Stone is ecologically friendly too, and it lasts longer," she retorted. "I also liked the wall of mirrors and the fuchsia tables and chairs. It added a flash of color. My only regret is that we used such cheap materials. This time I'd like to use better quality furniture, get the tables and chairs professionally painted."

I heard an imaginary ka-ching as I thought of how Toni could easily drop a bundle when it was for something she wanted. If she had her way, I'd be paying her back for decades. And it would be years before we saw a profit. That might not be a problem for my rich girlfriend, but I needed my paycheck. "Let me point out that even though this place you like so much spent a fortune on their decor, it didn't prevent them from going out of business. Quite the opposite I expect. It probably accelerated their failure. The first rule of starting any new enterprise is to keep expenses low, at least until you start showing a profit."

She continued as if she hadn't heard a word I'd just said. "That wall of mirrors was a great idea of yours, but I wish we'd gone for nicer mirrors."

Ka-ching.

"I also liked the individual chandeliers over each table, but again, I'd rather something a bit more elegant than tin."

Another ka-ching.

Judy must have been thinking much the same as me because she said, "That all sounds expensive."

Toni glanced at me and saw the concern on my face. "Don't worry so much. We have insurance money coming in, and whatever it doesn't cover I can front."

My heart sank. I still hadn't told her that we'd had no insurance. "Uh, Toni. There's something I think you should know."

"What?"

"We didn't have any insurance."

Her eyes sought mine in the rearview mirror. "What do you mean—You thought—" She burst into laughter. To Judy, she said, "Of all people, Nicky should know me better than that. Of course we had insurance. I took care of it myself. It was the first thing I did when I loaned the company the start-up money."

"*You* took out insurance?" I stared at her, openmouthed. "Are you sure?"

"It was my money on the line. When it comes to protecting my money, I would never, ever take a chance."

It finally sank in. During the first months we were in business, Toni had been in charge of the bookkeeping, so it was possible. "Oh, Toni, I could kiss you."

She grimaced. "Oh, spare me the emotions, will you? Just co-sign the check when it comes in. That's all the gratitude I need."

"You've got it." And then, worried about her going crazy with the checkbook, I said, "All my life I've had to be careful with my spending. It'll be so much fun to just go out and spend as much as I want. I can't wait."

Judy laughed. "If you need help spending all that money, give me a call. I'm with you. I'd love not having to look at price tags for a change."

"Hold on there. Where did you get the idea I'd allow *limitless* spending," Toni said. "I'm not planning to go crazy. We'll set a budget."

I made an imaginary checkmark for the power of reverse psychology.

A strip mall came into view. Toni pointed to it. "I think that's the place up ahead."

I stared at the row of unattractive stores framed by two large office buildings. The only empty place I could see was a ground-floor space with wall-to-wall windows covered in graffiti. It didn't look anything like the kind of location we wanted for our restaurant.

Toni pulled into the parking and we drove by the store slowly. She didn't seem any more impressed than I was. "That's got to be about three thousand square feet—way too big. We'd always look half empty." She didn't state the more obvious, that it was ugly as hell.

Judy piped in. "Not only that, but look at the shops around here. Dirty windows, peeling paint, filthy sidewalk. There is no way this area will attract the kind of clientele you want."

Toni stepped on the gas and we headed back downtown, dropping Judy off at her hotel along the way. Not long after, we pulled up in front of my house.

"Would you like to come in?" I asked.

"We're supposed to have dinner with Judy and Richard tonight. She didn't mention it. I wonder if she forgot about it." She pushed up the sleeve of her alpaca coat and looked at her watch. "I'd better give her a call. I'll come in, but only for a minute."

She followed me down the walk, brushing by to

open the door for me. She hung up our coats and fumbled through her purse for her iPhone while I went to the kitchen and got a bottle of wine from the fridge, setting it on the counter.

"How about a glass of chardonnay?" I grabbed two glasses—as if I needed to ask.

"Sure," she called back.

I leaned my crutches against the wall and hopped around on one foot, preparing a platter of nibbles. A minute later, Toni appeared in the doorway and caught me struggling to reach a high shelf.

She strode over, swatting me away. "What do you think you're doing? Trying to break your other ankle?"

"I just wanted to reach that box of crackers."

She didn't even have to stretch—that was what five feet nine and four-inch heels would do. She placed a row of crackers alongside the cheese on the tray and carried it to the table. "Anything else I can do for you?"

"Why don't you do the honors while you're at it?" I asked, setting myself at the table.

She screwed the opener into the cork and pulled. It came out with a soft pop. She poured the wine and handed me a glass.

"Thanks. What did Judy say about dinner?"

"She said we should reschedule for tomorrow night instead. Thank goodness. I so don't feel like smiling all evening and making nice with someone I don't know."

"That's right, you haven't met him yet."

"No, but I've certainly heard a lot about him." She said this with a tight mouth, making it clear she'd already made up her mind to not like the man.

"Are he and Judy having problems?"

"No, not at all. According to her, quite the opposite. Good heavens, how she goes on about him. Richard this and Richard that, how good-looking he is. And you know what I always say, when it sounds too good to be true, you're about to get clobbered by a monkey wrench."

"Nobody can slaughter a perfectly good saying like you do," I said, chuckling.

She picked up the bottle and refreshed her glass. "Anyhow, all that gushing makes me suspicious."

"Maybe she's just in love."

"Nobody can be that much in love after ten years of marriage."

"You were."

"And look what it got me."

"But you're back together now. And you're happy, right?"

She didn't answer, concentrating on cutting small precise pieces of Gorgonzola. She placed one on a cracker and popped it into her mouth. "That is good cheese. Do you have any walnuts?"

I nodded. "In the cupboard next to the fridge."

She shook a bunch into a bowl and brought it back to the table. "I love walnuts with any blue cheese." She fixed another cracker with cheese, this time adding half a walnut, and handed it to me. "Taste it."

It was delicious but I couldn't help noticing that she'd avoided my question. "You are still happy with Steven, aren't you?"

Without missing a beat, she went right back to talking about Judy's husband, giving me the distinct impression she was avoiding talking about Steven. "I know I shouldn't judge him before I even meet him. But I can't stand the way she snaps to attention whenever he calls. Even when we're in the middle of something, she just drops everything and runs. One night we were at the Drake Hotel, and our drinks had just arrived when her cell phone rang.

Well—you should have seen how fast she got out of there. It made me wonder if he might be abusive."

"Surely you're exaggerating."

She shrugged, and some wine splashed out of her glass and onto the table. "I questioned her about him, in a roundabout way, of course, but the most she would admit is that he's fastidious." She looked around. "Where do you keep your dish towels?"

I pointed to the drawer. "That doesn't mean anything, except that he's probably a bit finicky."

She got a towel and wiped the table. "Anyhow—" she dismissed the subject with a swish of her hand, "—she said she'd make reservations for tomorrow night. I told her you'd come. I can't wait to find out what you think of him."

I chuckled. "I'm definitely more open-minded than you are. You probably wouldn't like him if he turned out to be Prince Charming himself." I snatched another cracker and then struggled to my feet. "If we're staying in, I might as well prepare us something to eat." I rummaged through the freezer until I found a container of frozen soup and ran it under the hot-water tap.

Suddenly, Toni was at my elbow. "What are you doing?"

"I'm heating us up some soup—fasolada."

"Fazoo…what?" she asked. Without waiting for an answer, she took the container from my hands and turned the block of frozen content into a pot. "I'll do that for you. You go sit." She turned on one of the burners and set it at low.

"Will you ask Steven to come along tomorrow night?"

"Of course, that's the whole point of the dinner—to get everyone together. I guess I can't put it off any longer. I have to tell him about Judy and Celia tonight."

"You still haven't told him? Why did you wait till now?"

"I wanted to, but…" She left her thought unfinished

and sat. "I can sure use another drink." She refilled the glasses, sliding one across the table to me, and raising hers. "What shall we drink to?"

"To you and Steven?" I suggested. "To hoping he likes Judy?"

She smiled crookedly. "How about we drink to the men in our lives? Here's to hoping it's not too late to fix them."

"How do you want to fix Steven?"

"Sometimes that man sure can be difficult." There was a pause before she added, "But he more than makes up for it in other ways."

I laughed, but her comment did make me wonder about the state of her relationship. Did she really think Steven was difficult? That he needed fixing? We drank in silence, both thinking our own thoughts, mine being that for someone who was so notoriously open about her sex life, she became completely closemouthed when it came to her emotions. Go figure.

The house phone rang, startling us both. I leaned across, snatching the receiver. Behind me I could hear the soup beginning to simmer. I pointed to the pot and Toni jumped up and turned down the heat. I covered the mouthpiece. "It's Jake." To him I asked, "How's Charles?"

"Not so good. He's even more depressed since we came back. He won't eat. He won't do anything but come up with different theories about who killed Jennifer."

"Who else does he suspect?"

"Atwood, of course, but he's also making a case for Jennifer's brother to have killed her."

"Why would her brother have killed her?"

"Jennifer won the lottery a couple of months after leaving her ex—a couple of million, enough to pay for that house and still leave enough for a nice portfolio of investments."

Ah, that explained the house.

"Her brother is an artist—a two-bit one, if you ask me," Jake continued. "He's been borrowing money from her nonstop. She cut him off financially a few weeks ago. Then, last Thursday, he called her again, begging for another loan. She'd already loaned him tens of thousands of dollars. She turned him down."

"So Charles thinks her brother might have killed her for the inheritance?"

"He thinks he might have killed her out of anger."

"Does he know the police think she was killed by mistake?" I knew Toni would not be pleased by what I was suggesting. I turned to her and mouthed, "I'll explain."

"I told him that, but he doesn't believe it. Also, it seems Jennifer and her brother had a huge argument when she told him she was marrying Charles."

"How do you know about that?" I asked.

"Charles told me. Why?"

I exhaled. "I was hoping someone else could testify to having overheard the argument. It would prove Charles was telling the truth, and that he and Jennifer were happy together." At least until the argument the night of the murder. "But the problem is, that's only hearsay and from someone who could eventually be a suspect himself. By the way, do you have any idea what Charles and Jennifer were arguing about that night?"

"Jennifer wanted to get pregnant, but Charles wanted to wait until he was more established financially. He didn't want to live off her money."

"I suppose a lot of men might feel that way," I said.

"I guess," he said. "Anyhow, Charles spoke to the police about Atwood. They said they would check on him."

It suddenly became very important that Atwood be the killer. I would be safe. Toni would be safe. And we could all go on with our lives without worry…except Charles. He would still be without the woman he loved. "I wish there was something I could do for him."

"Actually, that's one of the reasons I called. Marley and I have been thinking. The best thing for Charles right now is to keep busy. He needs something to do, otherwise he'll just be obsessing. But with the restaurant gone, he doesn't even have a job anymore. Isn't there some work you could ask him to do? Maybe you can get him to work on recipes, somewhere other than in his house. Right now everywhere he looks he sees Jennifer."

"That's a great idea. I'll suggest he work out of my kitchen. Or, if he prefers he can work at Toni's." I glanced at her, wondering how she'd feel about that suggestion.

She strode over, snatching the phone from my hands. "I have a better idea," she said without preamble. "Nicky and I found a possible new location for Skinny's. If we can lease it for a reasonable price, we'll want to reopen as soon as possible. We'll need everyone's help to make it happen."

She handed me back the phone. I picked it up.

"—count on Marley and me," Jake was saying. "And I'm sure Scott will pitch in too. If Charles isn't up to working on recipes, I'll make sure he gets involved somehow." His voice lowered. "What about that lunatic? What if everybody's wrong and she really is behind everything?"

"I haven't a clue," I said, chilled at the thought. "And there's no point in worrying about it. I'll call you the minute we know about the restaurant." We said goodbye and hung up.

Toni had found the bowls and was ladling in the soup. "This smells divine." She placed them on the table and added more crackers on the cheeseboard. "I take it Charles isn't doing so well?"

I nodded. "Jake said the cops are looking at Atwood." I pointed to the soup. "We need some feta cheese for garnish."

Toni took some out of the refrigerator and plonked it on the table. "Did I hear you say something about Jennifer's brother being a suspect?"

"That could just be Charles being paranoid, but he thinks the brother might have killed her because she refused to lend him money." I repeated the conversation.

She nodded along. "It sounds to me like we have two likely suspects."

I sprinkled a spoonful of feta on my soup. "This is the way it's served in Greece. Try it. It's delicious, you'll see."

She shrugged and followed suit. She sampled it and paused, savoring the flavor. She took a few more bites. "What's in this soup? It's delicious."

"All healthy stuff—tons of vegetables, beans, olive oil, vegetable stock and my secret ingredient—honey."

"Honey? In soup?" She looked down at her bowl and took another spoonful. "It sounds weird, but it's delicious. It definitely goes on our menu the minute we reopen."

This came out her mouth in such a firm tone that, it, more than anything, told me she was committed to reopening. I smiled to myself and casually said, "Good idea." And then I changed the subject. "What do you think of getting Charles to start working on the burger? It'll keep him busy until we know what's happening."

"Good idea."

"I'm glad you agree. I'll get him to come over and start as soon as he can."

Toni pushed away her empty bowl, polished off the rest of her wine and set her glass down. "Well, I might as well get this over with," she said scowling.

I wasn't sure what she was talking about until she

headed off to the mudroom and I overheard her talking to the little male.

"What do you say, Trouble? Will you still love me even if I don't leave you my fortune?"

She said this in a joking tone, but it gave me pause. How would it be to constantly wonder whether people loved you for yourself or for your money? It made me thankful that she had never mentioned her fortune to me until just a few months ago, and especially that I'd had no idea I was her beneficiary until yesterday. At least she could count on *my* friendship being sincere.

"So you're off to tell Steven?" I said.

She pulled herself up straight and nodded determinedly. "Wish me luck." I followed her to the front where she slipped into her coat. "If I call you in tears in the middle of the night, you'll know he didn't take the news well." She started turning away and stopped. "Why don't you put away those crackers on the table? If you leave them there, you'll polish them off in one sitting." And then she walked out.

Actually, she had that wrong, I thought, closing the door behind her.

I wouldn't bother sitting.

masked killers coming after me

AFTER TONI LEFT, I changed into my pajamas and called Charles.

"I hope this isn't an imposition," I said, couching my request as a favor to us, rather than the other way around, "but Toni and I could really use your help." I explained about wanting to reopen and told him we needed a few new dishes on the menu. Using my broken ankle as an excuse, I suggested he come work in my kitchen.

He didn't put up any resistance and I realized Jake had been right—Charles welcomed the opportunity to keep busy. "I can continue working on that low-calorie burger. How about if I come by day after tomorrow? I still have a few things I'd like to settle."

As long as they didn't involve guns, fire, or violence of any kind, I didn't mind one bit. "You'll have to bring most of the ingredients. Keep the bill and I'll pay you back."

He agreed to be here at ten o'clock, and by the time he hung up I thought he sounded a bit better.

I had just gone upstairs to my bedroom when the phone rang.

"Mitchell," I exclaimed, thrilled to hear his voice. "How's the editing coming along?" I leaned my crutches against my bedside table and lay down on the bed. When I closed my eyes and listened to his voice, it felt almost as if he was right there with me.

"Good. We're making progress," he said, going on about some technical stuff like voice and rhythm for a while. I had no more idea what he was referring to than he did when I talked about balance of flavors, colors and textures.

"You know, I've been home quite a lot since I got out of the hospital, and I still haven't seen a hint of a movie being shot in your place."

"Really?" Why didn't he sound more concerned?

"Nothing. If a movie was being filmed, there would be dozens of people, cameramen, sound guys, set designers. And there would be truckloads of equipment up and down the street."

"I told you. They're only shooting one scene, not a whole movie. I wouldn't worry about it." He changed the subject. "Any news from the police? Have they nabbed the arsonist yet?"

"Whatever they're doing, they're not sharing with me."

"I can't wait to get back," he said, his voice growing husky. I forgot all about the blonde and the movie that was not being shot. "I'm worried about you. And I miss you. I can't wait to come home."

My heart skipped a beat. "I miss you too. Any idea when that will be?"

"I'm hoping we'll be finished in a couple of days. But if I come back before the end of next week, my house will still be rented." He paused—waiting for an invitation maybe?

I supplied it. "That's not a problem. You can stay with me."

"I wouldn't be in your way?"

"In my way? No, of course not," I assured him. We chatted on for a few minutes, and I hung up feeling like a million dollars. Mitchell was coming back, and he would be staying with me. "What do you think of that, Jackie Chan?"

Jackie was lying in her favorite spot, at the foot of my bed, staring at me as if she understood every word I'd said.

"He still loves me," I told her. "All that insecurity for nothing."

Yap, yap, she barked, hopping off the bed and marching away haughtily.

"Aw, come on, Jackie. Don't be like that. You know you'll always be my favorite." She stopped and threw me a backward glance, almost as if she was trying to determine how sincere I was. "I mean it. I love you." She stood still. And then I said the magic words. "Want a treat?"

She went charging down the stairs. "That proves it," I said, following her to the kitchen. "You only love me for the treats I give you." She didn't seem in the least insulted, clawing at my good leg until I handed over the liver treat.

I clambered back upstairs, and before long I fell into a fitful sleep, filled with nightmares of masked killers coming after me. For all my brave talk to Toni and Mitchell, the truth was I was still scared.

on the bright side, we're already divorced

I WOKE UP the next morning feeling better than I had since my accident. I'd had a good night's sleep. The pain in my ankle had muted to an ache. I felt so well that I skipped the painkiller. My only disappointment came when I stepped into my favorite skirt and had to leave the waist button undone. I hadn't weighed myself in days, not since the hospital. I mean, I'd tried, but standing on one foot, I'd wobbled so much to keep my balance that I couldn't get a straight reading. Now, it seemed that getting around on crutches was not burning more calories as I'd hoped. Unless I started seriously watching my weight, I'd regain every pound I'd lost—*groan*.

After coffee and toast, I got to work. I opened my cookbook to a recipe I'd noted the night before—black-bean brownies. I preheated the oven, measured and assembled the ingredients. Soon, I had a first version of the recipe baking and the wonderful aroma of chocolate filled the house. For the next couple of hours I tested one version after another, improving, perfecting, until by my fifth batch, they were everything a decadent brownie should be, rich and chocolaty yet not too sweet. I poured myself another cup of coffee, cut myself another smidgeon of brownie—beans, what could be healthier?—and my mind wandered back to Charles. Hopefully he was feeling better this morning. I picked up the phone.

After half a dozen rings, his voice mail came on. "This is Charles," it said in an exuberant tone, "and Jennifer," a woman's voice continued in an even chirpier voice. And then together, "We're busy right now, so leave a message and we'll call you back." The cheerful message only made Jennifer's death seem all the more tragic. When the beep came, my throat was too constricted to speak. I hung up and punched in Jake's number instead.

"Nicky? What is it?" he asked sleepily. And then worried, "What's wrong? Why are you calling me so early?"

I looked up at my wall clock—a quarter past eleven. "You were still sleeping? Sorry."

"What's up?"

"I'm worried about Charles. I tried calling him but he isn't picking up."

"Unless you just woke him up, my best guess is he's still sleeping. You won't believe what happened yesterday."

"Now what?" I asked. "Not more bad news, I hope."

"It's bad, all right." He sounded outraged. "Charles got a call from Jennifer's brother. This time he announced that Jennifer never bothered changing her will after she and her ex split up."

"That means Atwood inherits everything? That's certainly a motive for murder. Have you heard from the police? Did they check whether he had an alibi for the time of Jennifer's death?"

"He claims he was at the fire hall with a dozen other firemen who can vouch for him. But he wouldn't stand to inherit anyhow. Wills are automatically voided when couples separate, so technically, Jennifer died intestate."

"But we don't know for sure whether he really was there or not?" I asked. And then before he could answer I continued. "Mind you, he'd be stupid to lie about something like that. The police would find out." I paused. "How do you know so much about testamentary law?"

"I'm just repeating everything Jennifer's brother told Charles. He also said that, legally, Charles and she weren't living together long enough to make them common law spouses."

"Then who—"

"Her entire estate goes to her next of kin—namely, the brother. And if that isn't enough, he wants Charles out of the house before the end of the month."

"But that's only—" I stopped and counted the days till December, "—two weeks away. That's terrible."

"It's disgusting, is what it is. He's got to find a place, pack all his stuff and get out. And the brother said he wants to see receipts for anything Charles takes out of the house. He's claiming that all the furniture, the art, everything belonged to Jennifer. And he wants to keep it all."

"What? But that's not fair."

"What's 'fair' got to do with anything? As long as the law is on his side, that's all that counts."

"That might not be entirely true. I bet the guy is trying to intimidate Charles."

"He's a bastard," Jake continued, incensed.

As appalling as it was, I wasn't all that surprised. When it came to fighting for inheritances, people were often shameless. "I hope Charles didn't agree to any of this. He's got to fight."

"That's exactly what I told him, but he's so depressed I'm afraid he might not have the energy for a battle."

I thought quickly. There had to be something I could do. I thought of Toni's husband, but he was not the right lawyer for this kind of case. "Make sure he doesn't agree to anything until he hears from me."

"What are you planning?"

"First thing I have to do is find him a good lawyer. I'll make a few phone calls and get back to you. Tell him to not let Jennifer's brother intimidate him, no matter what he tells him. I think he's trying to pull a fast one." I hung up and glanced at my watch—not quite eleven-thirty.

I scrolled through my contacts list, pressed the speed-dial for Steven's office, and a minute later his receptionist put me through.

"Steven Lawford," a gruff male voice answered.

"Hi Steven. It's Nicky Landry. I hope I'm not disturbing you."

His voice mellowed. "Well, well, if it isn't my favorite client. How are you doing, Nicky? You must be staying out of trouble, otherwise I'd have heard from you." And then as an afterthought, he added, "You're not in some kind of trouble now, are you?"

I chuckled. "No, but a friend of mine has a problem. I'm sure Toni told you about the restaurant fire and about Jennifer being murdered?"

"Yes, of course—tragic."

I went straight to the point, giving him the gist of the situation. "Can Jennifer's brother really kick Charles out like that?"

His answer was quick and firm. "No, he can't. As for Charles's rights to the house, he might have a good case, however it will depend on a number of things. How long were they living together?"

"Er, I don't know exactly."

"Do you know if Charles contributed financially to the house?"

Not significantly, I thought, considering how little we paid him. But all I said was, "I'm not sure."

"How long did Jennifer own the house before Charles moved in?"

"I have no idea."

There was a long pause. "You don't know much, do

you?" he said with a smile in his voice. "Tell you what. I'll make a few calls and find out who's the best lawyer for that kind of situation. I'll call you back with a name and phone number. In the meantime I suggest you call your friend and tell him to get his paperwork together. The lawyer will want—do you have a pen and paper? It's a long list."

"Hold on." I rummaged through the catchall drawer in my bedside table and pulled out a well-chewed pen—probably from a diet-induced moment of desperation. "Okay, got it."

"The lawyer will need to know when Jennifer bought the house and when Charles moved in. If Charles contributed financially to the house, he should gather all receipts or evidence of this. If there were any financial arrangements between them, he should note them and show proof. Receipts, bank statements, income tax statements—he'll need to find all of those and any other records of his income and expenditures."

I was taking down the information as fast as I could, feeling more hopeful about Charles's situation. "Thank you, Steven. That's great help."

I hung up, and punched in Jake's number again.

He picked up on the first ring. "I just heard from Charles. It seems the police checked on Atwood's alibi. He's in the clear."

"So that leaves us with only Jennifer's brother as a suspect," I said.

"Unless Jennifer was killed by mistake. Or simply because she happened to be at the wrong place at the wrong time."

I'd been thinking the same thing. I changed the subject. "I just spoke to Toni's ex-husband. He'll find out who's the best lawyer for Charles to see."

"Does he really think Charles stands a chance?"

"So it seems. He said Charles needs to put together a file of documents to help his case." I was about to suggest he get a pencil and paper when my house phone rang. "I'll email you the list, and you get it to Charles. Make sure he does it." Jake promised he would see to it, and we hung up. I picked up the house phone. It was Toni.

"I told Steven about Judy," she blurted, sounding distraught.

"How'd it go?" I asked. Judging by the tone of her voice I already had a pretty good idea what the answer would be.

"On the bright side, we're already divorced, so I won't have to go through that again."

"That bad? I just spoke to him and he didn't sound upset—just his usual charming self."

She snorted. "Steven is too much of a professional to let personal matters affect his work. He could be bleeding to death, but as long as he's on the phone with a client, he'll take care of business before dialing 911."

"What happened?"

"Oh, he pretended everything was just dandy. He went into this whole what-a-surprise thing, and then went on and on about how happy he was for me. But I could tell that underneath it all he was furious. He has this vein that pulsates in his forehead whenever he's angry. It was going so fast I thought he might have a heart attack." She hesitated. "But, here's the weird part. The whole time I had the strangest feeling that the whole surprise thing was an act, and that he already knew all about my sister and my niece."

"But that doesn't make any sense. How could he? You didn't know about her yourself until—what—two weeks?"

"Actually, closer to a month."

A month? And she had kept this to herself all this

time? "What about the will? Does he know you didn't change it?"

She gasped. "Are you kidding? I didn't tell him *that*. I swear, he'd kill me if he ever found out."

Of course she was just joking, but a horrible thought came to me in a flash. What if it was *Steven*? If he was under the impression that she had already changed her will in *his* favor and then found out about Toni's sister and niece, he might worry that she would change her will again, this time making *them* her principal beneficiaries. As Inspector Crawford put it, it gave him seventeen damned good reasons to want Toni dead.

Why else would Steven have insisted he be her principal beneficiary? In hindsight, the more I thought about it, the more his behavior seemed suspicious. Steven was about ten years older than Toni. If he was intent on inheriting her fortune, it could only mean he was counting on her dying first. There was only one way he could make sure of that—he was planning to kill her. I felt ill at the thought.

I kept my voice calm. "Er, Toni, are you sure that Steven didn't already know about your money when you got back together?"

"What? Why would you—" And then she got it. She gasped. "You think Steven—That's the most ridiculous thing I've ever heard in my life. Steven might not be perfect, but he is not a killer. Next you're going to tell me that the woman who came barging in, making all those threats, is his girlfriend. Trust me, he likes them younger than she was."

"No, of course not," I said, wishing my thoughts weren't always so transparent. Toni was already paranoid enough. The last thing she needed was to be fed more suspicions to obsess about. "I wasn't thinking any such thing."

There was a long silence, and then her next words took me by surprise. "You're right," she said, her voice trembling with emotion. "It's got to be him. How could I have been so blind? Steven is trying to kill me."

i must have a photogenic memory

I MANAGED TO calm her, and suggested she come over.

"I'll be over in fifteen minutes," she said and hung up.

She must have been driving like a maniac because I hardly had time to email Jake when the doorbell rang.

"Is the coffee ready?" she asked, as she came charging in.

"I'll go make some right away."

"No, no, don't bother. I'll make it myself." She tore off her coat and went straight to the kitchen. Grabbing the jar of coffee beans from the cupboard she dumped a capful into the grinder in stony silence. She turned on the coffeemaker and then faced me. "How did Steven sound to you?"

"I told you. He was pleasant and courteous, as usual. Don't you think you're jumping to conclusions here?"

She scowled. "Sometimes I swear, I must have photogenic memory."

"You mean photographic memory."

"No," she insisted. "I mean photogenic. I seem to remember the past as being much nicer than it actually was."

I chuckled. "That's a good term you just coined." And then seeing her expression I realized she was being serious. "But why would you say that?"

She shrugged. "While we were apart, I used to fantasize that if we ever got back together things would be just the same, as if they were ever great to begin with. I'm not saying I'm unhappy with him. It's just that I'm not as happy as I thought I'd be." She cocked a hip, planting a hand on it. "You know, maybe it's true that sometimes we fake orgasms, but men can fake whole relationships."

I held back from laughing. "I doubt he's faking anything. I know he loves you."

"Or maybe he doesn't love me the way he used to. And if he doesn't, then why would he have wanted to reconcile—unless it's for my money?"

"Toni, you're jumping to conclusions."

"Of course it's him. Who else could it be? He's the only one with a motive. He thinks he's going to inherit everything." Grim-faced, she placed mugs on the table and went to the fridge for milk. "Turns out you were right. I was the intended victim all along. And that even explains the hit-and-run."

"What do you mean?" I had a bad feeling I knew just what she was about to say.

"When he asked me who my beneficiary was, I told him. I bet he tried to kill you just in case I was still leaving you an important amount. Well, he's got another surprise coming. If he kills both of us, all my money goes to charity. He won't get a dime."

That didn't make me feel one iota better. I swallowed hard. "I still think Steven has nothing to do with it," I said, hoping this was true.

She poured milk into a creamer and set it next to my cup. "Who else could it be?"

"There are probably a dozen other possibilities we haven't considered yet."

"Name me one." She leaned against the counter with her arms crossed. Behind that stubborn stare, I knew, was a scared little girl, praying I would convince her otherwise. Toni loved Steven. If Steven really was planning to kill her, I wasn't sure she would ever recover.

"There's still Jennifer's brother." I repeated the conversation I'd had with Jake earlier. "You might not have been the intended victim after all. Now that we know Jennifer also had money, the same motive you're so intent on applying to Steven, also works for her brother. He could have wanted to get rid of her before she changed her will and named Charles as her beneficiary."

Hope flickered in her eyes and then died. "There is no way Jennifer's brother could have predicted that the hit-and-run would send you to the hospital." Great, now Toni was using my own argument against me.

She was quiet, looking into her cup as if it was a crystal ball. "I have no idea what I should do." She looked so miserable my heart went out to her.

"Toni," I said softly. "You can't say or do anything until we know for sure what's going on. If you accuse Steven and he turns out to be innocent, which I'm sure he is, you won't be able to just smile prettily and say, 'Oops, my bad.' There won't be any going back. Steven will never speak to you again."

She looked dazed. "You're right. There's only one thing I can do. I have to find out who killed Jennifer. That's the only way I can prove Steven is innocent—or guilty," she added. She looked at me. "Got any bright ideas how I can do that?"

I was all out of bright ideas.

The coffeemaker beeped. "Thank goodness I talked you into reopening the restaurant," she said pouring the coffee.

"Thank goodness," I said with a crooked smile. My sarcasm went ten feet over her head.

"If I didn't have that project to keep me busy, I'd go out of my mind." Taking a seat across from me, she announced, "By the way, I've decided we should take the place on Avenue Road."

Talking about her plans for the new restaurant lifted her out of her foul mood. She picked up the phone and handed it to me. "Call the agent and tell him we want to see it at his earliest convenience."

AN HOUR LATER we were standing in front of what might soon be our new restaurant. The real estate agent—a tall thin man with a mouthful of large and overly bleached teeth—introduced himself as Barry Peters. He walked around, leather folder under one arm, pointing out all the special features.

"This used to be a combination bakery and coffee shop, so the kitchen area in the back is perfect for your needs," he said eagerly.

I stepped through a swinging stainless-steel door and stood in the middle of the kitchen area, gasping. The spacious room had counters all around, an old-fashioned professional stove and a row of wall ovens—too many for our needs. In the center of the room was a long baker's table with a ceiling rack crying out for a few dozen pots and pans. I looked around, mentally checking off all the items we could strike off our shopping list. The only expensive piece missing was a walk-in refrigerator.

Toni strolled around, running her hand along the stainless steel counter. "How come all the equipment is still here?"

"The landlord insisted the previous tenants put up their equipment as guarantee." He shrugged. "Turns out he was right. When they went belly-up six months later, they were already four months behind in their rent. Everything reverted to him. If you're interested in purchasing it, why don't you make him an offer?"

I looked around again, this time trying to determine the value of the equipment. "Do you have any idea how much he wants for the lot?"

He furrowed his brows, thinking.

Before he quoted a price I said, "What if we gave him the equivalent of the four months' rent he lost?"

He nodded slowly. "That might work. Let me give him a call."

I put up a hand. "Before you do that, maybe you should confirm the rent."

He quoted us a price per square foot, adding that this was net-net-net, which in commercial real estate leases, meant the tenant paid for all services, every single one of them—property taxes, electricity, taxes, maintenance and insurance—the list goes on. The total of those extra charges could amount to as much as double the rent.

I almost choked. "You can't be serious."

He shrugged. "This location is prime. That's what places around here cost."

"I was under the impression the price quoted in the ad was gross," I said. "If it isn't, that changes everything. Will you give us a minute?"

"Sure. I'll just step outside and let you ladies talk."

Toni and I followed him back to the dining area, and he continued on outside. I circled the room, assessing the advantages of this location. "This is a good location, and, true, we wouldn't need to spend much on decorating."

"We can probably fit twenty tables in this place," she added. "And with dress shops on both sides, that means we'll get lots of foot traffic. Those tables will be full all the time."

As much as I loved this place, I worried Toni might want it at any price. "We have to be firm on this," I said. "There is no way we can afford the price he quoted unless it's a gross lease." I looked her firmly in the eye. "You're with me on this, right?"

Toni kept glancing at the agent, who was having a whispered conversation on his cell phone—probably conferring with his client. He had turned his back on the building, making it impossible for us to read his expression.

She dropped her stare and looked around again. "Double the number of tables means double the number of customers and double the income."

"And double the amount of work, double the number of employees and double the cost of ingredients."

She rolled her eyes.

"Don't you dare agree on that price," I insisted.

"We can find a restaurant supply place and get everything we need in one fell swoop."

At that moment I noticed the agent slip his cell phone into his pocket. "He looks about ready to come back in. Whatever I say, you agree with me," I said.

He came back in and flashed his pearly whites. "The owner is open to selling the equipment. He said to make him an offer. So, regarding the space, do we have a deal?" He looked so full of suppressed excitement he was probably itching to rub his hands in anticipation.

"We can't seem to agree on this place," Toni said, much to my relief. "I like it, but my partner thinks it's too expensive."

I nodded. "There another place we saw that could also work for us, and the rent is considerably lower." I headed toward the door. "We'll get back to you."

I had my hand on the handle when the agent called, "Wait," just as I'd hoped. "Maybe we can come to some agreement."

"If you can give my partner what she wants, I'll be

happy to sign on the dotted line." Toni opened her purse and pulled out a checkbook. "And you'll have a five-year deal before the end of the day."

And, again, just as I'd expected, he opened his folder and pulled out a sheaf of papers. "Why don't we put together an offer? I'll present it to my client and put in a good word for you."

Forty-five minutes later, we were on our way back to my place. The day had turned from cloudy to sunny. I took it as a good omen. Toni grabbed her sunglasses from the pocket above the visor and slipped them on.

She threw me a glance. "Do you really think we can get it for so little?"

"In the present economy and with the number of places available out there, I bet we'll get a great deal."

"I hope you're right." She didn't seem convinced, which only made me appreciate all the more how cooperative she'd been.

We'd actually made two separate leasing offers for the same place. On the first one we'd asked for a three-year lease at a slightly lower amount per square foot than the asking price. For the second offer, we asked for a five-year lease at an even lower price, hoping that the longer lease would make that deal seem sweeter. We had also made a stand-alone offer to purchase the kitchen equipment. If we didn't get the store, we would at least have the equipment, which would be great no matter where we set up.

She glanced at me with admiration. "You could give lessons in strategy. I thought I was good, but you're a master. I can't believe you asked for the place to be repainted." I'd also asked for a few minor things like a month's free rent, new light fixtures and outdoor lighting.

"It's always a good idea to ask for a few things we

don't really want. It gives us room for negotiating. For every demand we drop, they have to make a concession."

"Smart," she said.

Minutes later we pulled up in front of my house. At the same time, the blonde I'd seen two days earlier stepped out of Mitchell's place.

"There she is," I exclaimed, just as Toni said, "That's her."

The girl dashed across the street to a gray Audi and hopped in. A moment later she was roaring up the street.

"What do you suppose she's doing in his place?" Toni asked, staring at the house. "It doesn't look like there's any filming going on. If there was, there'd be trucks and RVs parked all the way up and down the street. There'd be cables running in and out of the house, equipment…"

"Funny, that's exactly what I was telling Mitchell last night."

She frowned, looking at me. "What the hell is that girl doing in there?"

"I think it's high time we find out." I pushed open the passenger door. "Come." I shuffled up to my front door, handed my key to Toni and she did the honors. I led the way down the hall, ignoring Jackie's enthusiastic greeting, and went right back out again through the mudroom entrance.

"Where are we going?"

"I told you. We're going to find out what the hell is going on."

Moments later we were in Mitchell's backyard and I was turning over rocks in his planter.

Toni watched, horrified. "Sweetheart, I have nothing against breaking into his house." She whispered, glancing around, "But, please don't smash a window, at least not in broad daylight."

"Relax. I am not breaking in. Mitchell once told me he keeps a spare key back here. Ah, here it is." I located the fake rock and palmed the key.

She planted a hand on her hip and raised an eyebrow. "If we're not breaking in, then, why are we whispering?"

She had a point. Even though Mitchell was my boyfriend, he had not given me permission. Also, as long as his house was rented, it was not his to use. So technically, no matter how I looked at it, I was trespassing. I kept this to myself.

I climbed the back steps, unlocked the door and walked in.

"It's dark in here. Turn on the light," Toni said in a low voice.

"Give yourself a minute and your eyes will adjust." Sure enough, after a few seconds, it didn't seem so dim anymore. I made my way as silently as my crutches allowed, crossing the mudroom into the kitchen. I looked around, surprised at how tidy everything was. The floor was scrubbed clean. The counters were spotless. Even the refrigerator and stove had been polished until they shined. I couldn't help but notice that all the decals had been removed from the decades-old fridge. Was this the work of Mitchell or of the production crew? Maybe something *was* going on in here after all.

Toni stood in the middle of the charmless kitchen, her mouth hanging open. "You mean to tell me a production company wants to use *this* dump for a set? What are they filming, a horror movie?"

Funny, I'd had the same thought. "Be quiet. There might be somebody here."

"Don't you think we'll look even guiltier if we skulk around? We should act naturally. If we run into anyone, we'll just tell them the truth—that you're Mitchell's girl-friend and that you're just checking on his place."

I paused. "You're right," I whispered. And then said it in a normal tone, repeated, "You're right."

We continued on through the dining room and then to the living room. "What's that?" Toni asked.

I followed her finger to where she was pointing. There, against the common wall that divided Mitchell's home from mine, was something that looked like an audio system. There was a rectangular black box—a receiver—with dozens of blinking lights.

"That's not usually here," I said, coming closer. A number of wires were running from the receiver down to the floor. One continued along the baseboard, until it split, one part disappearing into the wall. Underneath was a fine dusting of white powder—plaster dust? The other part ran along the floor into the dining room. Others continued up the staircase to the second floor. I stepped closer and reached over to touch it. Toni slapped my hand away.

"Ouch! Why—"

She placed a finger to her lips and leaned in close. "That's surveillance equipment."

I gasped, turned and stared at the contraption again, taking new notice of the dozens of buttons and flashing lights. "How can you be sure? Maybe it's just movie-making stuff," I whispered.

"Believe me. I know what I'm talking about."

All at once I remembered the drilling sound I'd heard a few nights ago. Surveillance? Who was spying on who?—surely not on me. But even as I was trying to come up with some other possibility, I knew that was it. Somebody had been listening in on all my conversations. A wave of nausea washed over me. Toni tapped me on the shoulder and gestured for me to follow. She tiptoed up the stairs.

I crept up behind her as quietly as I could, which wasn't very. Crutches were not made for tiptoeing. Reaching the landing, I noticed one wire going off toward the front bedroom. We followed it until it stopped in the middle of the room, where it once again disappeared into the wall above a small pile of plaster dust.

Why in the world would somebody want to spy on me? Toni nudged me, taking my mind off the questions whirling in my mind. "Let's get out of here," she mouthed.

I nodded. We were just about to walk out, when from downstairs came the sound of a door opening and closing.

"She's back!" I glanced at Toni. "We have to get out of here."

All color drained from her face. She looked around frantically, and crept to the closet, swinging open the door. The inside was jam packed with boxes and piles of clothes. So that was how Mitchell had cleaned up. He'd just stashed everything in closets. Toni shut the door, her eyes darting from one possible hiding place to another.

"Toni, *do* something."

"I am. I am." In a nanosecond she'd scooted and disappeared behind the bed's dust ruffle, leaving *me* in the middle of the room.

What if the blonde's toting a gun? Oh my God, I'm dead! I went from panicked to terrified.

The footsteps reached the bottom stair and I swung into action. I dropped to all fours, hoping whoever was on the stairs hadn't heard the thump of my knees as it hit the floor. I pushed my crutches under the bed, lay flat on my back and—*damned cast*—began to worm my way under the bed, sliding and undulating as fast as I could, and making a lot of scratching noises in the process. *Dear God*, please *don't let her hear me.* The footsteps reached the landing, no more than fifteen feet from the bedroom. I wiggled faster. Half my body was still in full view. The footsteps were getting closer. Another few seconds and she would see me. Beads of perspiration moistened my forehead. I was so fucked. At just that moment, Toni grabbed my arm and pulled hard. In the next instant I was behind the bed skirt. Not a moment too soon.

The footsteps marched into the bedroom, coming within inches of where I had been a second ago. Now I was panting so hard I was certain she could hear me. Suddenly the theme song for *Sex and the City* began to play—Toni's cell phone—and my heart nearly exploded. All she had to do was lift the dust ruffle and she would catch us. And then, as suddenly as it started, the phone stopped ringing.

"Hello?" A woman's voice spoke from a few feet away, almost startling me out of my skin. Shit! She'd answered Toni's phone. We were so screwed. I looked at Toni. Her eyes were big as quarters, her pupils tiny in all that white. She mouthed something I couldn't make out, and then she tapped my arm with…*her cell phone*? How…? And then I understood. The ringing had come from the blonde's phone. I almost wept with relief.

Meanwhile she was still talking. "I forgot to adjust the volume in the upstairs bedroom. I had to come back. You said yourself you couldn't make out anything she said when she was in her bedroom…I am not…Besides, you heard her yourself. She never even saw whether the driver was a man or a woman. Even if she notices me, she'd never recognize me in a million years."

Toni's hand gripped mine and squeezed.

The blonde was the one who had been behind the wheel of the hit-and-run car. But evidently, she wasn't alone in this plot. Whoever was at the other end of that phone was at least a co-conspirator. Who the hell was it?

I listened hard, trying to hear what was being said at the other end. It was faint—too faint to make out any words. Was it my imagination or did the voice sound male? Steven's? I couldn't tell.

"Don't worry, I'm finished. I'm leaving right now. I'll be there in half an hour." There was a faint click followed by the sound of footsteps walking away. A few seconds later the front door opened and closed.

I stayed frozen in place, my heart still racing madly. I almost wept in relief.

Next to me, Toni exhaled. "I think it's safe to go now," she whispered. "But be quiet, that equipment can probably pick up sounds from this side too."

I scrambled out, scooping my crutches under my arms. I brushed dust bunnies from my coat and my hair, and hoofed it over to the window, hoping to get the license plate. Too late. The Audi was already halfway up the street.

"What are you waiting for? Let's go," Toni whispered urgently from the doorway.

I scampered after her, down the stairs and through the kitchen, with my heart still pounding against my ribs. I closed the back door and locked it, replacing the key in the fake rock. Only then did I breathe normally. We high-tailed it back to my place.

I was about to open my back door, when it dawned on me. "We can't say anything inside," I said. "Everything is being recorded."

"You look sick. Are you all right?"

I didn't feel well. My stomach was in turmoil. Somebody had been listening in on my every word. It felt like such an invasion of privacy. "I'm fine," I said.

She gave me a half smile. "Just thank your lucky stars

lover boy is in New York, otherwise they'd be entertaining themselves with porn audio."

"Toni," I said sharply, blushing. "This is no time to joke."

She looked at me wide-eyed. "Who's joking?"

"I don't even want to stay in my own home anymore. I feel violated."

"You don't have to stay here. We can go to my place if you like."

"You wouldn't mind? I'd have to take the dogs." An idea came to me. "Oh my God. That was probably her, wearing a wig."

Toni looked at me, confused, until a light lit her eyes. "You mean the crazy woman? You think that was her?"

"It must have been."

"You could be right," said Toni. "We already know she was driving the hit-and-run car."

A dozen questions crowded my mind. "But why? Who is she? Do you know her from anywhere?"

"No, other than seeing her go into Mitchell's place, I never saw her before in my life." She planted a fist on her hip. "If that bitch comes anywhere near us, she is so dead." She gave her pocketbook an ominous pat.

"You're not still walking around with that gun in your bag, are you?" I whispered, darting glances around.

She ignored my question. "Should we call the police?"

My mouth dried with dread. The thought of having to deal with the gruesome twosome again was more than I could handle right now.

"Bad idea." I shook my head. "I can tell you what they'd say. They'd accuse us of breaking into my boyfriend's house, which is illegal, and they'd say that Mitchell put in the listening devices. Then *he'd* be in trouble.

I say we have to figure out who this woman is, and how she's involved in all of this."

Tears sprang to Toni's eyes. "It's got to be Steven. She's just his type—blonde and gorgeous, and a decade younger than me."

"What makes you think she's younger? As far as I'm concerned she doesn't look a day younger than you. And for all we know she might have been involved with Charles or with Jennifer's ex. You realize what this means, don't you? Even if they have alibis, either Jennifer's ex or her brother could have planned this." I was thoughtful for a moment. "What I can't figure out is, why the surveillance equipment?"

"Somebody obviously wanted to listen in on your conversations. Tell me, are you certain Mitchell trusts you?"

"Don't be ridiculous." I didn't even want to imagine that possibility. It would be just too awful.

She shrugged. "Just a thought. You know, if I really am the intended victim, Steven knows I confide everything to you. He knows I tell you things I'd never tell him, like how I'd change my will."

"Supposing you're right, how would he have known to use Mitchell's house?"

We mulled this over until Toni said, "If we look at all the people who know you and Mitchell live next door to each other, that's practically everybody we know—Charles, Jake and Marley, Scott, and Steven."

"But why would any of them want to listen to our conversations?"

She thought about this, wrinkling her forehead. "Maybe to find out if we suspected them?"

I was happy to know Toni was considering somebody else than Steven, although as far as I was concerned, finding the surveillance equipment had changed everything.

I was now convinced somebody wanted Toni dead, and very possibly me too. "You're right," I said, deciding to keep my opinion to myself.

"There's one other person we never considered," she said.

I wasn't sure I wanted to hear this. "If I die, and you inherit, and later marry Mitchell…" She let that thought unfinished.

"That's the most ridiculous thing you've ever said," I snapped. But even as I said this, I couldn't help remembering how unworried Mitchell had sounded when I told him it didn't look to me like any movie was being shot in his place. What if the blonde was his co-conspirator? What if she was his girlfriend? It wasn't as if I'd never been made a fool by a boyfriend before. I was notoriously bad at picking good ones. I chased those thoughts away. That was in the past, I told myself. Mitchell was different.

Toni had been watching me in silence. Now, she said, "Some people would go to a lot of trouble to inherit the kind of money I have."

I remembered Crawford's words, "seventeen awfully good reasons." But Mitchell? "Come on, Toni. It's got to be somebody else. What about Jennifer's brother?"

She paused. I could see how much she wanted to believe that, but she shook her head. "You're only trying to make us feel better. One thing we can be pretty certain of is that Charles had nothing to do with any of this. And, just between you and me, I doubt Jennifer's ex or her brother are involved either. I mean, with the hit-and-run, the restaurant connection, and now the spying equipment, it's just too farfetched." She frowned. "We have an even bigger problem now. Whoever has been listening in knows everything we know, everything we even suspect." She gasped. "Oh my God. If it *is* Steven, he knows that

I suspect him. Not only that, he knows I lied when I told him that I met with my estate lawyer."

"Well then," I said, "if he knows, doesn't that prove he's innocent? Why would he kill you if he knows he's not in your will?" Her panic was starting to rub off on me. "Hold on. The woman said something about having to adjust the volume a few times. So, if he couldn't hear clearly, maybe he thinks you kept your appointment with your estate lawyer."

She grabbed my hand and almost shrieked, "That's even worse. If he thinks I did, and then overheard me talking about making Judy my beneficiary, that means he'll have to kill me before my next appointment with my estate lawyer—" she calculated quickly, "—next Thursday. I only have about a week to live." She looked ready for a meltdown. She gave my hand another bone-crushing squeeze. "Oh my God, Nicky, I'm too young to die."

"I have an idea," I said, with a conspiratorial smile. "Maybe we can use that recording device to our advantage. Here's what we'll do."

if i die you get it all

WE WALKED IN not a minute too soon. Any longer out there and my feet would have turned to ice. We headed for the living room, where the microphone was sure to pick up.

Toni spoke loudly and clearly. "I forgot to tell you, we're meeting Judy and her husband at seven for dinner."

I continued with the conversation we'd rehearsed. "That's nice. I look forward to seeing her again."

At the same time, she pulled out her phone and punched in my number. My cell rang. I let it ring a few times before answering.

"Oh, hi, Jake, what's new?"

Toni smiled and turned her cell phone off. I continued my pretend conversation.

"I know. I feel so awful for Charles." I paused for a few seconds. "What do you mean the police suspect him? Why?" I gave a dramatic gasp. "They found evidence? Oh, my God. Toni and I thought it was—never mind what we thought. We were obviously wrong. Is Charles under arrest?" Another pause. "I just can't believe it. No, I'm not suggesting you're lying. It's just such a shock. Let me know if anything else happens." I waited a beat and said goodbye. And then I said to Toni, "You'll never believe what Jake just told me."

"What?" Toni asked, playing her role to the hilt.

"The police found evidence that Charles killed Jennifer."

"You mean I was wrong thinking it was…"

"See? I told you, you were just being paranoid."

"Do you think it's a good idea for me to leave an inheritance to my sister? Maybe I *should* make Steven my principal beneficiary. After all, I do love the man. I plan to spend the rest of my life with him."

"You don't have to decide anything right now. Your appointment isn't for another week."

She gave a hearty laugh. "And in the meantime you remain my principal beneficiary. If I die, you get everything." We had decided that if Steven really was behind Jennifer's murder, it would be safer for him to know that Toni had not yet changed her will in his favor. He couldn't very well kill her until she did.

"Ha-ha, very funny." I waited a beat and then said, "What are you wearing for dinner?"

"I haven't decided. I'd better get going. Why don't you come over to my place? We can get ready together."

"Okay. Let me get my things together."

As conversations go, this one wasn't exactly worthy of an Academy Award, but hopefully it did the trick.

I limped around gathering all the stuff I needed—an outfit for this evening, my makeup and toiletries. I packed the dog food, some wee-wee pads and all the dog's accoutrements, including—most important—their playpen, a foldable wire-fencing system. I could not allow the dogs to run around loose in Toni's fancy condo. And then I went in search of Jackie.

"Jackie? Where are you, little girl?" No answer. "Jackie, come and get a treat." The puppies came galloping over and I fed them each a liver treat. But there was still no sign of Jackie.

"I found her," Toni called out from the front hall. She pointed to my bag, where Jackie had huddled inside, hiding her face under her front paws.

I burst out laughing. "Jackie, you little rascal. Just because you can't see us, doesn't mean we can't see you." I scratched the top of her head. "You wanted to make sure I took you with me, didn't you?"

Toni picked her up. "Is that what she was doing?"

"She does that sometimes. She sees me getting ready to leave, and if I happen to have left my bag open, she sneaks inside."

Jackie squirmed excitedly, trying to jump from Toni's arms into mime. "Don't worry, baby," I told her. "You're coming too." She threw me a grateful look.

We packed the car and fifteen minutes later we were in Toni's BMW with Jackie and the puppies, and on our way to Hazelton Lanes.

"Tell me one thing," I said as we drove into the underground garage. "If you're so sure it's Steven, how do you know your place is not bugged too?"

Toni cranked the wheel, narrowly avoiding the parking garage wall. She was maneuvering down the circular drive a bit too fast for my taste.

"I'm not," she said. "But what I do know is that nobody could have bugged me from a next-door apartment, at least not without attracting an awful lot of attention. The walls are concrete and any drilling would have caused a flurry of complaints from other condo owners." She threw me a wink. "I normally can't stand condo associations. They're usually made up of a bunch of old ladies with nothing to do but spy on their neighbors, looking for any excuse to lodge a complaint. But in this case, I guess it's a good thing."

"What if you were bugged from inside your apartment? Nobody would have had to drill. Steven could have planted bugs while he was visiting. It's not as if you follow him around every minute he's there." And then I added quickly, "Not that I believe for one minute that he's the one behind all this."

Her mouth tightened. "If there's a bug anywhere in my place, I'll find it." She came to a tire-screeching stop in front of a parking space, threw the gear into reverse and backed into it.

"And then what will you do? You can't take it out. If you do, he'll realize you know."

"Audio equipment is very sensitive to water. I'll just accidentally spill water all over it."

"How do you know so much about listening devices?" I asked. "You recognized the equipment in Mitchell's place in a flash. Until you told me, I thought it was just a regular sound system."

She turned off the motor and pocketed the key. "You forget. I used to be an actress." From the way Toni told the story, she was a major movie star. I didn't bother pointing out that, as far as I knew, she'd only acted in one movie and had only had a secondary role in it.

She continued. "I know how sensitive microphones are because the boom operator was constantly screaming at everyone to be careful not to get them wet. As for the spy equipment, I've used some myself." She grabbed her purse, opened the door and climbed out, leaving me dumbstruck.

I snapped out of my astonishment and clambered out. She helped the doggies out, and handed me the leashes. Each of the three dogs was pulling in a different direction. "Er, Toni. I won't be able to handle the dogs with my crutches."

She hurried away, calling over her shoulder, "Stay there. I'll be right back." A moment later she reappeared pushing a shopping cart. She opened the trunk of her car, transferring the bags into the cart, and then picked up the dogs and set them on top.

"Ready?" She headed for the elevator and I hurried along.

"What do you mean you've used that kind of equipment yourself?"

She pushed the elevator call button and gave me her get-real look. "What do you think it means? When I first suspected Steven of having an affair, I went shopping for a few listening devices of my own."

"You did? Is that how you caught him?"

"No, Steven is smart—much too smart to get caught." The elevator doors slid open and we entered. "But this time," she said, giving me a knowing smile, "I have a plan."

To my surprise, instead of pressing the button for the twentieth floor, where she lived, she made a stop at the ground floor. "Hold the elevator for me. I'll only be a minute." She disappeared down the hall. I heard her speaking with someone. A male voice answered. A moment later she was back.

"What was that all about?"

"I checked with the doorman. If there had been any noise complaints lately, he would have heard about it. I made up a story about putting up a couple of paintings and hoping I didn't disturb any of the neighbors."

"Good thinking."

A minute later we were in Toni's gorgeous condo apartment. I looked around in surprise. The entire decor was changed. The white walls of only a month ago were now taupe. The white silk-covered sofas were coffee-colored chenille. The white lacquered coffee tables were gone, in their place dark wood tables. And the wall-to-wall white carpet was now a travertine floor. All this work had been done in record time.

The first time Toni had invited me to her place, about a year ago, I'd jokingly asked her why this predilection for white didn't extend to her wardrobe. Toni had laughed and quipped that white was a bit too virginal for her. She'd had a point. Now, there wasn't a spot of white left anywhere.

"What did you do? Did you get rid of absolutely everything?"

She picked up the dogs from the cart and then set them on the floor, handing me the leashes. "It wouldn't have been very smart of me to keep my white rugs with an un-trained puppy, now would it? And you know me. If I'm going to redecorate, I won't do half a job." She took the cart back out to the elevator and reappeared. Until now I'd had my doubts about how much she really wanted Trouble—no more.

She gave me a lopsided smile. "You look surprised."

I slipped out of my coat. "I never imagined you'd go to this much trouble."

She hung my parka in the entrance closet, chuckling. "I told you I'd get ready for Trouble." She picked up the dogs' bag. "Now let's get those wee-wee pads down be-fore one of those mutts has an accident." She rummaged through it until she found them, and marched off toward the living room, dozens of pads in hand.

I followed, still holding on tight to the dogs, who by now were pulling on the leads, eager to explore. I sat be-fore they toppled me over, and watched as she covered nearly the entire floor in wee-wee pads.

"Don't you think you're going overboard?"

She shrugged. "I just want to make sure they don't pee on my beautiful travertine floor." She soon had set the pen over a second layer of pads. I bit my lips from laughing.

"Now," she said, brushing her hands together. "There is no way these puppies can do any damage." She dropped the dogs in their pen, gave them each a head scratch and turned to me.

"How about something to drink?" She left the room, returning from the kitchen a moment later with a large pitcher of water. She put a finger to her mouth. "I'll just take a few minutes and check for bugs," she whispered in my ear.

She carried the pitcher across the room to the sound system, turned it on and upped the volume. She inspected the back of the unit, turning it over and checking underneath, her forehead furrowed with concentration. "Nothing," she mouthed, and moved on. She searched every piece of furniture, looked behind paintings, inside her silk flower arrangement. Next she examined the inside of lamps shades, curtain hems, even the television. She felt along the baseboards, window frames and doorframes. And then she paused, scanning the room. She snapped her fingers, picked up the pitcher and marched off to the air conditioner. She stopped, hand on hip and studied it. She left the room, reappearing a moment later with a screwdriver.

Toni owned a screwdriver? Not much could surprise me about my girlfriend, but this did. I watched, fascinated, as she removed the cover and examined the inside. If I hadn't known better I might have believed Toni had been doing this all her life. At last she replaced the cover, and turned to look at me. She shrugged.

"What about the telephones?" I asked in a low voice.

"Good idea." She hunted down all the house phones, and set them on the table. One by one she removed the battery and carefully probed inside each cavity. Replacing the last battery, she shook her head. "I think I've looked everywhere," she whispered.

"If there's nothing here, doesn't that suggest Steven is innocent?"

She looked thoughtful—thoughtful and hopeful. And then she shook her head. "I told you. He's smart. He'd know better than to bug my condo. He probably figured that if he did, and I happened to find it, I'd know it could only be him."

She brought the pitcher back to the kitchen, pausing in the doorway. "Did you really want something to drink?"

"Yes, please." And before she offered me something alcoholic, I said, "Water is fine."

She came back with a tall glass a moment later. "I'm glad you're staying overnight. It'll give me a good excuse to not invite Steven over. I don't know how I'd be able to pretend everything is fine, knowing he'd just as soon murder me."

"I'm still convinced Steven is completely innocent, just as I am Mitchell is. Don't forget, Jennifer's brother stands to inherit her estate." I paused for a moment and then blurted, "I really hoped you and Steven would get married."

She smirked. "Ha! Like I always say, marriage is like a deck of cards. In the beginning all you need is two hearts and a diamond. But before you know it, you're stuck with a joker, and you're praying for a club and a spade."

I laughed. "How you can joke at a time like this is beyond me."

"Who's joking?" she retorted.

My cell phone rang. I rummaged through my bag and was still laughing as I answered. It was Jake.

"The police have just arrested Charles."

I gasped. "What?"

Toni stared at me, repeating my question. "What?"

"You heard me," Jake said. "They hit him with a search warrant and they found a holographic will Jennifer wrote just a few days before she was killed. She left everything to Charles."

"I don't believe it," I said.

"It seems it's authentic."

Toni came closer. "What? Tell me."

I shushed her with my hand. "Please tell me he hasn't confessed," I said into my cell.

"Who?" Toni asked.

I covered the speaker with my hand and whispered, "Charles just got arrested."

Her eyes widened.

"Where is he?" I asked.

"They took him to the station on College. I'm going there now. I'll let you know what I find out."

I had no sooner hung up that it rang again. This time it was the real estate agent calling to let us know he had a counter offer. "He wants to know if he can come over right now," I told Toni.

She nodded grimly. Suddenly the new restaurant didn't seem so important anymore.

i just hope it's not a true-crime drama

BARRY PETERS WALKED in smiling jovially. He got right to the point—good thing, because I was not in the mood for small talk. "The landlord made a few minor changes to your offer, but all in all, I think you'll be happy with it." He pulled out copies of the contract with a flourish and handed one to Toni and one to me.

I stared at the first page. My eyes swept down and zeroed in on the price. The owner had initialed the amount we had offered. I could hardly believe it. He'd accepted our offer. But on the next line he'd changed the term back to triple net. Judging from the frown on Toni's face, she'd seen it too.

"He still expects us to pay for all the services?" I looked across the coffee table at him. "That's a bit too rich for our blood."

He shrugged. "He did accept the lower price you offered. That makes the rent very reasonable. You know, on Avenue Road, the cost per square foot is—"

"I also know that in this economy, a five-year lease is no small deal." I turned to Toni. "What do you think? You're the one fronting the money."

"I agree. It's too much."

"Unless..." I pretended to ponder this for a moment. "Do you think the landlord would meet us halfway with the terms? Let's say we paid the water and electric bills, and he paid the property taxes, insurance, maintenance and repairs."

Toni answered as if I'd directed the question to her. "Yes, I think I'd go for that. But that's the most I'd go."

I turned back to the agent. I sensed that he knew our earlier mood had soured. "What do you think?"

He shrugged, looking nervous. "There's nothing like trying." He made all the changes on the document, making sure all the initials were in place.

I handed the pen and copies back to Barry Peters. "Let's keep our fingers crossed."

He slid the modified offers into his folder and smiled. "I'll get back to you as soon as I have a sign back." The door closed behind him.

Toni ran a hand through her hair. "At this point I'm so depressed I don't even know if I want to reopen or not."

"About Charles?" I asked, already guessing what she would say.

She nodded. "The worst part is that I'm almost hoping it is him, because it would mean…" She shook her head morosely.

"I think you're allowed some mixed emotions."

She gave me a weak smile. "How much do you want to bet we'll get the deal?"

"If we do, it'll be destiny," I said, citing the one thing she couldn't argue. She gave a slow nod. "You know, I really do love that space. You were right. It is perfect."

"If the agent calls us back in a few hours, it will be right in the middle of dinner. I'll have to tell Steven about our reopening." She hesitated, and then, "I can't wait to see his face. If he's been listening in on our conversations, he won't be able to pretend surprise. I can read him like a novel. I just hope it's not a true-crime novel." Her cell phone rang. "It's Judy," she mouthed.

At that moment, my own phone rang. I fished through my purse for it. "Hello?" I answered, hoping it was

Mitchell. I so needed to hear from him right now. But to my surprise, it was Inspector Crawford.

"What can I do for you, Inspector?" I asked. I listened for a moment, and then said, "You mean right now?" I glanced at my watch. "Okay, I'll be right over."

Toni, who had just hung up, sighed. "And where, exactly, are we going?"

"You don't have to come with me if you don't want to, but that was Crawford. The police have just picked up someone they think might be our crazy woman. He wants me to come down and see if I can identify her."

She hopped to her feet. "Let's go."

to the hospital for a psych evaluation

TONI PARKED A few doors down from the station. I'd been playing ping-pong with scenarios in my mind during the entire drive. I'd been convinced the crazy woman had been the blonde in disguise, but now...

Toni helped me out, holding my crutches for me. "What if she turns out to be the blonde woman? Do you think she could be involved with Charles somehow?"

"I don't know what to believe anymore," I said. "Do you really think he could have orchestrated the crazy woman's threats, the hit-and-run and the fire, just to disguise Jennifer's murder as a mistaken identity?"

"I'm like you," she replied. "Totally confused."

I nodded. "First, let's see if she is the same woman. Then we figure out who she's working with."

INSIDE THE POLICE STATION, we were greeted by Crawford, who was being surprisingly polite for a change. Standing next to him was a female officer.

"This is Detective Menard," he said pleasantly.

I found myself shaking hands with an attractive woman somewhere in her late thirties or early forties. She had dark brown hair, intelligent eyes, and a quick smile—completely opposite what I'd come to expect from a cop. And from the way Crawford was looking at her, he very much wanted her to like him.

"I'm sure you've heard that we've arrested someone for

the arson on your business and your employee's murder," she said sympathetically.

"We have," I replied. "How certain are you that he did it?"

"Sure enough to mount a solid case. If we weren't sure, we wouldn't have arrested him." She cleared her voice. "I know it's not easy, but at least you can rest assured that nobody is after you. I'm sure everything that happened must have felt like a harassment campaign."

"That's one way to describe it," I said.

She nodded. "Well, if this woman turns out to be the one who made those threats, that'll be one less thing for you to worry about."

"Where was she picked up?" Toni asked.

"She was going through trash cans on Tecumseth," she said, naming a street a few blocks from Skinny's. She looked from Toni to me. "Are you both going to identify her? I thought—"

"No," Toni said. "I'm only here as Nicky's ride."

I shook my head. "Toni wasn't there when she barged in."

"I see. In that case, you can have a seat," she said to Toni. "It shouldn't take long." She smiled at me and explained how the line-up procedure would work. "Ready? Let's go."

She and Crawford led the way down the hall and ushered me into an empty room with a one-way mirror looking into another starkly bare room. There was nobody but one bored-looking officer standing by the door.

She moved toward the wall, turned off the light in the room. "Don't worry. They won't be able to see us from the other room." She spoke into a microphone to the officer. "You can let them in now."

He nodded and disappeared through the doorway,

reappearing, followed by half a dozen ill-attired women. He directed them to stand in a row facing a mirror, and then handed them each a numbered card.

My eyes immediately fell on the second from the left. "That's her," I said. "Number two."

"Look at each one carefully before you decide."

"I don't have to. That's her."

"Are you absolutely certain?"

"Absolutely."

She spoke into the microphone again. "Thank you, that'll be all." The women trailed back out. The entire procedure had taken no more than two minutes, leaving me with an anticlimactic feeling. *Now what?*

The officers and I went back out and rejoined Toni.

"How did it go?" she asked.

"Good. It was her, all right." I sat beside her, shocked. We fell silent as we each contemplated what this would mean to the case.

"Thank you for coming over so quickly," Officer Menard said.

"It was no problem. By the way, was she wearing a disguise?" I asked.

She frowned, puzzled. "What are you talking about?"

"I thought she might have been wearing a disguise when she stormed into our store—that maybe that she was only pretending to be..." I tapped my temple as explanation.

"Oh no, she's not pretending anything. She's been in and out of a mental hospital for years."

"Do you think she was the one driving the car that hit me?"

"Not a chance." She hesitated. "We've questioned her and she's admitted to threatening you." She made a dismissive hand gesture. "According to her, you were conspiring to keep her from what's rightfully hers."

"Our restaurant," Toni said, rolling her eyes.

Crawford, who had kept quiet until now, nodded. "That's right. But, as it turns out there's an explanation for her delusion. Her family used to own the restaurant that was on those premises before you took over the lease. It went out of business three years ago."

"Oh," I said. "So there is some logic to her madness."

Officer Menard nodded. "It seems that way."

"Does that mean there's no link between her and anything else that's happened?" Toni asked, looking dumbfounded.

"None that we could find," she replied. "I'm convinced she had nothing to do with the fire or with the death of your friend."

"So, regarding the hit-and-run, where do we go from here?" I asked.

"We've contacted body shops all over the city and the surrounding areas. We'll be notified the minute any dark imports come in for collision repairs. In the meantime we now think your accident had nothing to do with the murder of your employee."

At that point I almost told them about the equipment in Mitchell's house, but I kept my mouth shut.

Standing next to me, Toni opened her mouth, and I just knew she was about to tell them. I elbowed her.

"Ouch," she cried. But luckily she got my message and kept her mouth shut.

"I still can't believe Charles did it. What about Jennifer's ex? Did you check on him? I understand he was stalking her."

She shook her head. "He was at the fire station all night, with twelve witnesses to confirm his alibi."

"What about her brother?" I asked. "He probably expected to inherit her estate."

"Her brother was in Kingston that night," she said. "That was confirmed by four witnesses who were at a bar with him that night."

"What about a hired killer?" I said. Without telling them about the blonde we'd seen going in and out of Mitchell's house and the surveillance equipment, I knew it sounded as if I was grasping at straws, but I didn't want them to stop investigating.

"The bullets were from a small-caliber gun. Whoever killed her was not a professional."

"Could we see Charles while we're here?" I asked.

"I'm sorry, he's been moved to the main branch." She gestured toward the hallway. "I'll walk you out." She escorted us back to the entrance and we left the building.

Toni and I got back in her car and headed to her condo in stunned silence. I didn't say a word until we were at Queen's Park. A new idea was brewing in my mind.

"You and I both know it wasn't Charles," I said.

"Well," Toni said. "If it wasn't him, her ex or her brother, then that leaves the blonde or Steven," Toni said, sounding like doom. "And something tells me it's Steven."

"There's somebody else we never considered," I said.

"Who?" She tried to chuckle, but it came out strangled. "You?"

"I'm serious, Toni."

I tried to think how I should couch my suspicion so it wouldn't come as too much of a shock. "Think. Who else would gain from your death?"

"Until I change my will, you."

"What if somebody else believed you had already changed your will?"

There was a long silence. And then she gave a brittle laugh. "Don't be ridiculous."

She knew exactly who I was talking about. "Tell me something, did you tell Judy you're planning to change your will and make her your primary beneficiary?"

Her smile wavered. "Not directly. I may have mentioned that I was meeting with my estate lawyer."

"You may have? Tell me the truth, Toni, did you, or didn't you?"

She took her eyes off the road, glancing at me, exasperated. "Oh, for God's sake, will you leave it alone? It's not her, and that's final."

That was when it hit me. "You already suspect her. Admit it. When did it occur to you that it might be Judy?"

She turned to me abruptly, almost swerving into the oncoming traffic.

"Watch out!" I yelled, grabbing onto the dashboard. She corrected, and my pulse went back to normal.

"I don't *suspect* her," she said at last. "But I'd be stupid to not have at least considered the possibility."

I didn't point out that was just another way of saying the same thing. "You never even hinted as much to me."

"There was no point. It's too farfetched."

"No more farfetched than Steven wanting to kill you." I let her digest this before continuing. "She could have planned the whole thing. She could have organized the hit-and-run to throw the focus off the real motive—your will."

"You're forgetting about the blonde woman," Toni said soberly. "If somebody is working with a sexy blonde co-conspirator, I think it's more likely Steven than my sister."

A moment later we descended into the underground garage at Hazelton Lanes, once again in tense silence. She pulled into her parking space, threw her stick shift into park and turned to face me.

She looked so miserable that I realized this was her worst nightmare—the two people she loved most in the world conspiring to kill her for her money. And until she'd actually denied the possibility, I hadn't even considered it. Now, I was stunned to find that it made sense.

Toni stepped out of the car, slammed the door shut and marched away, leaving me to struggle with the door and my crutches. I caught up with her seconds before the elevator doors slid shut.

I cleared my throat, but before I could utter a word, Toni cut me off. "I don't want to hear about it."

I was treading on sensitive ground. "Mitchell told me that a location scout just showed up at his door, asking to rent his house to a production company. I didn't think anything of it at the time, but now, I have to say it's quite a coincidence. Don't you think?" I looked at her. She was staring blindly at the stainless-steel door.

"Coincidences do happen you know."

"It's interesting that nobody came to my door to ask about renting my house. Don't you think it was a bit convenient that the scout happened to show up at his door, just before he left town?" She gave me a dirty look. I ignored it and forged on. "Judy knew that Mitchell was planning to go out of town. I mentioned it the day we met, and you told her that Mitchell and I live in a semi-detached. She had all the information she needed to plant that audio equipment."

She snorted. "And what would be the point of spying on you?"

"You said it yourself. Whether it was Judy or Steven, they had to make sure you'd changed your will." I didn't add that if Judy and Steven were working together, it didn't matter which one she left her money to. They would just split the inheritance.

She was quiet, studying her nails morosely. I continued. "And what better way to find out than to bug your best friend's house? You and I talk all the time. They knew you'd tell me about it, and that way she would know exactly when to plan the hit."

Her eyes widened. "The *hit?* Do you hear yourself? My sister is a *housewife*, not some hit man." The elevator doors opened and she stomped down the hall to her apartment.

I chased after her as fast as my crutches permitted. "Toni, I'm not saying I'm one hundred percent convinced she did it. All I'm saying is, we have to consider the possibility, just as we considered it could be Steven."

She unlocked the door and we walked in to a cacophony of yip yapping. "I'll take the dogs out," she said, her face tight with pent-up emotion. "I'll be back in a minute, and then we'll have to hurry if we want to get to the restaurant on time."

The door closed behind her.

I settled into one of the down-filled armchairs. A few minutes later, when Toni returned, Jackie ran straight to me. She jumped onto my lap, covering me with wet kisses.

Toni stood in the entrance, hand on hip. "That dog of yours refused to walk. She kept trying to drag me back." Her tone was a tad less bitchy. I hoped she'd get out of this mood before we got to the restaurant.

She took off her coat and joined me in the living room, grabbing the cashmere afghan artfully displayed on the sofa and spreading it over the seat.

"Come, dogs," she called. Both puppies came running.

She sat on the floor, petting them. "All right," she said, sounding calmer. "I admit I did mention to her that I was renewing my will, and I did hint that I was planning to leave her some money."

"How much of a hint?"

She shrugged. "We were just chatting, and she happened to mention how expensive it was to raise a child, and how she was she and Richard might never be able to retire. That's when I told her I was planning to redo my will, and I added, jokingly, that if I happened to die first she would be a very rich woman."

I was silent for a moment while I searched for the appropriate words. "Does she have any idea of your worth?"

"Anybody who can do a Google search would have a pretty good idea. She knows my grandparents' name. She knows I inherited from them. And I gathered from some of the things she said that her father's parents resented my mother's parents for their wealth and for the way they treated my father."

"At any time, did you happen to mention when you were going to the lawyer's?"

She scrunched up her forehead and then nodded. "I think I might have mentioned I had an appointment last week. I was referring to the one where I was planning to leave my estate to Steven, but she might have thought I was changing it in her favor."

"Did you know you missed that appointment?"

She shrugged, looking exhausted. "I have no idea. But after our little performance in your living room, she knows now." She headed for the kitchen, calling over her shoulder, "I could sure use a glass of wine right about now. Want to join me?"

"No, thanks." I looked at my watch. "We have to be at the restaurant in forty-five minutes."

Toni turned around and headed for her bedroom

instead. "Seven o'clock, who ever heard of such an uncivilized time for dinner?"

I guess that made me less than civilized, because I didn't care what time we ate, as long as we ate.

TEN MINUTES BEFORE the hour, I was ready. I was dressed in my favorite dress, an emerald green shift that made me look pounds thinner. Toni surprised me by wearing a simple black dress with a high neck and long sleeves. If not for the side slit that ended mid-thigh, I'd have described it as conservative.

"You look amazing," I said. "You're so elegant."

"You don't think it makes me look like an old lady?"

"No, you look…classy."

She chuckled. "Me, classy, that'll be the day." But I could tell she was pleased. She gave me an appraising look. "You look terrific too." And then, frowning, she added, "Something's missing. Oh, I know." She took off toward her bedroom, reappearing a moment later with a pair of earrings and something woolly draped over her arm. "Try these. They'll be perfect with your dress." She then unfolded the garment, which turned out to be a beautiful black cape. "You shouldn't wear your parka over your beautiful dress."

"Are you up to this?" I asked, struggling with the hinge-back earrings while keeping my weight on my crutches.

She nodded. "One thing I can't figure out is, if my sister is involved, who's the blonde and what is her relationship to her?"

It was a damn good question, one for which I had no answer.

She squared her shoulders. "No matter what, tonight

we have to behave like normal. I don't want Steven to know we found the equipment."

"Or Judy," I said.

"Er, actually, she already knows about that."

My jaw dropped. "But…how?"

"She called just before we left for the police station. She was surprised to find out you were here, so I told her about the surveillance equipment."

"Shit." I'd been on the phone with Crawford at the time and hadn't been paying attention to what she was saying. A million new thoughts rolled through my mind. "Shit," I said again. "This is not good."

"I told her I suspect Steven."

"If they're working together you can bet he already knows too." I thought quickly. "How'd she react when you told her?"

"She kept insisting that I must be wrong, that the equipment must be something else." She opened the door, and we left for an evening that should have been a happy occasion. I couldn't shake a sense of impending doom.

"WE'RE RIGHT ON TIME," Toni said as we reached the restaurant door twenty minutes after seven. "It's polite to arrive a few minutes after the appointed hour."

This helped explain why my friend kept me waiting so often. She was so rarely on time that, when by some weird chance she was, I checked my watch to make sure it hadn't stopped.

Toni threw her shoulders back and strode in, exuding charm and confidence. People from nearby tables turned to look at her.

I scanned the restaurant and spotted Steven at a table in the back. Next to him was—my heart skipped a beat, and I almost gasped out loud. It was the blonde from the fake production company.

"Nicky? Are you all right? You look as if you've just seen a ghost." Toni was staring at me, worried.

"I—I..." I turned toward the back of the room again, and almost wept in relief. The blonde was just Judy. It must have been a trick of the lighting, but what an uncanny resemblance. I looked at her again, and all at once, it hit me.

The maître d' suddenly appeared, arms wide open. "Welcome to Bacci Bacci. Do you ladies have reservations?"

Toni pointed toward the back of the room. "We're joining our friends over there."

"May I take your coats?" he asked. Toni took hers off and handed it to him.

I tapped her on the arm. "Er, Toni."

She ignored me and smiled at Judy, who was waving us over.

"Toni, listen to me," I whispered.

She turned to me. "What?"

"I just thought of something."

Having hung up our coats, the maître d' said, "If you ladies will follow me."

"Not now," Toni said to me, already turning away. "You can tell me later."

"It's important."

The maître d' picked up two menus from the reservations desk and led the way. Toni followed. There was nothing I could do but plaster on a smile and go along.

The men stood as we approached. Richard stepped forward, grinning. He was tall, probably close to six feet, with dark hair, dark eyes and an easy smile. His gaze rested on Toni. "You look so much like my wife that you can only be Toni." He turned to Judy. "Honey, I know I always said you were the most beautiful woman in the world, but now I have to admit that you have to share that title with your sister."

Judy's eyes crinkled in laughter. I squirmed under his studying stare.

"And Nicky, so happy to meet you." He held my hands between his, and for a moment I thought he was going to kiss them.

"You didn't tell me your husband was such a charmer," Toni said, grinning. She was being so pleasant that if this was an act, it would fool anyone.

The maître d' pulled chairs for Toni and me.

I wasn't nearly as good an actress as Toni. I struggled to keep my smile as I nodded to Judy. Could my suspicions be correct? Could Judy be the mastermind? I glanced at Steven. He was watching Toni. Judy or Steven? Or Judy *and* Steven. No matter which, Toni would be devastated. I looked at one and then the other again. They looked… normal. Not innocent, not guilty—just normal. I was completely confused.

"We took the liberty of ordering a bottle of chardonnay," Judy was saying. "I know you both love your chardonnay."

"That we do," Toni replied. "But, you know, I've been thinking. I've been drinking way too much wine lately." She turned to the waiter, who had just appeared at her side. "Make mine a martini."

Steven laughed. Toni flicked back a strand of hair, preening for him.

The waiter filled my glass, handed us menus and left, reappearing a moment later with Toni's martini.

Judy raised her glass. "I'm so happy you're all finally meeting. I propose a toast, to friends and family."

We all raised our glasses. I turned my attention to Judy's husband again. He was a handsome man. He and Judy made an attractive couple, just as Steven and Toni did.

Richard caught my eye. "I understand you are an amazing chef. How does it feel to go out to other restaurants? Do you enjoy it, or do you keep comparing to your place?"

"Both, actually. I enjoy it, but there is a part of me that analyzes and compares. I often find new ideas this way."

"It's too bad your boyfriend couldn't be here," Judy said.

"I understand he's an author," her husband said.

"He is. He would have loved to join us, but he's in New York right now, working with his editor."

"I'd like to meet him when he comes back. I'm an avid reader."

"He'll be happy to," I said, as questions crowded my mind. Judy had told us that she was raised as an only child, yet she and the blonde looked enough alike to be sisters. I grappled for an explanation. If Toni's grandparents had been correct in their opinion of Toni's father being a womanizer, he might have had multiple affairs, maybe fathering more children. Was this too farfetched? We'd considered so many crazy possibilities that this one didn't seem any nuttier than the others.

My ponderings were interrupted by the waiter hovering to take our orders. I hadn't even thought about what to order—totally unlike me.

"What are you having?" Judy asked.

I focused on the menu and settled on the first item in the pasta section, spaghetti marinara.

"Not very adventurous of you." Judy gave her order to the waiter, smiling. I'd always prided myself on my ability to read people, but if Steven or Judy turned out to be guilty, I could strike that talent off my list.

"Nicky?"

I startled, realizing that Steven was speaking to me.

"I got the name of a lawyer to help your friend," he said. "I don't know why I didn't think of her when we spoke, but Toni used her." He mentioned a name and turned to Toni. "You saw her last week, didn't you?"

Toni almost choked on her martini. "Er, yes, I mean no. I was supposed to meet with her, but I had to cancel at the last minute. I've rescheduled for next week."

While Toni studied Steven's expression, I watched Judy's. Was it my imagination or did her smile waver when Toni said she had cancelled her appointment?

Toni turned to me. "Steven's right. She is an excellent lawyer. If anybody can help Charles in estate matters, she can. Mind you, an estate lawyer isn't the kind of lawyer he needs right now." To Steven, she said, "The police just arrested Charles for Jennifer's murder. They think he then set fire to the restaurant to cover it up. How anybody can imagine Charles as a killer is beyond me."

"What's your theory?" Judy said.

Wouldn't you like to know? Something told me I should not mention that the crazy woman was now in police custody. And just in case Toni opened her big mouth, I said, "I wish the police would find that woman. I still think she's behind the whole thing."

Toni's eyes widened, and then noticing Steven staring at her, she chuckled. "Honestly, Nicky, you change your mind more often than you change your socks. Five minutes ago you thought it was Jennifer's ex."

Bless her, she'd gotten my drift. "I think it's more likely her than Charles. And, honestly, the fact that the police arrested him is enough to convince me he's innocent. In my

experience, you can count on the cops getting it wrong."
I turned back to Steven. "Would you be interested in taking his case?" I searched his face, waiting for his reply.

"I'll see what I can do," he said vaguely.

Was he trying to avoid helping Charles? If so, did that
mean he was guilty?

"Thank you. I'd appreciate that," Toni said.

Soon the food arrived and Judy brought the conversation around to the restaurant space she'd visited with us.
"Have you signed a lease on that store yet?" she asked.
"Toni and Nicky took me along to look at some restaurant sites and one of them, on Avenue Road, is perfect."

Steven's face fell. He stared at Toni. "Are you serious?
You never told me you're thinking of reopening. As long
as that lunatic is out there, you could be in danger. I'd hold
off on doing that if I were you."

She raised her eyebrows. "I thought you said she wasn't
dangerous."

"I didn't think so initially, but if you think she burned
down the restaurant and killed Jennifer, then it's a completely different story. Are you absolutely sure Charles
had nothing to do with any of this?"

Toni nodded. "One hundred percent."

"In that case, why don't you wait before making that
kind of decision, at least until we're sure the police got
the right guy?"

Other than being sincerely worried for Toni and me,
I couldn't think of any other reason Steven would care
about the restaurant.

"God forgive me for saying this," Toni said, "but what
if they convict Charles and the real guy goes free? Do you
really expect me to sit around and do nothing?" At that
moment, the theme of *Sex and the City* began to play. She
rummaged through her bag and glanced at the call dis-

play. "I have to take this. I'll be right back." She hurried toward the washroom.

Steven turned to me. "Please, Nicky, if she won't listen to me, maybe she'll listen to you. Talk some sense into her, will you. Why don't you hold off on reopening? There's already been one victim. I don't want to see anything happen to either one of you."

I looked into his eyes and saw nothing but sincerity. I didn't care what Toni thought, Steven simply could not be guilty. He loved Toni.

Before I could answer, Toni reappeared and gave me the thumbs up. "We got it," she announced, grinning. "The landlord accepted our offer. We now officially have a new location for Skinny's."

"Is it the place on Avenue Road?" Judy asked eagerly. And then noticing Steven's grim look, her smile melted.

"That very one." Toni nodded, avoiding Steven's eyes. "That was the agent calling to let us know the landlord signed our offer."

"He did?" I grinned, then said in a more subdued tone, "Without making any changes?"

"That's right. I've been thinking, we can't keep the name Skinny's on Queen for the new place." She continued with forced cheeriness. "What does everyone think of Skinny's on the Avenue?"

"Sounds good to me," I said. "What do you think, Judy?"

"I think I like it." She raised her glass. "To your new restaurant, Skinny's on the Avenue."

Richard raised his glass. "May your new business bring you success and happiness."

Reluctantly, Steven raised his. "And may you live to not regret it."

AFTER COFFEE AND DESSERT, Judy excused herself. "I hate

to break up the party, but we have to get going. I promised our daughter I'd call her and read her a story over the phone, and it's already way past her bedtime."

"Actually, Toni and I should get going too. If we don't walk the dogs soon, there's likely to be a mess when we get back."

Steven raised his hand for the bill, insisting that the evening was on him. "Can I give you ladies a lift?" he asked Toni and me.

"We drove over," Toni said. "I know it's only a few blocks, but with Nicky's cast she's in no shape to walk. Did I mention? She's staying over at my place tonight. She brought little Trouble over and she's helping me get set up with my new puppy."

Steven's smile almost reached his eyes, but not quite. I guessed he'd been hoping Toni would invite him back to her place.

THE FOOD AND drinks had been wonderful, and the news of the lease being accepted was even better. But there had been an undercurrent during the entire evening, and the stress had worn me out. Now, I was oddly dispirited. I couldn't imagine how much worse Toni must be feeling.

"I'm totally exhausted." Toni's jaw was set, her knuckles white on the steering wheel.

"Suspecting everyone is hard."

She turned into the underground parking. "On a brighter note, Judy's husband seems nice."

"I thought so too," I said, wondering if I should share my latest suspicion. She'd already suffered a few emotional blows today. But if I was right, that meant Steven was innocent.

"I don't know about you, but I thought Steven was behaving very strangely," she said, looking miserable.

I hesitated. "I'm not sure I agree. He seemed so surprised about our reopening. If he'd been listening in on our conversations, he would have known about our plans. If that was an act, it was worthy of an award."

She harrumphed and pulled into her parking spot. "He's good, I'll grant you that." Without further discussion, she hopped out of the car and came around to give me a hand.

We rode up the elevator in silence. Soon, we were back in her apartment, the dogs had been walked and Toni was opening a bottle of wine.

"Not for me," I said. "I thought you were cutting down."

"Just one glass. As a nightcap." She poured and, ignoring my objection, handed me a glass. "So, what were you trying to tell me when we walked into the restaurant?"

I cleared my throat. "Well," I started, searching for the best way to say this. "I had a bit of an epiphany. Maybe it was just the lighting, or maybe the angle, but when I walked in, I happened to spot Judy at the table and it hit me how much she looks like that blonde in Mitchell's house."

Toni's eyes clouded with confusion. "What in the world are you talking about?"

"Just bear with me for a minute." I took a swig of wine—liquid courage. "You know how shocked I was the first time I saw you and Judy standing side by side? Well, I had the same kind of shock earlier, when I spotted Judy at the table." My eyes sought hers. "Toni, she looks just like that blonde. They don't wear their makeup the same, and they don't dress in the same style, but they have the same bone structure."

"Whatever you're thinking, I just know I won't like it."

"Remember what Judy said about your grandparents

being set against your mother marrying your father? They thought he was a womanizer, right? Didn't it strike you as odd that they would say that about a man just because he happened to have been married before?"

She frowned. "What are you getting at?"

"It's the kind of thing somebody might say of a person with a string of relationships. Do you think it's possible he might have had other children, not just Judy and you?"

Toni's forehead furrowed. "You think I might have more than one sibling."

"Actually, I'm thinking another sister."

She took a sip of wine. "And you think Judy and her are in this together?"

"I think it's a possibility."

She shook her head in disbelief. Jumping to her feet, she marched out of the living room. "I've had enough for one evening," she called over her shoulder. "You can do whatever you like, but I'm going to bed."

As I watched her leave, I had the strangest feeling that things were about to get much worse.

doing some surveilling of our own

THE NEXT MORNING when I got up, Toni had already walked and fed the dogs, and had coffee ready and muffins waiting for me.

She handed me a cup. "Thank goodness those dogs are small. I'd hate to pick up the poop of a Great Dane. Having dogs is like having babies, only worse because they never grow up and move away."

"At least you don't need to set up a university fund," I said. To my surprise, she laughed out loud. "You're in a good mood this morning."

"I am. I've been thinking about it and if you're right, that means Steven has nothing to do with it." Her eyes moistened as she said this. "It's too early to know for sure, but—" she held up one hand, fingers crossed, "—here's to hoping." She set down her cup and slid the basket of muffins across the table. "Cranberry orange. I know you like them."

I had just bitten into one when my cell phone rang. Toni reached over and picked it up. "Charles," she exclaimed. "Where are you calling from?"

I waited, almost holding my breath until she covered the mouthpiece and whispered, "He just made bail." And then into the phone she said, "Let me put you on speaker." She pressed a button and put down the phone.

"Oh, Charles, thank God you're out. How are you?"

"I'm all right," he said, sounding anything but. "If it wasn't for Toni's husband, I'd still be in jail. He represented me at the arraignment and put up the money for my bail."

I was stunned. I sought Toni's eyes. "Did you know?" I mouthed.

She shook her head, a dozen emotions playing over her face.

To Charles, I said, "Are you all right? Was it totally awful?"

"I feel better now that I'm home. I showered. I changed. Now I feel almost human."

"Is there anything we can do for you?"

"You asked that I come over to your place and work on the hamburger recipe. Is that offer still good?"

"You bet," I said.

"I can come over today if you like. I'll bring everything I need, be at your place in a couple of hours."

"I'm not home. I'm at Toni's. Do you have her address?" I gave it to him. "But soon you'll be working in a brand new restaurant kitchen."

"You found a location?"

"Yep, and it's official. We're reopening as soon as we can."

"Let's just hope I'm not in jail by then."

"Of course you won't. Don't even think that way." I said this, knowing that when I was suspected of murder, I'd felt exactly the same. The threat of imprisonment was a powerful one. It brought out claustrophobia one never even knew they had.

"Well, that's something to look forward to," he said, sounding relieved. "It will be good for me to keep busy. How long do you figure it'll take to get ready?"

I explained that the place was already near perfect. "Still, everybody will have to pitch in. I'm counting on you to take care of the cooking equipment—pots and

pans, utensils, sieves, and all the rest. Jake can take care
of all the service items—trays, china, utensils, glassware.
I haven't discussed it with Toni but I think she'd be great
at sourcing the furniture, tables and chairs and everything
else we might need in the dining room." I looked at her
and she nodded. "As for Scott and Marley, I can make lists
of all the little things that don't necessarily fit in any of
the other categories. I'm hoping a month and a half or so."

He was quiet for a second. "You might just be able to
swing it," he said at last.

"One question, Charles. I know you have other things
on your mind right now, but you wouldn't happen to have
copies of all our regular recipes by any chance?"

"Yes, of course. I always backed up the recipe files on
my computer."

I breathed a sigh of relief. I hadn't even dared tell Toni
that I'd been worried about this.

He continued. "I even have all those we worked on but
thought weren't quite good enough for the restaurant."

"You do? That's so great. I could kiss you." I explained
about our upcoming column.

His voice went from mild interest to full attention.
"That's cool. That'll be great publicity for the new place."
The conversation wound down and we hung up.

"I'll call the paper and tell the editor about our reopening," Toni said. "Then, we can start working on that
column."

While Toni was on the phone with the newspaper editor, my thoughts wandered back to the blonde and the surveillance equipment. Suddenly it occurred to me. The best
way to find out who had set up the surveillance equipment
was to turn the table on them. We would spy on them for
a change. But if Judy was involved, we had to act fast. For
all I knew, it might already be too late. The blonde could

have gone back and already cleaned the place of everything. I reached for my cell phone and called Charles back.

"Change of plan. We'll meet at my place. I'm going there now." I hung up, just as Toni was ending her own conversation.

She gave me a thumbs-up. "It's all done. The editor said she'd schedule the article about Skinny's to coordinate with our reopening."

"That's great," I said. "Something tells me there's bad news. What is it?"

"They want the recipes for the first column day after tomorrow."

"In two days? I just hope Charles has at least that many recipes ready to go."

She put up a hand. "If he doesn't, we can make the following week all about low-cal breakfasts. There's those Skinny pancakes you like so much. And if we add the strawberry syrup recipe, we've got two recipes right there."

I had left the table and hop-clopped to the bedroom.

"Where are going?" she called out.

"My place, and you're coming with me. I'll explain on the way."

TWENTY MINUTES LATER TONI, the dogs and I were driving south.

"If you were Judy," I said, "and you knew we'd just discovered the surveillance equipment, what would be the first thing you would do?"

She was darting in and out of traffic, driving at her usual breakneck speed. "I'd get it out and fast. There might be fingerprints on it. And it could be used by the police as evidence."

"My thoughts exactly. Well, this time I plan on us doing

some surveilling of our own. You and I are going to be ready for whoever shows up to get the equipment—probably that blonde again—and when they leave, we'll follow. If I'm right, they'll lead us right to whoever is behind this."

Toni nodded, her eyes on the road. "Good plan," she said with determination, and then stepped on the gas even harder.

AFTER RUNNING UP and down the hall, excited at being back home, the dogs had quieted at last. Toni had taken her position behind the living room curtains. A few minutes later she called out, "Charles is here with Jake and Marley."

A moment later, the doorbell rang and I hurried over, with Jackie at my heels, sounding the alarm.

"I know, Jackie. I heard it too. Now be quiet." She threw me a dirty look as if to say, "Hey, I'm just doing my job here."

"Hope you don't mind we tagged along," Jake said, stomping his boots on the doormat.

"Not at all. I'm glad you're all here. I wonder if you guys can do me a favor. Come with me."

Jake picked up Jackie. "Hey there, gorgeous." Jackie licked his chin. She always was a sucker for compliments.

The guys followed me to the mudroom. "I'm having trouble with the back door lock." We stepped outside and I closed the door behind us.

"I would have kept my coat on if I'd known we were going back out," Marley said.

"It's only for a second." I turned to Jake. "Would you mind if Toni borrows your car?"

He looked at me perplexed. "My old heap? Sure, why?"

I explained about the surveillance equipment we'd discovered and that Toni was hoping to follow the blonde when she showed up again. "But just in case the woman knows Toni's car, I thought it better she used somebody else's." I pointed to my own on its pad few yards away. "Mine is not exactly inconspicuous."

"You mean, someone's been listening in on every word you say?" He looked at me as if I was certifiable. "I don't get it. Why?"

"That's what we're trying to figure out. You can have Toni's car in the meantime."

He pulled out his keys, smiling. "That's the kind of exchange I like."

I turned to go back in, but stopped. "By the way, whatever we talk about while we're inside, we can't make any mention that we think Toni was the intended victim." I looked at Charles. "I hope you don't mind."

"Sure, anything to catch the bastard who killed Jennifer."

We stepped back in, and Charles set to work preparing his low-cal burger, Jackie sniffing the air appreciatively.

"She can smell the meat." I bent down and scratched her behind the ear. "Don't worry, we'll keep a little for you." She did her doggie version of a happy dance, barking happily. "Now, get out of our way. We have work to do." She stalked off in a huff, her feathers—or rather her fur—ruffled.

I turned to Charles. "By the way, did you remember to bring those recipes?"

"Yep, got 'em right here." He picked up his pack sack and riffled through, producing a small stack of index cards. "I brought over the hard copies but I can email them to you if you prefer, and here's a list of recipes we discarded for the restaurant."

"Wonderful." I counted them. "Eight recipes—that's

enough for three or four weeks of columns." I leaned in and gave him a big kiss on the cheek. "You're a lifesaver."

"Glad to be of help." He returned to the counter. "I'll make two burger versions for everyone to test, a beef burger and a turkey burger."

I helped him set up the equipment, bowl, measuring cups and spoons.

"With the beef," he said, "I start with extra-lean ground beef with no more than five percent fat. I add one cup of old fashioned oatmeal to every pound of beef." He did this as he spoke, mixing the cereal and the meat along with one egg, one tablespoon of Dijon mustard and one-quarter cup chopped scallions. Using a half-cup ice-cream scoop, he made a row of burger mounds on a cookie sheet. "All you have to do is flatten them, and you've got eight perfect patties." He set it aside and started on the turkey version.

"I use ground turkey breast. It's lower in calories." He added chopped scallions, chopped celery, tabasco sauce and mango chutney, and mixed it well. "Also, if we use thin buns, we save a ton of calories. They're only one hundred calories each."

I left the guys to finish cooking the burgers and joined Toni, who was still at the living room window, watching the street like a hawk. "No sign of her yet?" I asked.

She shook her head. "And I'm getting cross-eyed from staring at the same spot for so long."

A few minutes later, Charles brought in a couple of sample burgers. "Hope you like them," he said, handing us the plates. "The beef burger is three-hundred-and-sixty calories. The turkey burger is only three hundred. Which means we can serve them with half a cup of fries and the meal will still come to under five hundred calories."

Toni took a bite of the beef burger. Her eyes widened.

"This is good." She set it down and took a bite from the other one. "Oh my God. This one is to die for."

"I guess that tells me which one you prefer."

"There she is," Toni whispered, putting down her plate. I peeked out from behind the curtain. Sure enough, the blonde was hurrying up Mitchell's walk. I darted back before she saw me.

Toni jumped to her feet and threw on her coat. "Where are Jake's keys?"

I searched through my pocket and handed them.

"Here are mine," she said, dropping them in my hand. "Remember, the minute you see her leave, call my cell, let it ring twice and hang up." She checked out the window to make sure the woman had gone inside, then she hurried to Jake's car. A moment later she was scrambling into the old Buick, slinking down in the seat until the top of her head was barely visible. At the same time I noticed scratching sounds coming from the common wall between Mitchell's place and mine. We'd been right. The woman was getting rid of the evidence. This proved it. She was working with either Steven or Judy. I prayed it wasn't both.

I returned to the kitchen with Toni's unfinished food, and fished through my purse for my cell phone. "Somebody just went inside Mitchell's house," I whispered.

"What do we do now?" Jake asked.

"You go about your business until she's gone. I'll tell you when." I hurried back to living room, taking up Toni's earlier spot. A few minutes later, the woman stepped out, carrying two large shopping bags. She glanced directly at my front window. Even though I knew she couldn't see me behind the curtain, I snapped back.

The woman ran down the steps and hopped into a silver Audi. Her car roared to life and she drove off. I punched Toni's number, let it ring twice and hung up. From the window I saw Toni sit up and a moment later she was racing up the street in hot pursuit.

I returned to the kitchen and nodded to the guys, beaming. "And let the games begin."

"So that means we can talk now, right?" Charles said.

"We sure can." For all my outward confidence, in truth I was worried for Toni. What if the woman noticed her? What if Toni got hurt in the process? I had to keep busy until I heard from her. Or I'd go out of my mind worrying.

"What do we do now?" Jake asked.

"Maybe we can go over the different chores that need to be done to get Skinny's ready to reopen."

"Good idea," Marley said, turning to grab another burger from the plate on the kitchen table. To my surprise, the meat in the three remaining buns was gone. "How can that be?" he asked. "They were here a minute ago."

I checked around the room. Sure enough, the dogs were chewing on burgers. Jackie threw me a furtive glance, as if to say, "Hey, I only took what you'd already promised." She returned to her meal, eyeing me suspiciously. I didn't have the heart to scold her.

"Maybe she'll tell us which she likes best," Marley said, laughing.

The kitchen was clean and we had already gone over the list, dividing it among the guys, when my cell phone rang. It was Toni, at last.

"Where are you?" I asked. "I was getting worried about you."

"I'm in front of the Hyatt Regency," she said. "The blonde woman is heading inside."

"Isn't that where Judy is staying?"

"Yes," she said in a tight voice. "I want to go in and see if I can find her. It's lunchtime, so maybe they're meeting in the restaurant. Can you come sit in the car? It would be just my luck that they leave by the side entrance while I'm running around in the hotel trying to catch them."

"I'll be right over."

"I'm parking on Avenue Road, just north of Bloor. The keys will be in the exhaust pipe."

I hung up and called to the guys. "I need a lift right now."

We piled into Toni's BMW with Jake at the wheel and drove off in a screech of rubber.

"I always thought Toni was a cowboy behind the wheel," I said, as he took a corner so fast I thought we'd roll over. "But she has nothing on you."

"Hold on. It's going to be a rough ride," he said.

"Oh, shit. Now you're dropping quotes too. I think you're spending way too much time with Toni."

He laughed, and I was pleased to note that Charles was chuckling too.

We crossed Bloor and Jake came to a rubber-burning stop inches away from his car. "I'll find a parking spot and join you inside," he said. Before I could argue, he had driven off.

I got out and felt around the exhaust pipe, and came away with the key. I settled in for what could be a long and boring wait. But to my surprise, moments later I spotted Judy walking down the sidewalk. I slipped down in my seat. When I pulled myself back up, she was walking into the hotel.

Shit. I had to notify Toni. I grabbed my cell and pushed the speed-dial button.

"What is it?" she answered in a harsh whisper.

"Judy is just walking into the hotel."

"Uh-oh. Thanks." She clicked off and I imagined her ducking behind a potted palm or column. I was just putting my cell away when I noticed a man walking down the street. Could it be? He was still some distance away, but I was almost sure…I squinted. *Damn.* It was him. I grabbed my cell again.

"What is it now?" Toni whispered.

"It's Steven. He's headed toward the hotel. No, wait, he's stopping." I prayed that he would walk on. He was looking around. *Shit.* "He's just walked in. Oh, Toni, I'm so sorry."

"So he's involved too. Great." She hung up. I snatched my bag, dropped in my phone and scrambled out of the car. Whatever was going on in there, Toni should not have to handle it alone. I hurried over as fast as my crutches could carry me, and luckily a bellman opened the door for me. I looked around. No sign of any of them.

"Excuse me. I'm trying to catch up to my friend. She just walked in. I was trying to keep up, but…" I gestured toward my cast. "She's a good-looking blonde. Judy Donaldson. She told me which room, but I can never remember numbers."

"I'm afraid I can't tell you her room number. You'll have to call her from one of the courtesy—"

"Oh, there she is," I lied, just as an elevator door started closing. "Judy," I called out, waving.

Just as I'd hoped, by the time he swiveled around, the doors were fully closed. "I guess there's no harm in telling you," he said. "She's in Room 717."

"Thank you," I said, already hurrying to the elevator. While I waited, I called Toni again.

"What?" she whispered.

"Judy's room number is 717."

"How'd you—" she started, and then stopped. "Thanks," she said.

After hanging up I made the same call to Jake. "We're only a block away," he said. "I'll catch up with you there."

An elevator opened and I climbed in. I went up and seconds later the doors opened. I stepped away from the bank of elevators and sneaked a peek down the long hall-way. There she was, strolling away as if she didn't have a care in the world—the murderous bitch. At that moment, the emergency exit door facing the hallway flew open and Steven stepped out. I ducked around the corner before he could see me.

When I dared peek out again, he was racing after Judy. My heart was pounding. That was close. Too close. Poor Toni. Not only her sister, but her husband as well. She would be devastated.

The elevator doors slid open again and Toni stepped out. "There you are," she said. "I looked all over the hotel, the restaurant, the bar. I never found her. And the front desk refused to give me her room number. How did you get it?"

"The bellman told me."

She looked at me with new respect. "Wow. All he told me was to use the courtesy phone." And then seeing the worry in my eyes, she said, "What's wrong?"

"Er, Judy just went down the hall and around the corner—to her room, I guess. Steven was right behind her."

All at once her eyes narrowed and her jaw set. "Oh, yeah? Well, we'll see about that." She marched down the hall, ready to kill. I galumphed after her.

She was about ten feet ahead of me when she turned the corner. In the next instant I heard her gasp, and then a crack, followed by a thud. I worked my crutches faster. I came around the corner half expecting to find Steven splayed out on the carpeted floor. But to my horror, Steven was holding Toni from behind, his right hand covering her mouth. He was whispering something in her ear.

"Stop," I yelled. I fumbled for my phone, dropping

my purse. "I'm calling the police right now." I waved my phone menacingly.

"Will you shut up?" he whispered harshly, glancing back over his shoulder. "What are you trying to do? Let them know we're out here? Now, if you promise to be quiet, I'll let you go."

Toni nodded, and he slowly took his hand away.

As soon as her mouth was uncovered, Toni took a step back and ground one of her five-inch stilettos into Steven's foot, all the while screaming "Fire!" at the top of her voice.

Steven was hopping on one foot, muttering a long string of expletives, when suddenly the door to Room 717 flew open and Richard stepped out. His eyes fell on us and shock filled his eyes. He took a step back, trying to close the door, but it was too late. Toni had already jammed her Vuitton purse in the doorway.

"Not so fast," she said, shoving him out of her way. One thing about Toni. She never let anyone stand in her way.

"No, Toni," Steven called, running in after her. I hurried over, working my crutches as fast as I could. I got to the door, and stopped, staring at a scene straight out of *Law and Order*. Steven was frozen in place, an expression of horror on his face, as Toni was held with a gun at her head by none other than the blonde woman.

"Come one step closer and she dies," the woman warned him. Judging from the steely glint in her eyes, she wasn't fooling.

Standing across the room, Judy looked stricken. "What's going on?" She looked at her husband, who had backed toward what I figured must be the bathroom, an irritated expression on his face. "Richard? I don't understand."

"Aw, shut up." He turned to the blonde. "Got any suggestion as to how we can get out of this one?"

"Hey, don't blame me," she said. "You're the one who came up with the foolproof plan."

Judy's eyes went from the blonde to her husband. "What is she talking about? Please tell me she isn't talking about—"

"Close the fucking door," the blonde shouted, jabbing the barrel of the gun into Toni's head. "Unless you want your friend here to take a trip six feet under."

Judy ran to the door and closed it.

Toni, who had remained quiet until then, said, "Isn't that what you're going to do anyhow? I have bad news for you. I still haven't changed my will. So neither you," she said to Judy, "nor you," she said to Steven, "will get my money. It all goes to Nicky."

"Wrong," the blonde said. "Because Nicky is going to be dead too. And then the whole amount goes to your sister, as your closest living relative."

Judy gasped. "Richard, what is she talking about? Tell me you're not a part of this. I would never accept the money under those circumstances."

"You won't have to," the woman said, chuckling. "I will."

"You? But you're not related to Toni."

Richard walked over to the blonde and smiled. "Judy, meet your other sister, Susan."

I was too stunned to utter a word. So my farfetched theory that Toni might have more than one other sister had proven true. And neither Judy nor Steven had anything to do with the plot. It was a small consolation, considering we would all be dead soon.

"There are a couple of problems with your plan," Steven said. "First of all, how do you propose to kill us? We're in a hotel, surrounded by people. A gunshot won't go unnoticed. And you have only one gun against four of us. You won't be able to kill all of us."

I couldn't believe the man could be so calm under this kind of pressure.

Toni cut in. "And even if you did, you'll never see a penny of my money."

"Oh, and why not?" asked Susan, smugly.

"Because," Toni said, as smoothly as Steven. "If Nicky doesn't survive me, all my money goes to charity. And my will is solid. No lawyer will be able to overturn it."

Steven picked up from there. "So, unless you'd enjoy spending the next twenty-five years in jail, I suggest you get the hell out of Dodge while the going is good. Actually, twenty-five years would be the minimum you'd get. For premeditated murder, you'd get life."

Susan looked at Richard, dumbfounded. "This was all your idea," she shrieked. "I will not go to jail because of you." She pulled the gun away from Toni's head and slowly backed her way to the door, waving the gun around the room. "Nobody come close or I swear I'll shoot."

"Wait for me. I'm coming too." Richard grabbed a laptop bag and pulled the room phone from the wall. "Everybody give me your cell phones, now."

He hurried around the room, grabbing everybody's phone and stuffing them in his case. He joined her at the door. Susan's gun was still trained on us. "If any one of you tries to come after us, I won't hesitate to kill you," she said, and just as she was about to open it, a knock came at the door.

"Open up. This is the police," a deep voice said from the hallway.

And then everything happened very fast. While Susan swiveled around, Toni dug into her purse, coming out with her own gun. The door flew open and Charles, Jake and Marley came charging in. There were no police, I realized—Jake had uttered the command. In the ensuing madness, Susan tripped and fell, dropping her gun.

Before she could get it, Toni yelled, "Don't move, or I'll shoot." Everybody froze.

Steven walked over to Toni. "Well done, sweetheart." He gently put a hand over the gun. "How about I take over from here?"

"Don't worry, I've got it." She threw him a confident smile. "Why don't you call the police, sweetheart?"

Two months later

It was eleven-thirty in the evening the night of our official reopening. After our last clients left, the gang congregated into the dining room for some champagne. To Toni's and my delight, Steven and Mitchell joined us.

"I can't believe we did it." Leaning my crutches against the table, I let myself collapse into a chair. "We got the restaurant open in record time."

"I wish Judy could have been here." Toni slipped off her five-inch heels and massaged her sore feet. We were zonked from a two-month marathon of hard work and a few too many margaritas.

"But under the circumstances, I can understand that she doesn't feel much like celebrating. Imagine being betrayed by your husband that way."

It had taken a long time, but under questioning by the police, at last the details of the plot had been revealed. Detective Menard had called earlier and given me an update. It seemed that Susan Bentley and Judy's husband had met years ago—ironically, it was when Susan had showed up unexpectedly, looking to meet the half sister she'd just found out about. But Judy was not home that day and Richard opened the door. He and she fell in instant lust and had been having an affair since. Richard had been on the point of asking Judy for a divorce when she found Toni. That day, she'd come home to tell him breathlessly how rich her sister was. A few weeks later, when she mentioned that Toni was talking about changing her will in her favor, Richard saw this as his opportunity to get rich.

"I can't imagine how she must feel," Charles said. "Losing someone you love is hard enough. But finding out he was planning to kill her has to be a hundred times worse. At least I know that Jennifer loved me, and that knowledge eases the pain."

Steven shook his head. "I still can't believe you thought I would be capable of murder."

Mitchell wrapped a protective arm around my shoulders. "You know what I don't understand is what that homeless woman had to do with everything."

"As it turns out, nothing," I said. "But because Susan told Richard about the way she stormed in and threatened me, he thought it would be a great idea to use her as a red herring. It was Susan who called the restaurant the day of the television interview. Then, because she ran me over just a couple of days later, we all concluded that the crazy woman was behind it, just as they'd planned."

"But why kill Jennifer?" Mitchell asked.

"In this case, the police were right. Jennifer's death was a mistake. Susan was in your house earlier that night, listening in on Toni and me," I told him. "When Toni mentioned she'd forgotten something at the restaurant and had to go back, Susan decided to go after her. But by the time she got there, Toni had already left. A few minutes later, when Jennifer showed up, Susan followed her inside and shot her. Susan and Richard didn't even know until the next day that she'd shot the wrong person."

Mitchell gave my shoulders a squeeze. "I can't believe I left you on your own to cope with all of that."

"How could you have known?" I said. "Judy was so excited at finding her sister that she told Richard everything she knew about Toni. She happened to mention that you're a writer and that you were going out of town to work on your manuscript. Richard came up with the idea to learn more about Toni's plans by planting that equipment."

"What I still don't get is why the hit-and-run?" said Jake.

"Added security," I explained. "Toni had mentioned to her that I was in her will. They wanted to make damn sure Judy got everything, and the only way they could be sure of that was if I was dead too. The plan was for Richard to stay with Judy until she inherited, and only then get rid of her.

"They didn't expect her to go back to the hotel that day. She was supposed to go have her hair cut, and should have been out for hours. If not for the hairdresser overbooking, she would never have walked in while Susan was there. Even then, if not for us barging in, Richard might have been able to explain Susan away. And Judy would never have been the wiser."

"She was crazy about that husband of hers. She believed everything he told her." Toni took a sip of her drink. "All I can say is I'm glad that is behind us. Now, all we have to worry about is making this new restaurant successful."

"You better be careful," Steven said. "That soon-to-be wife of mine is a slave driver."

I squealed. "You're getting married?"

"Don't be ridiculous," Toni said. "I'm much too pragmatic. Second marriages are nothing more than ignoring experience in favor of hope. I trust experience." I couldn't help but notice the amorous look she threw Steven as she said this. She set her glass on the table. "Hit me again."

"You're looking pretty perky," I said, "for someone who was exhausted a minute ago."

"I always wake up at the crack of ice." She winked.

Steven leaned over and filled her glass. "Nicky, refill?"

"Not for me, thanks." I looked at my watch. "I don't know about you guys, but I'm wiped."

"Come on, live a little," Mitchell said.

Suddenly the front door opened and, for the briefest of moments, I was sure we were having a repeat visit from our crazy lady. The woman who walked in was disheveled from the wind. She finger-combed her gray hair and I suddenly recognized her as Edna Jamieson.

"Oh, my God," I said, rising from the chair and grabbing my crutches. "I'm so sorry, Mrs. Jamieson. I completely forgot to get back to you. And that was months ago."

She stepped toward me, smiling and extending her hand. "I'm partly to blame too. I'm not always the easiest person to get a hold of."

"Won't you come in, Mrs. Jamieson?" Toni said.

"I don't want to intrude. I heard you were reopening and decided to drop in." Edna Jamieson went through her purse and came out with a business card. "You may not know this, but I'm CEO of Lanson Publishing," she said, naming one the country's best-known publishing houses. "From the very first time I ate at your restaurant, I felt strongly that you two young girls should write a cookbook."

From the corner of my eyes I saw Toni suddenly brighten at being called a young girl.

"And if you decide to do this, I'd be thrilled to publish it. I know your skinny recipes concept is a sure winner. If you're interested, give me a call."

I took the card and glanced down at it, noticing the handwritten number at the bottom.

"That's my private number," she said. "Call me, any time."

And as suddenly as she had appeared, the woman was gone, leaving everyone in the room with their heads spinning.

"Did I just hear her right?" I asked Toni. "She wants us to write a book?"

Toni nodded. "That's right."

"You know what that means, don't you?"

"We're going to be authors!" she exclaimed. "You'll be rich too. And I'm going to need a whole new wardrobe."

* * * * *

White Wine Spritzer

Serves one
48 calories

Every person has their favorite white wine. When selecting a white wine for a spritzer, I suggest choosing a dry one with an earthy flavor, such as a very oaky chardonnay.

Ingredients:

2 oz. dry white wine
1 oz. soda water
2 ice cubes
Slice of lemon

Directions:

Sip slowly and make it last.

Eggplant Parmesan

Serves four
284 calories per serving

Ingredients:

Nonstick cooking spray
2 egg whites
2 ½ lbs. eggplant, peeled and cut crosswise into
¼ inch-thick slices
½ cup garlic-flavored croutons
½ tsp. olive oil
1 cup tomatoes, chopped, with their juice
¼ cup chopped fresh basil or 1 tsp. dried
½ tsp. black pepper
1 cup shredded part-skim mozzarella cheese
(about 4 oz.)
¼ cup grated Parmesan cheese
4 cloves garlic
½ cup onion, chopped

Directions:

Preheat the oven to 400°F. Line baking sheet with foil. Spray foil with nonstick cooking spray.

In a shallow dish, beat the egg whites and 2 tbsp of water until foamy. Dip eggplant into egg whites, then into bread crumbs, pressing crumbs into eggplant.

Place eggplant on prepared baking sheet and spray oil over eggplant slices. Bake 30 minutes, turning eggplant over after 20 minutes, until golden brown and cooked through.

In a stove-top pan, sauté the onions and garlic in olive oil until onions are soft and just beginning to turn golden.

In a medium-size bowl, stir together tomatoes and their juice, basil, salt, pepper, garlic, and onions.

Spoon 3 tbsp. of tomato mixture into bottom of 9" square glass baking dish. Place half of eggplant over sauce, spoon half of remaining tomato mixture over eggplant, and sprinkle half of mozzarella on top. Repeat with remaining eggplant, tomato mixture, and mozzarella.

Sprinkle Parmesan on top and bake for 20 minutes, or until eggplant is piping hot and sauce is bubbly.

Skinny French Toast

Serves two
187 calories per 2-slice serving including yogurt and
strawberry syrup.

Ingredients:

Four 1-inch slices of day-old French bread *(1 oz.
each)*
Three eggs
3 tbsp. skim milk
1 tsp. Splenda
1 tsp. cinnamon *(optional)*
Cooking spray
½ cup strawberry syrup
½ cup 0 fat vanilla Greek yogurt

Directions:

Spray your frying pan.

Beat eggs, Splenda and cinnamon together in shallow
pan *(I use a round cake pan)*.

Dip your slices of bread into egg mixture and fry in
frying pan on medium heat until golden, then turn over
to fry other side.

Serve with ¼ cup vanilla yogurt and ¼ cup strawberry syrup.

Strawberry Syrup

This entire recipe will contain 270 calories and should measure 1½ cups of syrup. Each serving of ¼ cup contains 13 calories.

Ingredients:

1 package frozen unsweetened strawberries, about 2 cups *(allow to thaw overnight in refrigerator before cooking)*
1/8 cup Splenda

Directions:

(Should be made the night before to allow time to cool)

Mix strawberries *(including juice)* with Splenda in a pan and, stirring frequently, cook on medium heat until it begins to boil. As soon as it boils, take off stove and cool overnight. Skim off foam before serving.

Fasolada (Greek Bean Soup)

Serves 8
253 calories per serving

I had this soup for the first time at a local restaurant and loved it so much I had not two, but three bowls. My husband couldn't believe it. I begged the owner for the recipe and he kindly gave me the ingredients. I went home and experimented until I got it right.

To eat this soup is to fall irrevocably in love with it. I've made it once a week for the past three weeks.

Ingredients:

1 16-oz. can of navy beans
1 16-oz. can of stewed tomatoes
2 tbsp. tomato paste
3 carrots, peeled and sliced
½ cup chopped turnip
2 parsnips, peeled and sliced
1 large onion, chopped
2 stalks celery, chopped *(leaves included)*
½ cup extra virgin olive oil
1 garlic clove, minced
1 to 1 ½ quart water (*I like to add two tablespoons Better than Bouillon vegetable base)*
¼ to ½ tsp. cayenne pepper (*according to how much heat you want in your soup, although it still won't be very hot)*
Salt and pepper to taste
And the secret ingredient is 1 tbsp. honey
¼ cup feta cheese for garnish

Directions:

In large soup-pot, sauté vegetables and garlic in olive oil at medium.

When all vegetables have become sweaty, rinse beans thoroughly and add to pot, along with canned tomatoes, tomato paste and seasonings. Add salt, pepper, cayenne, liquid and Better than Bouillon vegetable base. Bring to a boil for ten minutes, then lower the temperature to a simmer and continue cooking for one hour.

Add the honey, stir, and serve with 1 or 2 tsp. crumbled feta for garnish. Yummmmm.

Low-fat Mulligatawny

6 servings of about 1½ cups each
230 calories per serving

Approximately 1 hour and fifteen minutes
from start to finish.

Ingredients:

1 tbsp. olive oil
1 large yellow onion, chopped
3 cups celery, chopped
1 cup sliced carrot
3 large cloves of garlic, minced
2 medium granny smith apples, peeled and diced
4 cups chicken broth
1 tsp. hot Madras curry powder
(If you don't like it too hot, use regular curry powder, or for hotter, use 1½ tsp.)
½ tsp. of ground cumin
½ tsp. of ground coriander
½ tsp. powdered ginger *(or 3 tbsp freshly ground ginger)*
½ cup white basmati rice *(rinse rice thoroughly before adding)*
¾ lb. chicken breast, cut into bite sizes
1½ cup lite coconut milk
1 tbsp. lemon juice
Salt and pepper to taste
3 tbsp. toasted sliced almonds

Directions:

Heat oil in your stockpot over medium-high heat. Add all vegetables including garlic; cook, stirring often, until softened, about 5 minutes. Add apples and spices and cook, stirring often, until the apples begin to soften, about 2 minutes. Add broth and rice; bring to a boil. Reduce heat to a simmer and cook, uncovered, for 12 minutes.

Add chicken, return to a simmer and cook until the chicken is fully cooked and the rice is tender, 8 to 10 minutes more. Stir in coconut milk and return to a simmer for three or four minutes.

Remove from the heat; stir in lemon juice, salt and pepper. Garnish with almonds.

To toast almonds, cook in a small dry skillet over medium-low heat, stirring constantly, until fragrant and lightly browned, 2 to 4 minutes.

Perfect Butternut Squash Soup

Serves 4 to 6
250 calories per portion, if serving 4.
167 calories, if serving 6.

Start with this basic butternut squash soup recipe and add your own flair—to create your own version of the perfect.

Prep Time: 15 minutes
Cook Time: 35 minutes
Total Time: 50 minutes

Ingredients:

1 large butternut squash *(about 4 ½ lbs.)* or 4 lbs. peeled and cubed butternut squash
2 medium onions
3 cloves garlic (optional)
3 tbsp. butter or vegetable oil
½ tsp. salt plus more to taste
8 cups chicken or vegetable broth

Directions:

Halve, seed, peel, and cube the butternut squash. Set aside.

Halve, peel, and chop the onion. Mince the garlic, if you like.

Heat a large pot over medium-high heat. Add the butter or oil and the chopped onion. Sprinkle with ½ tsp.

salt. Cook, stirring occasionally, until the onion is soft, about 3 minutes.

Add the garlic and cook until fragrant, about 1 minute.

Add the squash and the broth. Bring to a boil. Cover, reduce heat to a simmer, and cook until the squash is very tender, about 20 minutes.

Transfer small batches to a blender or food processor. *(My personal favorite is a submersible blender.)* Hold a kitchen towel over the top *(to prevent burns)* and whirl until completely and utterly smooth, 2 to 3 minutes per batch.

Return the soup to the pot and add more salt to taste.

Pear Salad with Blue Cheese Dressing

Serves 4 as a light lunch
394 calories per serving

Ingredients:

2 hard Bosc pears, cored and sliced
2 oz. walnut pieces
5 oz. blue cheese of your choice
1 tbsp. olive oil
1 tbsp. walnut oil
½ tsp. butter
2 tbsp. whipped cream
yolk of one large egg
2 bags of mixed spring lettuces *(about 6 oz. total)*

Directions:

In a bowl, mix 1 tbsp. blue cheese with walnut oil, beating until almost smooth.

Next, heat the walnut oil in a large frying pan over a medium heat and lightly sauté the walnuts, tossing them around for about 1 minute. Now blot the oil off and transfer them to a plate. Add the butter to the pan at the same heat, then add the pears and sauté them for about 2-3 minutes on each side until they are golden. Drain the pears on kitchen paper, put them on a plate and set aside.

To make the sauce, place the cream in a small saucepan with the rest of the blue cheese, crumbled. Now whip them together over a low heat until the cheese melts and then forms a creamy texture. Drop in the egg yolk and continue to whip until the sauce thickens; do not quite bring to a boil.

Remove the pan from the heat and set it aside while you divide the salad leaves among 4 serving plates. Arrange the pears around the leaves, scatter with the walnuts, and pour the sauce over each salad.

Skinny Beef Burger

Serves 8
375 calories each

Ingredients:

1 pound extra-lean beef *(5 or less fat)*, preferably grass fed
1 cup quick-rolled oats
1 large egg
1 tbsp. Dijon mustard
1 jalapeno pepper, chopped very fine
¼ cup chopped scallions
Salt and pepper to taste
Pam cooking spray
8 thin buns *(the ones that are 100 calories each)*
8 oz. of cheddar cheese, sliced or grated to garnish

Directions:

Mix all ingredients *(except buns and cheese)*. Using a half-cup ice-cream scoop, measure out scoops on a cookie sheet and flatten to desired thickness.

Spray a large skillet with Pam and cook at medium heat until done. While these are cooking, heat buns whichever way you prefer. I like mine toaster crisp, but you might like yours heated in the oven for less crispness.

Assemble burgers, topping each with 1 oz of cheese. *Enjoy.*

Skinny Turkey Burger

Serves 6
300 calories each

Ingredients:

1 pound ground turkey breast
½ cup quick rolled oats
¼ cup chopped scallions
¼ cup chopped celery
¼ cup chopped tart apple
1 tbsp. tabasco sauce
½ cup mango chutney
Salt and pepper to taste
Pam cooking spray
6 thin buns *(the kind with 100 calories)*
Garnish with lettuce

Directions:

Mix all ingredients *(except buns and lettuce)*. Using a half-cup ice-cream scoop, measure out scoops on a cookie sheet, and flatten to desired thickness.

Spray a large skillet with Pam and cook at medium heat until cooked through. Turkey burgers, unlike beef burgers, cannot be served any way other than well done. While these are cooking, heat buns whichever way you prefer. I like mine toaster crisp, but you might like yours heated in the oven for less crispness.

Assemble, adding lettuce, *and enjoy.*

REQUEST YOUR FREE BOOKS!
2 FREE NOVELS PLUS 2 FREE GIFTS!

H HARLEQUIN®

INTRIGUE

BREATHTAKING ROMANTIC SUSPENSE

YES! Please send me 2 FREE Harlequin® Intrigue novels and my 2 FREE gifts (gifts are worth about $10). After receiving them, if I don't wish to receive any more books, I can return the shipping statement marked "cancel." If I don't cancel, I will receive 6 brand-new novels every month and be billed just $4.74 per book in the U.S. or $5.49 per book in Canada. That's a savings of at least 12% off the cover price! It's quite a bargain! Shipping and handling is just 50¢ per book in the U.S. and 75¢ per book in Canada.* I understand that accepting the 2 free books and gifts places me under no obligation to buy anything. I can always return a shipment and cancel at any time. Even if I never buy another book, the two free books and gifts are mine to keep forever.

182/382 HDN GH3D

Name _____ (PLEASE PRINT)

Address _____ Apt. #

City _____ State/Prov. _____ Zip/Postal Code

Signature (if under 18, a parent or guardian must sign)

Mail to the **Reader Service:**
IN U.S.A.: P.O. Box 1867, Buffalo, NY 14240-1867
IN CANADA: P.O. Box 609, Fort Erie, Ontario L2A 5X3
**Are you a subscriber to Harlequin® Intrigue books
and want to receive the larger-print edition?
Call 1-800-873-8635 or visit www.ReaderService.com.**

* Terms and prices subject to change without notice. Prices do not include applicable taxes. Sales tax applicable in N.Y. Canadian residents will be charged applicable taxes. Offer not valid in Quebec. This offer is limited to one order per household. Not valid for current subscribers to Harlequin Intrigue books. All orders subject to credit approval. Credit or debit balances in a customer's account(s) may be offset by any other outstanding balance owed by or to the customer. Please allow 4 to 6 weeks for delivery. Offer available while quantities last.

Your Privacy—The Reader Service is committed to protecting your privacy. Our Privacy Policy is available online at www.ReaderService.com or upon request from the Reader Service.

We make a portion of our mailing list available to reputable third parties that offer products we believe may interest you. If you prefer that we not exchange your name with third parties, or if you wish to clarify or modify your communication preferences, please visit us at www.ReaderService.com/consumerchoice or write to us at Reader Service Preference Service, P.O. Box 9062, Buffalo, NY 14240-9062. Include your complete name and address.

HI15

REQUEST YOUR FREE BOOKS!

2 FREE NOVELS
FROM THE SUSPENSE COLLECTION
PLUS 2 FREE GIFTS!

YES! Please send me 2 FREE novels from the Suspense Collection and my 2 FREE gifts (gifts are worth about $10). After receiving them, if I don't wish to receive any more books, I can return the shipping statement marked "cancel." If I don't cancel, I will receive 4 brand-new novels every month and be billed just $6.49 per book in the U.S. or $6.99 per book in Canada. That's a savings of at least 19% off the cover price. It's quite a bargain! Shipping and handling is just 50¢ per book in the U.S. and 75¢ per book in Canada.* I understand that accepting the 2 free books and gifts places me under no obligation to buy anything. I can always return a shipment and cancel at any time. Even if I never buy another book, the two free books and gifts are mine to keep forever.

191/391 MDN GH4Z

Name _____ (PLEASE PRINT) _____

Address _____ Apt. # _____

City _____ State/Prov. _____ Zip/Postal Code _____

Signature (if under 18, a parent or guardian must sign)

Mail to the **Reader Service:**
IN U.S.A.: P.O. Box 1867, Buffalo, NY 14240-1867
IN CANADA: P.O. Box 609, Fort Erie, Ontario L2A 5X3

Want to try two free books from another line?
Call 1-800-873-8635 or visit www.ReaderService.com.

* Terms and prices subject to change without notice. Prices do not include applicable taxes. Sales tax applicable in N.Y. Canadian residents will be charged applicable taxes. Offer not valid in Quebec. This offer is limited to one order per household. Not valid for current subscribers to the Suspense Collection or the Romance/Suspense Collection. All orders subject to credit approval. Credit or debit balances in a customer's account(s) may be offset by any other outstanding balance owed by or to the customer. Please allow 4 to 6 weeks for delivery. Offer available while quantities last.

Your Privacy—The Reader Service is committed to protecting your privacy. Our Privacy Policy is available online at www.ReaderService.com or upon request from the Reader Service.

We make a portion of our mailing list available to reputable third parties that offer products we believe may interest you. If you prefer that we not exchange your name with third parties, or if you wish to clarify or modify your communication preferences, please visit us at www.ReaderService.com/consumerschoice or write to us at Reader Service Preference Service, P.O. Box 9062, Buffalo, NY 14240-9062. Include your complete name and address.